To those who dream, and to those who have yet to fall asleep

SYMBOLS OF THE GODS

ANIMA
GODDESS OF AIR

AQUES
GOD OF WATER

LAPHARA
GODDESS OF STONE

TITANS
RULERS AND CREATORS
OF EVERYTHING

TAARIN
GODEN OF EARTH

IGNOS
GOD OF FIRE

Since the beginning of time, humans and Gods have co-existed in peace.
The Gods rule over elements of nature.
Humans worship the Gods.
New Gods are created when more control is needed.
The Gods can be temperate, they can be kind, even loving.
But they are never merciful.
There is no mercy at the hands of a God.
Remember this, child.
These are the fundamentals of the universe.
Wake up.
Change is coming soon.

Chapter One

EVER SINCE ERATHIEL WAS YOUNG, HE HAD always liked to play pretend. This is evident, through the stories of his childhood he told me over an autumn night's bonfire or through my own experiences with him, however fleeting they were. He would wander off, preferably somewhere quiet and colourful, and dream up whatever he could find in the expanses of his headspace.

His family liked to play pretend, too. His father, Chathan, a cold, bitter man, liked to pretend that his family would be financially stable after his father passed. Chathan liked to pretend that the nobility and fortune his father carried would be, by some miracle, passed down to him rather than his elder brother, a much worthier man for the role. Erathiel's mother, Myrinai, liked to pretend that she was content, unaffected by the tensions in their family. Erathiel's eldest brother, Florian, liked to pretend to be fond of their father. Pretending was not simply a game for them; it was a pillar that upheld life.

It did not bother Erathiel much, because whenever tensions escalated in his home, he escaped to the world he created for himself. He would imagine that he was a warrior who won every battle he fought, or an artist whose works were preserved for centuries, or a philosopher whose writings became timeless. He would imagine that he had the possibility of being remembered.

The Gods were remembered, humans were not. A human's legacy died out in mere generations, usually fewer if they were unexceptional. A God, however insignificant, was to be remembered and revered until the end of time. Until the day that humans lost the hands to build and the mouths to speak, temples and statues would be erected in the Gods' honour, and tales of their glory would be told for eternity.

He, like most, never saw this as unfair, necessarily. When human society upholds traditions for so long, it is hard to see them as changeable; rather, they are viewed as customs of the universe.

Still, he liked to pretend that he, a simple boy born to a family whose bloodline was sure to die out, had the capability of being comparable to the ranks of the Gods.

Perhaps it was the pretending that kept him sane.

"AEDIS HAS BLESSED US WITH AN EARLY summer," Chathan said.

Summer had just dawned on the kingdom of Lenethaus. As Erathiel was overhearing the conversation between Myrinai, Chathan, and Florian, the maids cleaned up breakfast, and it would soon be time to start the day.

"Excellent; we may be able to harvest the lemon balm soon," Florian replied. At the time, Florian was only eleven years old, but he had quite the mind and was anticipated to take over the family's apothecary once Chathan retired.

"The Wind Goddess's temple was recently remodelled," Chathan said, nodding at Florian's statement. "There is now a statue of Auroleus."

"I do not believe I've heard of him," Florian commented.

"He is Gala's newest Creation: the God of Ocean Winds. He is only around seven years old, I think. Still, perhaps we should leave an offering. It would be wise to stay on his good side." They never got around to leaving that offering.

"Nature will be at its finest during these months," Myrinai chimed in. "So long as Floratris has a favourable temperament, that is." Myrinai always had a special attachment to flowers. After all, she did convince Chathan to name their firstborn son after Floratris, the Goddess of Flowers.

Chathan tensed. "Yes, I suppose."

"Wouldn't you like to travel? We could visit the countryside, or the cliffs of Sheesera—"

"We have work to do, Myrinai. Time must not be wasted," Chathan said briskly. Myrinai and Chathan stared at each other for a long moment, then Chathan sighed and left the room.

In that day and age, marriages for love were distinctly rare amongst mortals, but with Myrinai and Chathan, one could see that they had no say in the matter. Their personalities clashed. Myrinai was sentimental, Chathan was down-to-earth. Chathan was hardworking, Myrinai was lazy.

Despite how frequent they were, Erathiel enjoyed his parents' disagreements. Typically, Chathan would leave the room, and Myrinai would dismiss Erathiel and his siblings, essentially giving them a free day.

That is exactly what happened after the quarrel surrounding travelling. Myrinai sent Florian to work and told Erathiel to "go play."

And thus, the day continued. Erathiel and his twin sister, Ciradyl, were entertained by one of the maids. At the time, they were only six years old, so they could not yet leave the walls of the manor unattended. Chathan and Florian left to work at the apothecary, and Myrinai spent the day weaving fabric. A mood hung over the household during supper, and the children were sent to bed early.

Essentially, that was the structure of every day during Erathiel's early childhood, give or take studying and helping Chathan at the apothecary. It was repetitive, rigid with order. Sometimes, he appreciated the structure; other times, he grew weary of it, but it was of no matter.

Everything was about to change.

Chapter Two

MY FIRST CLEAR MEMORY OF ERATHIEL originates from when he was around eight years old. Fisyn, the Goddess of Spring, had blessed Lenethaus with fair weather. The sky was fresh with newly painted shades of blue, and dew rested gently on the grass that brushed against his ankles as he ran. That year, Erathiel's father had allowed him to leave the manor during free time, and he would spend most of his time near the ocean.

One day, once he reached the ocean, he set his contraption in the water: a sailboat of sticks bound by twine, donning a sail made of a scrap piece of fabric. The tide was low, so the tiny boat was able to withstand the waves. However, the wind was still, and the boat was unmoving. His shoulders slumped. This was his third attempt at sailing the boat, and something had gone wrong every time.

Suddenly, he perked up. He remembered something his mother had told him.

If all else fails, ask the Gods.

He scrambled to his knees, scraping them against jagged rocks in the process, reached out towards the sky, and began to pray.

It was interesting; he had never directly asked the Gods for anything before this. He had gone with his family to lay offerings to the most powerful Gods, but the Karalors had never directly requested anything of them. After all, he was taught that it was rude to ask anything of the Gods unless it was absolutely necessary; alas, he was a young, dumb child, and he began to pray.

At first, he struggled to think of the God's name who could aid him, and then he remembered that conversation between Florian and his parents. "Auroleus," Erathiel said confidently. The name, in his voice, was silky and smooth, steady as the waves against the shoreline. He continued, repeating the phrase his instructor had taught him. "I plead with you to appear before me and aid me in this time of need."

Honestly, he did not expect the plea to work. Tales of Gods appearing before humans were few and far between, and said humans were typically heroes of grandeur, not eight-year-old boys.

However, a pale blue light appeared in the sky, drifting towards a rock in the ocean. From the light came a figure, and he knew that it could be none other than yours truly: Auroleus, the God of Ocean Winds.

I was a paradox when it came to my appearance. My hair, white with hues of blue and lavender, rested neatly upon my head. My pale blue skin seemed to glow in the morning light. White freckles shaped like tiny stars dotted my complexion. Although I was short, barely taller than Erathiel himself, I had a muscular build. I was wearing a white toga lined with golden fibres, and the Symbol of Aques, the God of Water, was implanted on my wrist. It was impossible to doubt that I was a God.

However, it was clear that although I was a God, I was but a child. I was around Erathiel's age, and it was evident. Gods age at around the same rate as humans do, and once they reach their peak ability, they Ascend and take on a higher form. At that point, I had only been Created around nine years ago. My toga was dishevelled and haphazardly worn, and the golden anklets I wore were chipped. My eyes, deep blue flecked with gold, were full of youthful joy and wonder, and quite honestly, I was amazed as he was.

After all, it was the first time I was summoned.

"You...you actually wanted me—er, who are you?" I asked.

It took him a moment to remember his name. "Erathiel Karalor," he muttered, eyes wide with wonder and awe. He had never seen a God. He did not quite seem to know what to do, so he offered me his hand to shake, but then, remembering that it was a great disrespect to touch the flesh of a God, he hastily withdrew his hand, face flushed red.

However, I took his hand with a jovial smile and shook it with enthusiasm. "Auroleus, God of Ocean Winds, Creation of Gala and Ocari! I—well, I must say, I never actually expected to be summoned by a mortal." I stared at him with fascination, as if he were an interesting animal. I reached out for his ear and traced its outline with my fingers. "They are so...short, are human ears always like that?"

"Er—yeah, I suppose so?" He looked quite uncomfortable.

"Fascinating," I muttered, slowly drawing my hand back. "Oh, er, I suppose I should be more formal, seeing as I am fulfilling a request from the mortal plane and all. What was it I was supposed to say..." At this point, I was just talking to myself. Erathiel did not seem to mind.

"Oh, it is quite fine, you have no need to be formal or anything, I just..." He stopped in his tracks, his face growing, somehow, redder. He seemed embarrassed by his request.

"Well?" I asked, eyes wide with patience.

"I was just wondering if you could, perhaps," here he gestured to the small boat in the water, "make it sail?"

I perked up. "Oh! But of course." With an almost careless wave of my hand, a gust of wind came from my fingertips. As I cast the wind from my hands, the Symbol of Aques on my wrist was illuminated, and a matching Symbol made of light lit up above my palm. The wind smelled faintly of salt, and it carried fibres of blue light. Within seconds, the wind hit the sail, and the boat was moving.

Erathiel smiled widely in victory, and I must admit: although I expected my first request to be perhaps more *high-stakes*, I was amused, and a bit proud of myself. Most other Gods had received requests, prayers, or offerings since infancy, and they constantly held that fact over my head. At last, I would be free from the mockery.

Erathiel turned to me, and a smile spread across his face. "Thank you," he said earnestly. "You have probably got to leave now, right? I'm sure you have more important things to tend to."

He was right; Gala, the Goddess of Wind and one of my Creators, expected me to appear for a feast celebrating the anniversary of the Creation of Aques. But the boy, however simple, was better company than the Gods; they were all egocentric and abhorrent people to converse with.

"No," I replied, deciding not to attend the feast. "You do not mind if I spend time here for a while? You seem like decent company."

Erathiel looked surprised, as if he had never heard such a basic compliment. He nodded eagerly. "Alright!"

So, we spent the rest of the day building another boat, one that was larger and stronger. Erathiel built the boat itself, and I, having no skill with anything related to building, gathered twigs and ivy to form the ship. I followed Erathiel's command; it was strange, a mortal ordering around a God, but I complied.

While we worked, Erathiel was very inquisitive. He was constantly asking questions: some about me, some about the higher-ranked Gods, some that seemed obvious, some that I had never comprehended myself.

When Vesa, the Goddess of Dusk, painted the sky with hues of orange and purple, Erathiel and I stared out at our work, proud. Two boats floated in the water: one larger, covered in ivy, and one smaller, the original boat that Erathiel made. "This was nice," I remarked. "Simple pleasures like this do not come often in the Immortal Realm."

"I would imagine," Erathiel responded.

I turned to face him. "You would not perhaps be interested in...doing something like this again sometime? I have never truly had someone to spend time with."

Erathiel's face lit up. "Oh, er, yeah, that would be lovely!"

I smiled back. "Great." I stared up at the sky. Night was starting to set in, faint stars dotted across the darkened purple airspace. "I had best be getting back. Gala will be expecting me."

"A good night to you, Auroleus."

"Farewell, Erathiel."

ABOUT A WEEK AFTER HE FIRST MET ME, Erathiel was shaken awake by Chathan. "Wake up, boy," Chathan snarled. "You will make us late for our arrival at the temple."

Erathiel woke up, his red sheets crumpled in the opposite corner of the room; he had overheated during the night. He stretched out his arms, yawned, and groggily said, "Wha—"

"To the temple of Ocari," Chathan snapped impatiently. "Get properly dressed. We are going to leave an offering."

"Wait," Erathiel called as his father approached the door.

"We don't have eternity, boy."

"Are we going to leave an offering for Ocari's Creations?"

"We will leave an offering for Aestalios, yes. It would be wise to stay on his favourable side during this season; he is the God of Tides, after all."

"And what of Auroleus?"

"What of him? His status means nothing; Gala does his work for him. Let the boy mature before we leave him our valuables." At the time, this is what most of Lenethaus thought of me.

Erathiel nodded in understanding, and Chathan left the room. Erathiel changed into a set of pale yellow and white robes, which were a bit oversized, then hurried down the staircase, where, out the window, he saw that three carriages were waiting outside.

Silver embellishments on the carriages gleamed in the morning light. The two horses drawn in front of each carriage, all white with long, well-combed manes, were pacing their hooves against the ground. The drivers fidgeted impatiently with the reins. Erathiel boarded a carriage with his siblings, his elder sister Sionia carrying her infant sister. His cousins boarded the carriage next to them, and Erathiel's parents, uncle, aunt, and grandparents were already waiting inside the third. This was tradition; once every two weeks, the entire family would visit a temple to leave an offering for the Gods.

Before he boarded the carriage, Erathiel collected a few handfuls of long grass that grew outside the manor. During the two-hour carriage ride, he twisted the grass into an anklet that he would later offer to me at the temple. It was not nearly as valuable as the gold, wine, or jewels that the rest of the Karalors offered the higher-up Gods. However, Erathiel believed that I deserved something, even if small.

Once the family arrived at the temple of Ocari, the God of Oceans, they were immediately enthralled by the beauty of the intricate statues depicting the Gods. The largest statue was Ocari, reaching out with an expression of triumph.

Next to him was Gala, hand on his spare arm in a comforting embrace. On either side of the pair were Ocari's two Creations: Aestalios and, well, myself. A large bowl was cemented in front of each of the statues. This is where the family would leave their offerings.

As members of the Karalor family broke off to leave gifts to Ocari, Gala, and Aestalios, Erathiel wandered off alone to bring me the anklet. Immediately after he set the anklet down in the bowl, it disintegrated into pale, blue light and floated upwards. Erathiel nodded in satisfaction.

From the Immortal Realm, I smiled.

Chapter Three

IN THE BLINK OF AN EYE, TWO YEARS PASSED. Erathiel and I became more acquainted, meeting up every month or so. I always wore the anklet he gave me, and I pretended not to notice him smiling to himself every time he saw it. We soon developed a meeting spot: Thyrin Cove.

. Thyrin Cove was a forgotten old place, a tiny area in the massive southwestern coast of Lenethaus. It was a quiet, serene turquoise cove lined with a coast of powdery sand. Rays of sweet summer sun shone through the canopy of the nearby black cherry tree forest.

Leading from the coast to the forest, there was a worn, weathered stone staircase that was overgrown with strands of grapevine. The stairs and pathway it was connected to had fallen into disrepair; clearly, they had not been used since the Ancients walked the earth.

After wandering down the old and chipped pathway one day, Erathiel discovered a cave, the entrance overgrown with thick, wilting ivy. When he discovered the cave, he was still quite young. Sometimes, he could have sworn he heard someone inside singing. He did not dare explore the cave out of fear for what may have lurked inside.

Thyrin Cove was a relatively abandoned location; hence, we did not need to worry about anyone else finding us. It was our little place, our beauty at the edge of the world, and it was more than enough for the expanses of our minds to roam free.

NORMALLY, WHEN HE DESIRED TO MEET ME, Erathiel would call to the sky and pray for me to visit the mortal plane. However, one day in early spring, I was already there when he entered Thyrin Cove, sitting on a rock in the forest.

"Auroleus," he said, a surprised inflexion in his voice. "What are you doing here?"

"I had a feeling you would be here today," I responded, distracted by something in my hands. A thwarted expression creased my face as I fiddled with the object.

"What are you—"

"The Gods are constructing a clock tower," I explained. "Every God is mandated to contribute, and I am building this." I held out the object in my hands: a small, mechanical bird made of gears and bolts. I waved my hand and blew a gust of wind inside the bird. Its wings flapped briefly, but the air passed right through. "It's supposed to fly. It's not working."

"Here, hand it to me." Erathiel took the bird out of my hands, sat on the ground beside me, and started making a few modifications.

"How are you—"

"Hush. Let me concentrate." After a few minutes, Erathiel was done and handed it back to me. "Here. It should be able to contain the wind now."

I flicked my fingers, and a gust of wind carrying blue light came out, along with the Symbol of Aques, which levitated and glowed above my hand. Unlike before, the wind was captured inside the bird, giving its interior a bluish glow. It spread its mechanical wings and took flight, circling above us. I let out a cheer of joy. "Erathiel, you are a miracle!"

He flushed red. "No, I simply have experience with mechanics."

I patted him on the shoulder. "Regardless, I thank you, dear human." I looked towards the sky. "Alas, I must get going."

He was disappointed. "So soon?"

I nodded. "Yes, Gala will be expecting me." I gave Erathiel a good, long stare. "It has been...too long since I last saw you."

"Yes, it has."

"Are you available to meet me here, this time a week from now?"

He paused. He knew he was unavailable; he had a mathematics lesson from his instructor. However, his instructor, an impatient man, was not someone Erathiel particularly enjoyed being around, unlike me, his only true friend at the time. Erathiel was conflicted, and he struggled to make eye contact. His eyes panned down, and he noticed the anklet he had made hanging limply around my ankle. A smile tugged at his lips. So, Erathiel nodded. "Yes, I believe I am."

I nodded. Not knowing what else to say, I gave him an awkward wave, distilled into a pale light, and floated to the Immortal Realm.

LATER THAT NIGHT, WHEN ERATHIEL CAME back to his manor, Florian was waiting for him in the main dining hall. Florian was a rather scrawny man, unimpressive when it came to his physique. He wore a set of dark lavender robes with golden lining, and his spectacles were perched on the end of his nose. The wrinkles of worry that creased his warm, freckled complexion were alleviated when Erathiel entered the room.

"Ah, Erathiel, you have returned," Florian said, ushering his younger brother to sit down. "Are you hungry? I've made us supper."

Erathiel was confused. "Why hasn't Mother made it?"

"She and Father are not home. I am not quite sure where they are, actually."

"What about the maids, then?"

"I did not want to bother them. Just eat, alright? I worked hard on it."

Erathiel nodded and examined the food. It was a mushroom soup; at least, he guessed it was such. He slowly took a bite, and it took every last bit of self-control not to spit it out. The dish was revolting. Florian looked at Erathiel with a hopeful expression. "So?"

With a great amount of effort, Erathiel managed to swallow it. He forced a smile and said, "It is quite good."

Florian grinned widely. "Great. I have been enjoying cooking; perhaps someday I will open a tavern."

"I wish you luck," Erathiel muttered.

"So, where were you all day? Oh, I am not upset, only curious," Florian hastily added after he saw Erathiel's expression of nervousness. Erathiel often found that his conversations with Florian were rather tentative. He was one of the few family members that Erathiel could tolerate, but their relationship was off-balance. Florian had fragile self-esteem, especially when it came to his hobbies (all of which he was poorly skilled at), so Erathiel often had to uphold Florian's self-image. However, Florian was also a sort of father figure to Erathiel, essentially filling the role of a third parent. Thus, their dynamic was strange.

"I was with a friend," Erathiel responded.

Florian warmly smiled. "Oh?"

"Well, I suppose we are friends, anyway. He and I have been spending time together for the last two years."

"I am quite sure you two are friends, then. Who is he? Would I know him?"

Erathiel paused, debating whether to reveal my identity to Florian. If it were Chathan, perhaps Erathiel would not have told him about me, but he trusted Florian more than anyone else in his household, so he said, "Auroleus."

Florian looked taken aback. "Auroleus, as in the God of Ocean Winds?"

Erathiel nodded, nervous. He felt it was necessary to gain Florian's approval of me.

Florian's smile returned. "Well, I would be delighted to meet him someday, if the opportunity comes."

Erathiel nodded. "Perhaps."

A loud clatter bounced off the walls as the dining hall door swung open. "There you are!" a loud voice boomed. "Eugh, it smells horrible in here!"

Erathiel and Florian exchanged a glance of annoyance. The man entering the room was Tallis, their eldest cousin.

He was a strong man with an impressive build, an uncomfortably square head, and a beard that had just started to grow in. Tallis was a loud, obnoxious alcoholic, and if Erathiel and his siblings could be unified over one thing, it was their distaste for Tallis. He was the golden child of the Karalor family, even though most Karalors wanted absolutely nothing to do with him.

Tallis flicked his wrist towards Erathiel. "Boy, fetch me a pint, will you? It has been a long day."

Erathiel stood up and poured the mead, muttering obscenities under his breath. When he placed the pint down in front of Tallis, he took great care to ensure that some of it splashed back on Tallis's robes.

"Pay more attention, boy!" Tallis barked. Erathiel nodded, stoic, and returned to his seat.

"I made supper for my siblings," Florian offered hopefully. "Only Erathiel was hungry so far; would you like a portion?"

Tallis nodded, and Florian placed a bowl down in front of Tallis. After one bite, Tallis spat the soup back into its bowl. Making a retching motion, he exclaimed, "This is terrible! Are you attempting to poison me?"

Florian looked hurt, and Erathiel gave his brother a look of reassurance. "Perhaps you simply do not have a refined palate," Erathiel said blankly to Tallis.

He turned to Erathiel, rage in his eyes, and slammed his fist on the table. "What did you say to me, boy?" Erathiel cowered in fear. Tallis stared at Erathiel for a long moment, then turned away. "No matter. I will get my wife to cook me something later."

Florian nodded curtly. He opened his mouth to say something, seeing as whenever Tallis mentioned his wife, there was sure to be a long rant, but it was too late.

"My wife's a real bitch, you know that?" Tallis proclaimed. Florian and Erathiel winced; it was uncommon to hear obscenities in even semi-formal settings. "She is useless. She refused to acknowledge me yesterday. Can you believe the audacity?"

"Consider me shocked," Florian responded. Tallis did not seem to pick up on the undertones of sarcasm.

Tallis sighed forlornly and shook his head. "Ah, I miss the days of freedom, before I was wed to Ciliren. She is pregnant now, you know."

"Is she?" Erathiel asked. He was tempted to ask if the child was Tallis's, but he held his tongue.

"Are you deaf as well as careless?" Tallis grumbled. He glanced at Florian. "You understand, Florian. You were so much...happier...before that fiancée of yours came along!"

Florian's posture tensed, his hands clenched tightly. "Ilyara and I are perfectly content, thank you."

"Preposterous!" Tallis exclaimed, spit flying out of his mouth as he spoke. Florian flinched away from the saliva projectiles. Tallis groaned, then said, "Our fathers may be good men, but they have horrible sense when it comes to choosing wives for their sons."

A chair creaked as Tallis stood up. He knocked over his bowl of mushroom soup as he made towards the exit. "Well, I'll be off to find a *real* supper." He clapped Erathiel on the back. "Take some advice, boy. Marry for love, or you'll end up haggard and miserable like us." He gestured to Florian with a smirk.

"That," Florian said through clenched teeth, "is the *single* thing we can agree upon." He stared at Tallis coldly. "You'd best be going, then."

"Alright, alright, I am leaving." With a loud crash, Tallis slammed the door closed behind him.

"He is a slob," Florian said promptly as he cleaned up the mushroom soup that Tallis had spilt. "I pity Ciliren."

Erathiel nodded in agreement, eyes widened in aggravation. "Are we the only sane men in this household?"

Florian gave Erathiel an incredulous glance, then let out a bitter laugh. "You are just now realising this?" Shaking his head in exasperation, Florian left the room.

SUMMER CAME, AND SUMMER PASSED. AUXRA, the Goddess of Autumn, was cold and unforgiving, so the season came with an early chill. The leaves of the forest bordering Thyrin Cove were morphing into a crisp red-orange, and small creatures were scurrying about, collecting food in preparation for the long, cruel winter.

On a particularly cold evening, Erathiel and I had gathered branches and stones, formed a makeshift fire pit, and started a fire. Erathiel and I sat next to each other on a log.

Erathiel was gazing at my face. It looked different in the firelight. A golden glow shone on my complexion, highlighting the perfectly carved features that were just starting to lose their childhood roundness. My eyes, blue as the deepest waters, reflected fragments of light. A faint smile spread across my lips. Every time our shoulders brushed, a feeling akin to electricity ran through Erathiel's veins. Out of—what, curiosity, fear?—he moved ever-so-slightly away. My smile lowered, almost unnoticeably. Despite the fire, I was cold again.

"Auroleus," he said slowly. I leaned my head towards him; it was evident he was soon to ask one of his 'questions.' "Do Gods have...families?"

I hesitated, confused. "What do you mean?"

"What I mean to say is, well, I mean, humans have families. We have parents, siblings, cousins, children, spouses...do Gods have families as well?"

"No, not really, I suppose. We have romantic partners, but nothing else. Since Gods are created as a concept and not through physical action like humans, we lack biological relations. A God's Creator would never treat their Creations like a parent would treat a child, if that's what you mean. Rather than a particular couple raising their Creations, an older generation collectively helps raise a younger one. And in terms of siblings, well, that concept does not exist among the Gods."

Erathiel nodded in understanding, then asked, "Does it ever get lonely? Without a family, I mean."

"Well, I would not exactly know what it is like to have one, so I'd say...maybe?"

What was that look in his eyes? Pity? "Huh."

As I stared into the fire, knees curled up to my chest, I could not help but picture it. A father, teaching his son how to build. A mother, comforting her children after they scraped their knees. Siblings play wrestling in the grass. A feast with extended relatives, where the food was warm and the laughter seemed constant. Meeting a partner, and despite the odds, marrying for love. The couple, building a home together. Children, playing around the house. There was peace. Loving. They grew old together. A man whispered to his beloved's gravestone, just before he left the Mortal Realm himself.

Tears stung my eyes. This was not the life of a God; therefore, it was not the life I would have the pleasure of leading. For a moment, while I mourned this beautiful fantasy, I felt rage at fate itself. Why must I have been born this way, when a better life was so possible? I could never have this 'family' Erathiel spoke of. Unless—

Perhaps if I was given no semblance of family, I could create my own.

I turned to Erathiel, a sad smile creasing my face, hope in my eyes. "Can you be my family?"

"I'm not quite sure what that means, but...yes." He took me in his arms, pulling me into a tight embrace.

We sat there for a while; I did not want to let go. After all, the night was cold, and his embrace was warmer than the fire itself.

Chapter Four

FROM THEN ON, WE WERE INSEPARABLE. WE met up in Thyrin Cove almost every day; although Erathiel was failing many of his lessons as a result, it was more than worth it. "Your instructor is going to murder you," I remarked when he missed an exam one day.

Erathiel simply shrugged. "So long as you can visit me in the Realm of the Dead, I see no issue with it."

Sometimes, we would talk for hours. Other times, we would invent games for ourselves. Every so often, when there was nothing better to do, we would sit and stare at the stars. Every so often, Erathiel would steal a glance at me. I rarely noticed at the time, but looking back on it now, part of me wishes I had seen.

ON A CRISP, WINTER DAY, WHEN ERATHIEL and I were fourteen, a decent stretch of the cove had completely frozen over. Erathiel and I were racing to the shore. Despite my status as a God, Erathiel was faster than I, so he was just in front of me as we ran. The gently falling snow rested upon his dishevelled dark auburn hair. His amber eyes, determined and full of concentration, stood out against his deep tan complexion. He was taller, broader, and stronger than before, his features sharper and refined.

Something was different about him, or perhaps something in my perception of him had shifted. His family—

and his people, for that matter—viewed him as simple. There was nothing simple about him. He was a lone ember amidst a dying fire, a wildflower in a barren field.

He must have noticed me staring, because he turned around and asked, "What?"

I shook my head. "I am about to win."

I put all my effort into running, and I finally surpassed Erathiel just before reaching the shoreline. He smiled, sweeping the hair out of his face. "Fine. You win."

Both panting and out of breath, we stared out at the ice. Erathiel picked up a stone and tossed it into the water. The stone broke through the ice and sank. His shoulders slumped. "Shame," he remarked. "I hoped we would be able to go out on the ice."

I turned to Erathiel and shrugged. "Who's to say we cannot?" I waved my hands, and the familiar Symbol of Aques appeared, hovering above my palm. A gust of cold wind that carried blue light swept through the area. A crackling sound of ice being formed rang through the air, and I turned to him with a smile. "Should be safe now."

He threw another stone for good measure, and this time, the stone simply slid across the ice. Out of the patchy cloth bag around his back, he took out two pairs of ice skates: horse bone sharpened to a point, tied to the bottom of a leather shoe. We pulled on the shoes in silence. Erathiel seemed to get his footing right away, whilst I was anxious.

With a stupid grin on his face, he turned around, noting my expression. "Are you...*nervous*, Auroleus?"

"Me? Never."

"Has Auroleus, the mighty God of Ocean Winds, never done something as simple as skating before?" I was silent, and his expression softened. "It is simple. Just follow my lead, and you should be alright." He outstretched his hands. With a look of wonder, I took them in mine. His palms were warm against winter's chill.

A light smile spread across Erathiel's face. For some time, we stood there, hands intertwined by the frozen cove. It could have been a few seconds, it could have been hours; if it had been forever, then we would have been ready to embrace eternity.

Erathiel stared deeply into my eyes, lost in thought. I cocked my head. "Is everything alright?"

He shook his head, clearing his expression. "Yes, quite well. Are you ready?"

I nodded. Erathiel stepped backwards onto the frozen cove slowly, guiding me along with him. "Follow my motions," he instructed.

My footwork was shaky at first, but within a few minutes, we were in sync. There was a certain rhythm to it, almost dance-like. I was confident enough to stop staring at his footwork and meet his eyes. Yet, I only got a glimpse of his amber orbs before I stumbled and fell.

"Oh!" Erathiel exclaimed, barely standing. "You told me you would try to be careful!"

"I am!"

He laughed, pulling me up. "If you were, then this would not have happened." After making sure I was stable, we started to skate again.

The sound of our skates and laughter rang throughout Thyrin Cove. The snow gently fell, piling on branches where two starlings perched. Out of all his memories, Erathiel seemed to closely treasure that quiet wintry afternoon spent in Thyrin Cove.

Inevitably, I stumbled again, this time pulling Erathiel overtop me. He seized the opportunity and pinned down my arms and legs. "Let me go!" I exclaimed, half-amused.

Smiling, Erathiel shook his head. "No, no, I don't believe I will."

I struggled for a moment under his grip, then (he underestimated my strength) I was able to roll over, pinning him down instead.

"Oh, Gods, this is cold!" Erathiel yelped, feeling the back of his head against the ice.

I laughed in response. "Got you."

We both let out a light chuckle, then our expressions grew much more serious, almost...longing?

There was something about him in that moment, something so pure and perfect...I wanted to be closer. I weighed the options, took the risk, and started to lean my head forward.

Erathiel, however, did not notice my advance and took his chance to escape my grip. He successfully pushed me off of him, then suggested, "Shall I race you to the shoreline?"

I cleared any semblance of disappointment from my face. I gave him a light smile. "You know I will lose."

"Is that not the point?"

I shrugged. "Fair enough."

We spent the rest of the day at the shoreline, simply talking about whatever came to our minds. I kept a comfortable distance from Erathiel; after all, I was worried that he did not see me the way I saw him.

Nothing about the air changed, and yet, the rest of that day seemed colder.

ERATHIEL PACED HIS SISTER'S ROOM, VISIBLY anxious. His parents were arguing over something, and it escalated to the point where Ciradyl, who was in the room at the time, was sent to her chambers, and Erathiel awkwardly followed along.

Ciradyl was sitting on the edge of her bed, kicking her feet. "I am so tired of this," she said, staring at her ceiling. "All this tension."

The twins could hear the echoes of their father's yelling. "It's always been like this; I have grown used to it," Erathiel responded.

She sighed in frustration. "Yes, but it's been getting worse. Do not pretend you have failed to notice."

Erathiel paused, then nodded solemnly. "I have observed." He stared at the door anxiously as the screaming got louder. "Can we speak of something else, please?"

Ciradyl nodded. She thought for a moment, then her face lit up. "Oh! Have you heard about the recent scandal among the Gods?"

"No?" Erathiel stopped pacing, suddenly interested. I typically stayed away from drama amongst the Gods, particularly because of how quickly the affairs grew complicated, and Erathiel knew this. However, he knew the chaotic nature of the Gods' scandals, and he was worried that I would be caught up in the crossfire.

"Alright, so, have you heard of Auri and Vesa?"

"The Goddess of Dawn and Goddess of Dusk...what about them?"

"They recently made their partnership public. They are courting," she added after she saw his confused glance.

"Oh." He was expecting one of the Second-Generation Gods to have committed adultery, or a new Creation idea to be abandoned. Something as simple as homosexuality was fairly common amongst the Gods.

She stared at his indifferent expression and scoffed with a smile. "It's insane, maybe the Gods' only flaw. How can a species so grand practise...*lesbianism?*" She shook her head. "I will never understand."

The people of Lenethaus typically dismissed homosexuality as 'unnatural,' despite that it was commonly practised amongst the Gods. Erathiel, even growing up, was particularly indifferent to the matter—there were more important subjects to care about—but most in his family were more opinionated.

"I believe I will retreat to my chambers," Erathiel remarked, making his way towards the door.

Ciradyl rolled her eyes. "I was simply trying to *spread the news,* my Gods, you're no fun!"

Once Erathiel walked to his room, he laid down, sprawled out upon his bed. His thoughts immediately wandered to me. It had been two months since we had gone skating, and we had barely seen each other since then. I always had an excuse: 'I had plans,' or 'Gala needed me.' In the few times we met up, I was more distant than usual. Even when I was there, he still missed me, in a way.

Out of some concoction of boredom, he called up towards the sky. "Auroleus," he began. "Can I speak with you? Please?"

He waited. There was no response. Just as he was about to give up all hope, a voice came.

"Erathiel? What is it?"

He took a shaky breath. "You have been...distant. Is it something I've done?"

I hesitated. "No, it is not your fault. I have just been busy."

"And I understand that, truly, I do. I have not seen you in a month, Auroleus, and even when I did see you, you weren't truly there."

I was silent. He was right, but I could not reveal why I was distant.

"I miss you, Auroleus. Where have you gone?"

These next words broke me. Light tears stung my eyes. It took all my effort not to let that show in my voice. "I miss you too. I am truly sorry that I failed to make time for you."

"Would you, perhaps, be available to join me at Thyrin Cove tomorrow?"

"I'll be there."

He sounded relieved. "Thank you."

"Of course."

With that, my voice faded, and Erathiel was satisfied.

ERATHIEL SAT IN A TREE, STARING AT THE forest. Spring was just dawning, and with it, life. The trees were starting to gain back their emerald hues, and newly blooming hyacinths clumped around their roots. Bugs and hummingbirds flitted around the overgrowth of lilacs. Squirrels scampered up the trees, their tiny bodies filled with rejuvenation after their long, restful winter. Only a few small, muddy patches of ice remained in the water, and snow no longer dusted the mossy boulders piled around the cave; Hithar, the God of Winter, had relinquished his grip on Thyrin Cove.

Finally, I appeared beside Erathiel. After my pale blue glow dispersed, I gave him a light smile. "Erathiel, it is good to see you, old friend! I do apologise for my late arrival."

"It's fine, I failed to notice." He did notice, and he was hurt deeply by it, but he intended not to let that show. Erathiel turned to me with a smile. "So, er, we have not met in a while."

I tensed. "Yes."

"Has anything interesting happened to you in the meantime?"

I shifted nervously, half-regretting coming at all. "Nothing in particular. You?"

He shook his head. A mundane answer to a mundane conversation. Expected, choppy, almost scripted, somehow rhythmic in a distorted sense. We used to be able to talk for hours, endless topics and limitless tangents, passion and excitement as we spoke. This was dull. This had no meaning. How did we fall this far?

Silence set in, as it always did during conversations like these. It was simply the norm for interactions that neither party wanted to participate in. I wanted to be there, though, and I assume he did, too. So why were we like this?

Desperate to redeem this fruitless encounter, Erathiel suggested, "Would you like to explore the caves?"

I was surprised. "I thought you were too scared to enter them."

"I am not eleven anymore, Auroleus."

I let out a light chuckle. "Fair. If you get scared, do not blame me for this."

He shook my hand in agreement, then paused for a moment. Electric sparks. It was perfect, and yet, could it have been more wrong? I wanted him gone, gone!...but I wanted so much more.

The moment passed, and he quickly climbed down the tree, expecting me to follow. I was left with a strange concoction of emotions.

This will be dealt with at a later time, I decided. I followed Erathiel down the tree, along the stone path laid by the Ancients, and to the cave, the entrance of which was still curtained with ivy.

Erathiel drew out a dagger and hacked away at the thick, gnarled ivy. When enough of the vines fell to create a gap large enough for an entrance, he stepped away. He wiped his forehead, which was glowing with sweat, and gestured to the opening. "Well? What are you waiting for?"

I stepped inside the cave.

The air was dense and heavy with moisture. Bioluminescent lichens made their homes in the cracked, grey walls of the cave. Agate with layers of deep blue and purple grew in clusters. A few tunnels ran deeper into the cave network; clearly, this was the entrance to a winding cavern. The sound of a distant waterfall echoed off the cave walls, giving the caverns a sense of serenity. Besides the lichens and a few frogs, we were the only life forms in the cave.

We need not worry, I thought, *about anything except ourselves.*

Erathiel and I explored the entrance of the caverns, not daring to go any deeper. He asked me a few questions in an attempt to make conversation, and I gave minimal responses. How could I do anything more?

Finally, he sighed. "You can leave now, if you wish."

I cocked my head. "What?"

"You clearly do not want to be here. I am not sure what this divide is between us, but it seems I'm the only one putting in effort to get rid of it."

I stared at him forlornly. "What happened to us?"

He threw up his hands in exasperation. "You tell me, you are the one creating this rift! Am I not worth as much as I used to be?"

I paused, affronted by this claim. "You do not realise that you are worth everything, Erathiel, you are-"

"If I am worth 'everything,' as you claim, then why have you avoided me?"

"I-there are complications-"

"Then fix it. Fix it, or leave, but we cannot keep pretending that this is normal!" His tone shifted from rage to sadness. "I miss you, Auroleus. Please come back."

There was a lump in my throat. It was a struggle to speak. "I...have much to contemplate. I have been cruel to you. I apologise. None of this is your fault."

He nodded. I could not tell whether he believed me. "You should go," he began slowly. "Think about what you need to. Return when you are ready."

I nodded. He gave me a sad smile. The years flashed before my eyes. No low point had gone this far. I lamented on what was, what could have been, if my emotions, my foolish, unrequited emotions, did not complicate everything. How could I destroy what was already so perfect? How could I, despite the distance, need more space?

However, I did recognise that if I was going to salvage this relationship, this was what must have been done.

With that, I left the caves, leaving Erathiel alone, as I always seemed to do.

It sank in: him and I, together, a partnership? It was simply impossible, nothing more. For how could he, the embodiment of perfection, settle for me, a terrible excuse for a God who could not help but neglect the person he cared for most?

I WILL NOW SHARE A BRIEF MEMORY OF MINE. I am aware that this is not my story; it is the story of Erathiel, but I feel this memory pertains to it.

I came back to the Immortal Realm, full of guilt and anguish. My emotions were torrential. I did not know how to cope or what to do. One thing was certain: I was incapable of handling this on my own. I needed advice, and I knew precisely who to ask.

Esolir, the God of the Sun, happened to pass by on the cobblestone streets where I stood. One could tell just by looking at him that he was past his lifespan's first cycle; in other words, he was going to Ascend soon. He presented all the typical signs: black scleras, growth in height, markings around the hands and wrists, and slow but sure transfiguration of the hair and skin. He wore a set of elegant gold and white robes and held a sophisticated demeanour. He smiled upon seeing me approach him. "Auroleus! Lovely day, is it not? How may I be of assistance on this fine evening?"

"Would you happen to know where Auri and Vesa are?"

"I may be mistaken, but I believe they are in the bakery."

"Thank you!" I shook Esolir's hand frantically and ran off towards the bakery.

The scent of warm, sweet pastries wafted through the air as I swung open the door of the bakery, gasping for breath. The quiet, comfortable atmosphere of the little shop was momentarily disrupted. Arberra, the Goddess of Trees and the owner of the bakery, stared at me with a concerned expression, then shrugged and continued scrubbing down the counter.

Auri and Vesa sat at a miniature table in the centre of the bakery, where a tree grew through the bakery itself. Fireflies floated around the tree, which was surrounded by small wooden tables and chairs painted with an aquamarine hue.

I pulled up a chair. "Do you mind if I join you?"

"Not at all, sit," Auri responded with a smile. Her hair, white with strands of red and orange, ran down her shoulders. Her skin was a pale reddish-pink, and she had wide amber eyes and similar starry freckles to my own. She wore a practical outfit with golden accents.

Her partner, Vesa, was a perfect contrast to Auri. Her white locks, dappled with pieces of purple, green, and blue, were tied up loosely. Her dark eyes stood out against her skin, a fair purple shade. Her robes were flowing and dramatic, lined with silver threads. "You appear troubled," Vesa observed. "Is everything alright?"

I nodded, then paused, then shook my head. "Lately, I have been having...moral strife, if you will. I am pushing away someone I care for dearly, and I feel terrible about it. Have I told you about Erathiel–"

"Is Auroleus going on about that boy again?" a familiar voice asked from across the bakery. It was Aestalios. Seeing as he was a fellow Creation of Ocari, his physique was similar to mine. However, he was burlier, taller, and his hair was darker than mine.

Auri let out an audible sigh. "Yes, he is. Pull up a chair." Aestalios came over, sitting between Vesa and me. "Auroleus, this is nearing the point of exhaustion. Just tell the boy you love him and move on with your lives, alright? It is *painfully* obvious."

"I wish it were that simple," I moaned. "He is a mortal, and I am a God. That difference alone will raise controversy. Besides, humans are typically less condoning of a relationship between two men. I have no idea whether he is attracted to men at all, let alone me. It would simply never work."

"Auroleus, any human, regardless of gender, should be honoured by the mere opportunity to court a God. Do not take this so seriously," Vesa said dismissively.

My expression tensed. "I would rather treat him like a person with complex emotions and preferences than an underling who will serve my every command, thanks." Vesa nodded, impressed by my unpopular viewpoint on this issue.

"Based on your description of him, he seems...you know," Aestalios remarked. "I would assume that it is at least possible that he is attracted to men."

"Yes, but assuming anything in this situation can be the difference between a relationship and a seven-year-long friendship growing cold, so I would rather not do that."

Aestalios shrugged. "Then I've got nothing."

"Auroleus, have some confidence," Auri said with a smile. "Regardless of your Godly status, you are quite a pleasant person to be around. It sounds like you and Erathiel are compatible. You may not see it, but there is a chance of a relationship, and that chance is more significant than you realise."

"What if he rejects me?"

"And what if he does not? You fail to see the positive side of this. You fear rejection so badly that you forget to think of the possibility of a relationship. You say you are pushing Erathiel away, and I agree, and I do not think you realise how much it hurts him. Do you actually want to court him, Auroleus, because if you did, then why would you waste all your effort on neglecting him?"

"I–"

"Let's make this simpler. Do you love him?"

I paused, my eyes flitting between Auri and Vesa. Their "love" was not the "love" I felt. Scandalous exchanges, lustful affection, and flirtatious banter, it simply was not the image that love gave me. Other sensations came to mind. Coy smiles. Sparkling eyes. Conversations about nothing, and conversations about everything. A gentle touch that meant the world. Vivid sunsets. Ivy growing up the sides of ancient buildings. A leather journal full of drawings and ideas. Fireflies resting in the summer grass. The light of a melting candle. The warmth of a steady flame. The scent of ink on paper. The stillness of a clear night. Mechanical whirs. Music drifting through the air. Gentle laughter. My name, which felt different in his voice, *special*. Memories of a simpler time.

His hands on mine, laughing at my clumsiness. "You told me you would try to be careful!" "I am!" "If you were, then this would not have happened." I thought back to that day on the frozen cove with distinct regret, yet an overwhelming sense of determination. I failed to make a move then. I would not let the opportunity slip again.

I recalled Auri's question. "Do you love him?" My love felt different, so was it truly "love?" Uncertainty coursed through me, but it quickly cleared. My love was mine, and the only one who could dictate its validity was me, and the object of my love would be, eternally, Erathiel.

"Yes," I answered. "I do."

Vesa smiled. "Then that is enough. If you love him, give more of your time to him. Show him your affection, and see if he reciprocates."

"If I may," Aestalios interjected, "perhaps refrain from being too blatant; you do not want to scare the boy off."

I nodded. I could, perhaps, see a future where Erathiel and I were courting. It was, indeed, a great future. Was that future worth risking the friendship we had worked so hard to build?

Perhaps it was.

Aestalios saw the expression on my face and smiled widely. "Good luck, kid. This will work out in one way or another, I promise."

I was shaky and unsure, but I managed to smile back. "Thank you, all of you," I gestured towards Auri and Vesa. "This truly helped."

Later that night, as I quietly observed the Mortal Plane from above, I noticed Erathiel in his chambers. After quickly making sure he was alone, I sent my voice down to him.

"Erathiel. Are you available to meet me at Thyrin Cove tomorrow?"

ERATHIEL AND FLORIAN SAT DOWN QUIETLY, eating dinner—rather, in Erathiel's case, pretending to eat. Florian had cooked up another interesting concoction, a dish vaguely resembling beef pie, that smelled almost plague-like. They were discussing Florian's recent wedding to Ilyara.

"—It was a nice arrangement, wouldn't you say so?"

"Yes, absolutely." Florian seemed distracted.

"Is everything alright?"

"Yes—well," Florian let out a deep sigh. "I am worried for the apothecary."

Erathiel's expression grew concerned. "I thought the apothecary was doing well."

"In sales, yes, but product, well..." He let out a sad chuckle. "Sotis is never favourable, is he?"

As soon as Florian mentioned Sotis, Erathiel understood the problem. Sotis, the God of Soil, was a powerful God and was once very benevolent. However, ever since his Ascension was recently completed, he had become harder and harder to please. He had a chaotic temperament and was anything but merciful. Thus, he had a tendency to punish the humans with poor harvests.

"Perhaps Sotis will be gracious this year," Erathiel said optimistically.

Florian scoffed. "Only in another universe." They were silent for a moment, then Florian perked up. He pulled a handful of items out of his pouch and gave them to Erathiel. "Here, I found a few trinkets around the shop. I thought you might like them."

Erathiel examined the items: small gears, bolts, and even a compass needle. He turned to Florian with joy. "Thank you!" he exclaimed.

Florian smiled. "Of course."

Erathiel excused himself from the table and went to his chambers. He took a half-built contraption—a mechanical insect designed to scout the caverns—out of his desk drawer and started fiddling with it.

He worked until his only light sources were a dying candle and the rays of moonlight from his window. He put the insect down and sighed in satisfaction. He had made sufficient progress, and he was growing tired.

As he walked over to his bed, he heard a voice call from the sky.

"Erathiel. Are you available to meet me at Thyrin Cove tomorrow?"

A grin spread across Erathiel's face. "Yes."

Chapter Five

WHEN ERATHIEL ARRIVED AT THYRIN COVE, I was already waiting for him. As soon as I saw him, I ran over and pulled him into a tight embrace. We stood there for about ten seconds, my arms wrapped around him. I took in his scent, his warmth, and I was whole again. I stepped away, worried. "Is this okay?"

He nodded frantically. "Yes." He pulled himself closer to me, his head resting against my chest. His breath synced with mine. "I missed you," he said, sounding choked up.

I smiled softly. "I missed you too. Now, I am back, for good.   Is   that   okay?"

"Okay—it is perfection."

After a while, I finally stepped back. There were tears in his eyes, and there were tears in mine. Neither of us acknowledged it. "Alright, alright. What would you like to do?" I asked. "I have no plans for the rest of the day, so I can stay as long as you like."

He gestured towards the caves and shrugged. A tentative expression creased my face. "Erathiel, truthfully, I doubt I have the will to explore the caverns right now."

Erathiel shrugged. "Perfectly fine." He squinted at the cave, which was embedded in a large pile of rocks. It had once been a cliff, we thought, but over the years, it had weathered and fragmented. "We could try to climb it?"

I smiled. "Perhaps we could stay until dusk?"

He returned my smile, light echoing across his face. "Perhaps."

We made our way to the cavern entrance. I viewed the fractured cliff as unscalable, but Erathiel seemed to think differently. "First, step here," he gestured towards a rock, "then head left for a while, until—well, see that string of moss-covered boulders?" I nodded. "We climb that, then, we should..." At that point, I was merely half-listening to Erathiel. It did not truly matter what he was saying, of course, I knew he would guide me through the process again momentarily. Simply hearing the sound of his voice was melody enough.

He had what I liked to call a mechanical mind. The way he thought was mathematical and precise, and he seemed to see shapes and solutions where they may have been invisible to the normal eye. I could tell when the gears of his mind were turning; there was a certain spark in his eyes that I always seemed to get lost in. *He would make a marvellous architect, or perhaps a chemist,* I thought. *Regardless, his intellect cannot go to waste.*

"Auroleus? Auroleus!" Erathiel asked, grounding me. He was standing atop the first stone, his hand outstretched. He appeared amused. "Are you awake?"

I shook the thoughts from my head, returning myself to the present moment. "Yes."

He laughed to himself. "Alright, then. Shall we climb?"

After approximately an hour of (failed) attempts and near-falls, we pulled ourselves onto the top of the cliff. Our knees were scraped and our faces were dusted with mud, but we smiled all the same. We felt like children again. I always seemed to get that sensation when I was around him.

We were far above the treetops, so we had a clear view of the cove. I closed my eyes and took in a deep breath of salty air, truly feeling, breathing, living in that moment.

Erathiel immediately wandered to the edge of the fractured cliff, desiring a closer look. He peered over the edge. "Do you think we would die if we fell from this height?"

"That...is quite a morbid thought."

He shrugged. "This is a morbid world. Keep up."

"We Gods are not particularly worried when it comes to the matters of death."

Erathiel sat down near the edge of the cliff, staring out at the water. "That seems like a foolish sentiment."

I sat beside him. "How so?"

"Gods may not die of old age, and they may not die from, say, a fall," he gestured to the cliff's edge, "but ichor flows through their veins all the same. A God can bleed, so he can die, am I wrong?"

I was hesitant. A God typically never pondered the possibility that they might be slaughtered. "No, you are not."

"I assumed as much. If death is a possibility, then why do you fail to worry?"

I picked up a stone and started fidgeting with it. "We Gods have our wisdom."

"You have wisdom, yes, yet you seem to lack intelligence. Practicality."

"And yet, we have all survived this long. Intelligence tells you to fear and avoid death; a natural response, yes. Wisdom tells you to seek wonder, to relish the finite, to *live*. You humans fascinate yourselves with death. It is, in the end, all you truly care about, no? I would consider us Gods–" I threw the stone. I heard it hit the ground, and yet I did not hear it break. "–to be well-versed in life."

He stared at me as if I had said something profound. I gave him a nervous smile. He returned it.

The next few hours seemed to slip away from us. Our conversation about death led to me asking Erathiel what he wanted to do with his remains.

"I must admit," he responded. "I thought about this a lot. I want my lover–" my heart leapt when he said 'lover,' not specifically 'wife,' "–to take my corpse up the hill behind my childhood manor, lay me to rest amongst the flowers, and bury me under the magnolia tree."

"It sounds...beautiful. It makes your death seem almost peaceful."

"Ideally, that *is* how my death would be, regardless."

The conversation then shifted to Erathiel's favourite flower (an orchid), then to Erathiel's family apothecary, which I had no idea existed until then. He then complained about his cousin, Tallis, who sounded like an abomination of a human. Amid a rant about his latest project, Erathiel paused sheepishly. "I apologise; I realise I was talking for a while."

"No, no, I love hearing you rant," I said, twirling a bit of his hair between my fingers. "You sound so passionate."

He gave me a bashful smile and pulled away. "I feel guilty for rambling, that is all."

I nodded in understanding, but in reality, I could not possibly grasp the notion. I wanted to know everything about him. I wanted to know his favourite colour. I wanted to know his perspective on the universe. I wanted to know him, to love him, to see the world through his eyes.

He gasped in excitement, pointing towards the sky. "Look!"

Dusk painted its hues of purple and pink across the sky. Lines of dark clouds contrasted the bright colours, and there was almost an ethereal shine emitted from the gently setting sun.

Erathiel stood up, smiling widely, entranced by the chromatic swirl. "Our view is so clear! It is beautiful," he said with awe.

I glanced at him. "It is."

AEDIS BROUGHT A PEACEFUL, TRANQUIL summer over the kingdom of Lenethaus. Erathiel and I spent plenty of time together: cloud gazing, climbing trees, and skipping stones over the water. However, the summer seemed to pass us by. Before we knew it, the leaves were growing orange and crisp, and the air had a pre-autumn chill. Birds were starting to embark on their southward flight.

Erathiel and I raced from the beach to the forest, laughing as we ran. Erathiel was intent on winning, which he did, but he was so fast that he ended up crashing into a tree.

He staggered back, clutching his head. "Agh!" he exclaimed.

I was immediately anxious. "Are you okay?"

Erathiel let out a jovial laugh. My expression softened. "Yes, yes."

I walked over to him, chuckling. "You are an imbecile."

He rolled his eyes, pretending to be annoyed, but the smile pulling at the corners of his mouth gave him away. "I am not."

I placed my hand gently on the place where he hit his head, examining his bruise. "Contest me all you want, you know the truth."

We locked eyes for a moment, then he gently pulled away from me when he looked up. The cherries growing from the trees seemed ripe. "My father will be pleased," he said with a smile. "I can gather cherries; that is the reason he sent me here, after all." He tried to reach for the cherries, but his fingertips could not grasp them.

I laughed and pointed at him as I grabbed the cherries with ease. "You are rather short."

He grumbled. "You're a pain today."

I flashed a large grin. He shook his head, sighing while trying to suppress his smile. Erathiel held out a woven basket. "We should get this over with, then."

I let out a dramatic groan. "Must we?"

He gently hit me over the head with the basket. "Yes, why would I have asked you here otherwise?"

"Because you enjoy my company?"

"Enjoying your constant teasing? Never."

I gasped, pretending to be offended. "How dare you?"

Erathiel smiled triumphantly.

"No, no, I refuse to believe this. You love my company."

"Do I, now?"

I took a step closer and stared down at him. "Mhm, yes."

He simply shrugged. "Perhaps I do."

We started to harvest the cherries, but because I grew bored extremely quickly, we decided to make a game out of it. Erathiel would climb the trees and throw the cherries, and I attempted to catch them in the basket. I only caught it about half the time, but it was entertaining nonetheless.

Dusk came and went quickly, and Erathiel and I were left to watch the stars. We laid out on the ground, pointing out shapes in the sky and the fragments of the universe we found most beautiful. "Stilis has done well tonight," I murmured, staring out at the sky.

Erathiel turned to look at me. "Do you know Stilis...personally?"

Stilis, the Goden of Stars, was an interesting character. Stilis was the physical embodiment of sophistication and elegance, and was so fiercely, unapologetically, free.

For starters, Stilis was what we Gods called Tryan, a concept outside the typical standings of 'male' and 'female.' Instead of the descriptors of 'he' and 'him' or 'she' and 'her,' Tryans used 'se' and 'sem,' and use 'Goden' instead of 'God' or 'Goddess.'

Stilis also did not seem to care about the affairs of Gods nor mortals, regardless of whether se was personally involved. Se spent most of ser time with ser inner circle (who typically spoke of subjects far too intellectual for me), guiding lost souls to the Realm of the Dead, and, of course, controlling the stars.

I was acquainted with Stilis during our childhood, but over the years, we grew distant. Still, we were connected through mutual friends, namely Auri and Vesa.

"I used to know sem better," I admitted. "Se is decent company, if a bit pretentious. I prefer spending time with Auri and Vesa, and perhaps Aestalios when he isn't so boisterous–" Erathiel let out an incredulous chuckle. "Does that amuse you?"

"No, well, yes, it is just interesting to hear you speak about the Gods, whom my family worships, mind you, as if they are mildly annoying childhood friends."

"Well, that is what they are to me, are they not?"

He shrugged. "I suppose." His gaze wistfully shifted upwards. "I have always loved the sky."

I finally turned to look at him. His face looked different in the moonlight. "Yeah?"

He nodded, tracing a constellation with his finger. "Yeah."

"We could chart the stars someday. Make the night sky our own."

A solemn laugh escaped his lips. "It would be nice...but we are too late. Stilis has already done that, has se not?"

I scoffed. "Erathiel, you speak like your father, a man who has already given up. Of course we can chart the stars. The universe could be ours if we wish it to be so. Here, let us start tonight." I gently held Erathiel's wrist, just under his hand, which was still pointed to the sky. I moved his hand so that it gestured to a particularly bright star westbound. "I name this star Auroleus." I had him point to a nearby star, so close to the first that they were barely distinguishable. "And that one is Erathiel."

ERATHIEL STUMBLED INTO HIS DINING ROOM, drowsy and sluggish. It was a strangely warm autumn day, and he and I spent the afternoon racing across the shoreline. He expected Florian to be there, most likely with a poorly cooked meal, but instead, he found Tallis.

"Supper at last!" Tallis exclaimed. His expression dropped when he saw Erathiel. "Oh. I thought you were a maid."

"Well, I am not," Erathiel huffed, taking a seat far away from Tallis. He stared out the window, briefly picturing himself as a great swordsman, conquering ruthless kingdoms and winning the hearts of civilians.

His daydreams were interrupted when, much to his disappointment, Tallis spoke. "Where have you been all day, boy?"

"I was with a friend," Erathiel said briskly.

A sly smile spread across Tallis's face. "Ah...courting someone, are we?"

Erathiel was instantly defensive. "No. The friend in question is male."

Tallis grunted, disappointed. "You really need to start conversing with women more. The time for marriage will come soon enough."

Erathiel quickly exhaled through his nose, stood up, and walked towards the door.

"Not going to eat, boy?" Tallis called after him.

"I have lost my appetite."

Tallis shook his head. "There must be something wrong with you, boy, I swear it."

ERATHIEL WAS AWOKEN IN THE MORNING'S
early hours. The sun was just beginning to rise, and the birds
nesting outside his window had not yet begun to chatter.

Tallis's words still rang clear in his mind. *There must be
something wrong with you, boy, I swear it.* At first, Erathiel
dismissed the statement as Tallis simply being rude, but
Erathiel had started to dwell on it. Was Erathiel, indeed,
broken?

Most other boys his age had their minds set on one
thing alone: women. The way they spoke of women not only
repulsed Erathiel, what with the boys' vulgarity, but the very
concept disinterested him as well.

When he pictured this so-called "love" the boys spoke
of, a submissive housewife did not come to mind. Instead, he
thought of deep laughter, a strong figure yet someone he
could hold in the hours of night, warm, firm hands, my
hands...

...*no. This is wrong,* Erathiel thought. *This is not the
function for which I am designed.*

Still, the thoughts came, some thoughts of the time we
had spent together, mostly thoughts of activities we had yet
to partake in.

As he grew lightheaded, he clutched his temples as he
shook back and forth. *You were not made for this. You were not
made for this.*

Erathiel stood up, needing an outlet for this newfound
energy.

He snuck outside the manor, towards the training
grounds. He strode over to the polished wooden rack where
many swords and spears were stored. He grasped the hilt of
the curved longsword farthest to the left, his blade of choice.

48

He positioned his right hand above the jade-encrusted pommel, then stepped out onto the training grounds.

If one thing separated Erathiel from the rest of his family, it was his proficiency in swordsmanship. Chathan often told him that if any son of the Karalor family were sent to war, it would be Erathiel (Florian was too slender, Tallis and his brothers were too brutish). Erathiel did not like to contemplate this; his purpose was mechanics, not murder.

Still, Erathiel's instructor vigorously trained him on swordfighting in particular. Erathiel enjoyed practising, but his instructor was far too harsh for his taste and often ruined the experience. Thus, Erathiel only put half-effort into his sessions with his instructor and used his full strength when he was alone.

Erathiel held out the sword, adjusting his form as he prepared to strike the invisible enemy. He took a deep breath, then swung.

The sword slashed the air, moving obediently as if it were merely an extension of his arm. His footwork was pristine, advancing and retreating almost as if he and the enemy were entangled in a dance. Erathiel and the blade were intertwined, in a sense, in perfect sync.

Slash.

As he swung at the air, Tallis's words were repeated in his mind.

You really need to start conversing with women more.
Slash.
You really need to start conversing with women more.
Slash.
You have not found a wife yet.
Slash.
You are a failure.
Slash.
What were you meant for?
Slash.

Do you matter?
Erathiel threw down the sword, screaming as loud as he could towards the open sky. He stood there for a moment, struggling to regain his breath, then re-entered the manor.
There is something wrong with you, boy, I swear it.

MY NEXT MEMORY COMES FROM A BITTERLY cold night in late autumn. Leaves, wrinkled with dying hues of orange, were barely clinging to their trees. It was rare to see any living creatures; birds had already flown south, and the animals residing in the undergrowth had begun their winter's rest.

Earlier that day, Erathiel and I pitched a fire in our makeshift fire pit. The flames were seldom strong enough to keep us warm. Erathiel sat on the log of a fallen tree, his legs spread out and his body leaning towards the fire. I sat on the ground, leaning against the log and wrapping the bottom of Erathiel's cloak tightly around my shoulders.

I think we would have talked more that night, but it was so cold that our lips felt numb. Perhaps the mere company was enough.

A bitter wind swept through the forest, bringing a freezing chill to the air. I shivered, the words 'So cold...' barely escaping my mouth.

Erathiel silently wrapped his legs around my shoulders. I looked up at him, and we exchanged a nervous smile. I rested my head upon his knee as I broke his gaze. We stared into the fire.

The numbness and cold were replaced by tension and electricity. There was something in his touch, something that made me question the basis of our relationship. Was it purely platonic? I could only be left to wonder.

That would be a question for another time, though. In that moment, we were at peace. It was only he and I, alone on a crisp autumn night, cold, but a little warmer because of the other's touch, and that was good enough. We were calm. We were content. We were silent, but there was so much spoken. We were young, in love, and wondering whether the other felt the same.

SUMMER'S WARMTH FILLED THE KINGDOM OF Lenethaus. The winter was long and unforgiving, and spring was plagued with thunderstorms. The summer heat brought a new sense of life and hope, and soon enough, the quaint kingdom's markets and town squares were bustling with commerce once more.

Erathiel and I laid on rocks near the shoreline, breathing slowly as we soaked in the summer sun. Our hands accidentally brushed a few times. He visibly failed to notice; thus, I pretended I did as well.

The lack of conversation was starting to bore me, and the sweat dripping down my forehead was becoming too much to bear. I sat up, with a dazed expression on my face. "The air is far too hot," I complained, causing Erathiel to roll his eyes. I gestured to the turquoise waters. "We should swim."

"Auroleus, it is barely summer. The water will be freezing, do you honestly expect me to–"

"Yes." I pulled off my linen shirt, grabbed him around the torso, and, with my Godly strength, picked the struggling Erathiel up with ease and carried him into the water.

I laughed jovially as he yelped. "Auroleus, this is freezing, how are you not—put me down!"

Once we were about waist-deep in water, he stopped squirming, and I loosened my grip. Erathiel dramatically gasped for breath, then pulled off his shirt over his head. "May I at least return my shirt to shore?" he asked. "Father will chastise me if I get it wet."

I considered it, then nodded. "Fine."

He nodded in return, then walked towards the shore. His pace quickly increased to a run as he neared the shoreline, preparing to make his escape. Just before he left the water, he stole a glance back at me.

"Woe betide you if you leave that shoreline!" I shouted. He flashed me a wily grin and sprinted away from the shore.

I lifted my hands and summoned a strong wind to push me towards the shoreline. Erathiel noticed the Symbol of Aques and the light carried by the wind, then grew visibly panicked. Just after Erathiel dropped his shirt on the sand, I grabbed him around the waist. Erathiel shrieked, and I was worried I had gone too far, but his smile and laughter were clear as day. Beaming, I pulled him away from the shoreline.

"You can let me go now," Erathiel said. When I gave him a pointed look, he added, "I promise I will not run away again. I am adjusted to the water now, regardless."

I eyed him suspiciously, then nodded curtly. "As you wish." I gently set him down in the water.

As we slowly waded across the cove, I noticed that Erathiel fell further behind. I turned around to make sure he did not intend to escape the water again, and I was met with a splash of salty water in my eyes.

"Agh!" I exclaimed, rubbing my eyes. "What–" Once my vision had cleared, I saw Erathiel staring at me mischievously. "You." I pulled my arm back and splashed him twice as hard.

"Hey!" he screeched, returning the favour. We ran around the shallow end of the cove, splashing each other as we went. The sound of our laughter mixed with the sloshing of water rang through the area.

Finally, when it seemed he had the advantage, I channelled a gust of wind to create a massive wave. It threw him aside like a leaf in a gale, and once he finally emerged from the water, he sputtered. After spitting out what appeared to be a clump of seaweed, he exclaimed, "Unfair!"

"This is the price of challenging the God of Ocean Winds," I said triumphantly.

Erathiel stared at me incredulously. "Did I say I have given up?" He dashed the water towards me.

I was half-impressed. The moment quickly passed, and I battered him with an array of torrential splashes as I chased him deeper into the cove.

Once the water was deep enough to submerge us up to our shoulders, Erathiel seemed more anxious. "Fine, I surrender, if you insist," he said. His breathing grew rapid as he stared at the water nervously.

My expression dropped. "Are you alright?"

He lost his footing and started to paddle. He confessed between breaths, "I cannot...exactly...swim..."

My first instinct was to berate him, but I decided against it. I gently placed my arms around his and held him up. He moved closer and gripped my shoulders, attempting to keep himself up. Erathiel was secure, but he could not tell as much, and his breathing grew shallower.

"Hey, hey, it is alright," I said soothingly. "Hey, Erathiel, look at me. Everything is okay. Breathe in, breathe out."

He took a few deep breaths, then met my eyes. Heat coursed up my body the minute our gazes locked. It was only in that moment that I could comprehend how close we were. If he were only a smidgen closer to me, we would have been intertwined, and I would have been by no means opposed to that.

I watched him as he relaxed his muscles, yet he still seemed nervous. He stole a glance at me now and then, then his eyes moved downward, and his face flushed a bit more. Once his face was thoroughly red, I could not help but chuckle to myself.

"Something amusing?" he spat defensively.

"Nothing, nothing." Part of me enjoyed seeing him flustered, but I could also recognise he was struggling, so I suggested, "Shall we return to the shoreline?"

"Please."

His muscles were numb from flailing about in the water, so I carried him to shore. I set him down gently, then laid down in the sand. He lacked the energy to sit up, so he collapsed, his head falling upon my chest. Either he was bereft of the energy to move, or he simply did not mind.

A smile spread across my face. My breathing synced with his, and for a moment, we were one. For that moment, I felt at home.

Breathe in.

Breathe out.

The world was safe.

Chapter Six

AS SUMMER NEARED ITS END, AN IMPORTANT event approached in the Immortal Realm, leaving the Gods excited. Every conversation worked its way around to one topic: the Starlight Ball.

The Starlight Ball, hosted by Esolir, the God of the Sun, and Lunix, the Goddess of the Moon, celebrated two things: the anniversary of Esolir and Lunix's partnership, and the anniversary of Stilis's Creation. It was a formal event, and nearly every God was in attendance.

I was not particularly looking forward to the event. I enjoyed donning stately attire and stealing a few sips of champagne whenever I could. Alas, the company of the Gods was not particularly pleasant.

I desired to invite Erathiel. The Gods were sure to be at their most pretentious on a night such as this, and Erathiel's presence would keep me sane.

I was waiting anxiously to invite him. Most of the day, he was assisting Chathan at the apothecary. When he finally entered his room, covered in grime and filth, I appeared before him. "Erathiel!"

"Agh!" He jumped back, startled. He regained his steady composure, then asked, "Why are you here?"

"I have come to ask you something important!"

After a long pause, Erathiel asked, "Yes?"

"Have you heard of the Starlight Ball?"

He huffed. "I have, considering it is the topic of every conversation, whether in the company of Gods *or* mortals."

"Precisely!" I exclaimed, mirroring his aggravated tone. Then I smiled. "So, I was wondering if you would be interested in attending with me?"

I pictured his response. *Yes, Auroleus, of course. I have dreamed of this moment. I love you. Can we run away from society, make a home for ourselves on the shoreline, adopt children, and watch every sunrise together?*

Instead, he replied, "Auroleus, I am not sure whether my presence will be...wanted...in an event of this calibre."

"Nonsense!" I practically shrieked. "We Gods quite regularly host mortals at formal events–" a mortal has never, in the history of the Gods, attended one of our events, "–and everyone in attendance is permitted to have another person accompany them–" I had to beg Esolir to let me invite Erathiel; invitations for these sort of events were *very* strict, "–I understand if the formality of it does not interest you, believe me, but I yearn for your company, Erathiel. I need someone there."

Erathiel paused; I had the sense that I rambled too much. I nervously awaited his response, every possibility cycling through my mind. Finally, he slowly nodded. "Why not?" He shrugged. "I suppose my father will allow it—rather, he will not notice my absence."

I had to restrain myself from bursting with joy. "Splendid! Wear something formal, preferably white, or gold, or deep purple or blue if you own it—do humans own formal clothes? You must, right? Yes, yes, just wear anything formal. I will meet you here in two days' time, and we will travel to the Lunar Library, that is where the event is held, if you were not aware, and I will have to introduce you to Auri and Vesa, and perhaps Stilis..."

Erathiel paused, then laughed nervously. "Alright. I will see you then, Auroleus. Now, I request you to depart so I can change out of these." He gestured to his set of clothes.

"Oh,   but   of   course!"

"Wait," I heard him call as I prepared to leave.

I turned back around, beaming. "Yes?"

"Will it be...*odd*...for us to be seen together in an event like this? We are two men, after all."

My smile faltered as my heart sank. I tried not to let dismay creep into my voice as I said, "Well, it is not as if we are romantically involved, is it?"

He looked down and nodded. "Okay." He looked up at me. "I will see you in two days' time, Auroleus."

I nodded, dissolved into light, and faded from the room.

I tried not to let Erathiel's last comment linger in my psyche. After all, he had agreed, albeit after some convincing, and that was all that truly mattered.

I ARRIVED AT ERATHIEL'S MANOR, DRESSED AS elegantly as I could muster. I donned a set of formal white robes, the waistband and cape of which reflected space dust and stars. Spiralling gold accents traced the neckline of the robes, and a single golden earring hung from my left earlobe. My hair rested perfectly upon my head, not a single strand out of place. I had to admit, I was quite stunning. I rather enjoyed formalwear, it made me feel more important than I was.

Erathiel walked down the steps of his manor, and my jaw dropped. He was stunning. He wore a set of black-and-purple formal robes, silver arm cuffs rested upon his wrists, and his amber eyes were winged with eyeliner. I took a deep breath, and once he was standing near me, I finally managed to say, "You look...yes."

He was confused, yet amused. "Thank you, I think."

I cleared my throat. "Shall we go, then?"

"I have a query."

"Yes?"

"How exactly do you intend to transport me to the Immortal Realm?"

"Ah, well, you see, the Lunar Library is in a space accessible to both mortals and Gods. Using a certain rift, humans should be able to travel there. It is separate from the rest of the Immortal Realm; getting there is complicated for humans, but you need not worry about that, do you? All I need to do is, here, let me just–" I closed my eyes, moved my hands in a particular pattern, and a flash of light erupted, along with the Symbol of Aques—golden in colour and large in size—and other scattered golden runes. The rift, although shaky, was projected a few paces in front of us. The light surrounding it was erratic, but its interior had the typical appearance of all rifts: not the location itself, but simply the cosmos.

"Are you ready?" I asked the terrified Erathiel. I outstretched my hand. He swallowed, then nodded, took my hand, and we stepped into the rift.

WE ARRIVED OUTSIDE THE LUNAR LIBRARY. The Library was a massive structure, a beige and golden building with a dome-shaped observatory. Trees lined the cobblestone courtyard, their leaves hues of blues, purples, and pinks, with flowerbeds filled with flora of every imaginable shape. The sky, unlike in the Mortal Realm, was a perfect view of the complexities of the galaxy, incomprehensible celestial bodies swirling in a sea of starry fractals.

Already, there were swarms of Gods entering the Library, their elegance complementing mine, if not overshadowing it. Erathiel seemed nervous in the large crowd, but I was confident; I was accustomed to gatherings such as these.

I realised that I was still holding his hand, so I grasped it tightly to get his attention. "Shall we go inside?"

He nodded. "Yes."

I guided him through the crowd as we ran to the entrance of the Library. We walked up the marble staircase, into the building, down the left hall, and into the observatory.

The whole room had been cleared of its usual bookshelves and study areas for the occasion. Instead, tables with gold-edged white cloths lined the wall, and most of the area was open for dancing to music that came from an unknown source. Floating candles with blue flames illuminated the observatory. The beauty was awe-inspiring.

I scanned the room, and every God I knew seemed to be in attendance. Naturally, Luxheia, the Goddess of Light, and Tenedius, the God of Darkness, could not be bothered to attend, considering that they were the highest-ranked Gods and rarely made a public appearance. However, I did notice all of the Creations of Luxheia and Tenedius, the Second Generation of Gods. Aques, the God of Water, and Anima, the Goddess of Air, were already dancing. Despite the formal occasion, they each wore their signature accessories: Aques's silver cuffs that covered his wrists, and Anima's necklace, the charm of which was a stone with blue and violet markings. Taarin, the Goden of Earth, was speaking to Esolir and Lunix, a light in ser eyes. Ignos, the God of Fire, and Laphara, the Goddess of Stone, were sitting at a table.

I felt an arm wrap around my shoulders. "There you are!" Auri's voice chimed. She and Vesa stood beside us. "We have been searching for you two. You both are dashing!" As her gaze shifted to Erathiel, she grinned. "This must be Erathiel, then. We have heard plenty about you."

"Plenty," Vesa added, looking Erathiel up and down.

"I do not speak of him too often," I protested.

Vesa audibly laughed. "Ha! Right."

"I really do not." I gave Erathiel an apologetic look, and he returned my nervous smile.

"Regardless," Auri said, deciding to halt her onslaught of teasing, "we are glad we found you both. The company of the higher-up Gods is not exactly…"

"Pleasant," Vesa finished. "Shall we find a table, then?"

We nodded, and I led the group to an empty circular table that could sit about eight.

"Correct me if I am mistaken, but I do not see any other humans here," Erathiel said after we sat down.

"Oh…" Auri said, trying to restrain her amusement. "It must be a coincidence." She knew full well that mortals were not expected to attend the Starlight Ball. However, she prevented herself from humiliating me any further.

"Yes," I added hastily.

"You two had best go off," Vesa remarked. "Many Gods have long awaited your introduction, Erathiel."

"We will stay here," Auri added. "You know, to ensure no one occupies the table."

"Go on, then." Vesa waved us off.

Erathiel and I stood up and walked around the ballroom. We came across Esolir and Lunix, who were mid-conversation, but stopped when they noticed us.

"Auroleus!" Esolir's voice boomed. He grasped my hand and shook it tightly. "It is good to see you, my boy! You two are stunning!"

"T-Thank you, sir," Erathiel stuttered, half-bowing to the pair.

"Nonsense! Call me Esolir," he said as he pulled Erathiel into a fatherly embrace.

"Pardon my husband," Lunix said with a smile. "He is particularly enthusiastic tonight."

"And why should I be anything otherwise?" Esolir exclaimed, letting go of Erathiel and holding Lunix's hands.

60

"Our Creation comes of age tonight! This is cause for celebration!" The few people in the surrounding area cheered. Esolir's voice lowered after that comment. "Although this may be more...personal, it has been seventy years since we started courting."

"Seventy years," Lunix murmured. "I would not trade it for the world." She and Esolir embraced with a gentle kiss.

As I watched them, a light smile spread across my face. To some extent, they treated the younger Generation like their children, and despite the decades since their partnership began, they were truly in love. They were the closest thing to a family when it came to the pantheon of Gods.

Lunix gently pulled away from the embrace, giving Esolir a light smile before turning back to us. Her gaze shifted to Erathiel, as if noticing his presence for the first time. "This must be the famous Erathiel!" This elicited a nervous laugh from Erathiel and an indignant huff from yours truly.

A new melody drifted across the room, and Esolir's eyes lit up. "We must dance," he pleaded to Lunix with a hopeful expression. She nodded, and after a brief cheer, his attention reverted to Erathiel and me. "Will you two be joining us on the dance floor?"

"Not right now," Erathiel responded.

"Perhaps later," I added.

Erathiel eyed me for a moment, confused, then shrugged. "Perhaps."

Lunix glanced between the two of us, barely able to contain her laughter. "We will leave you two be. Please, enjoy yourselves tonight."

I led Erathiel away. After a period of silence that lasted far too long for comfort, I remarked, "We should speak to Stilis, you know, to congratulate sem."

"Yes," he agreed. We scanned the ballroom, then Erathiel asked, "Is that sem?"

Sure enough, there se was, looking more refined than ever and holding a glass of champagne. Stilis smiled when se spotted us approaching sem. "Auroleus, is that you?" se asked. "You are so grown!"

"As are you," I responded. "Congratulations, or, er...I am not quite sure what to say at this sort of event."

Se chuckled, mirroring my awkward nature. "'Congratulations' will suffice; thank you." Stilis turned ser head to Erathiel, then looked back at me after letting out a light gasp. "Are you two–" Se noticed me twitch my head in warning, then offered me a knowing smile. "Ah. I see." After a long beat of silence, se said, "It has been too long since we last spoke."

"It has," I agreed.

Erathiel cleared his throat. "Would you like to sit with us, Stilis?" he asked, gesturing to our table. "Auroleus mentioned that the company of the higher-up Gods is irksome, to say the least."

"Yes, feel free to sit with us," I said, more of a formality than an actual offer. To my surprise, Stilis nodded frantically.

"Yes, I beg of you, please. Do you know how many half-hearted 'congratulations' I have received this evening? Too many. I need an actual conversation with people who are not too self-absorbed to communicate with, thanks."

"Of course," I replied understandingly. We led him to our table, where another God accompanied Auri and Vesa.

Haneræs, the Goddess of Sand, was sitting at the table, fidgeting nervously with the silver rings on her dainty hands. She had sandy brown skin, her forehead and slate blue eyes dappled by starry white markings. Her pale blonde plaits fell down her shoulders, and she wore golden-and-white robes with strings of pearls. She was a year or so younger than I, yet her behaviour was significantly more refined.

"I apologise if I am intruding," she said in a gentle, smooth voice.

"Nonsense!" Auri insisted. She explained to us, "Sotis was making her uncomfortable. He is rather drunk."

My eyes widened in surprise; it took a great deal of alcohol to get a God drunk, but I would hardly put the notion past Sotis, known for his erratic behaviour.

Just then, Aestalios came bumbling towards the table, four glasses of champagne in each hand. "Drinks, anyone?"

Most of us happily took the drinks, except Haneræs, who remarked, "Most of us are not are not legal yet."

"And who is keeping track of that?" Aestalios retorted. Erathiel and I exchanged a glance, shrugged, and tapped our glasses together before taking a large drink. Aestalios nodded. "That's the spirit!"

He glanced back at Haneræs, then confirmed in a more reassuring tone, "Of course, you do not have to drink if it makes you uncomfortable." She nodded at him appreciatively.

Aestalios walked around the table to Erathiel and thumped him on the back, causing Erathiel to spit out some of his drink. "This is the pretty boy, then!"

"Are you...flirting with me?" Erathiel asked, which evoked a deep laugh from Aestalios and chuckles from the rest of the group.

"Alas, my attraction lies with the fairer sex." Aestalios turned to me, and in a quieter tone, he said, "He's a funny boy."

Stilis, after watching the exchange, whispered, "I quite enjoy the company of your group."

"Feel free to spend time with us more often; we enjoy your company as well."

Se smiled. "I might take you up on that offer."

For the next hour, we talked, whether about the affairs of the Gods or the state of mortals. Since I was most familiar with everyone there, I led the conversation, and I must say, I was quite the charlatan. I provoked laughter, deep thought, and a strong sense of kinship between the seven of us. However, I failed to notice Erathiel growing quieter as the night progressed. I failed to notice the way he watched my emphatic gestures, how the look in his eyes changed. Worst of all, I failed to notice how, after his breathing grew rapid and his eyes went glassy, he stood up from the table and left.

ERATHIEL TORE THROUGH THE CONFUSED crowd, interrupting several couples' choreography, and emerged outside the ballroom. He wound his way through the bookshelves until he reached a quiet corner. Clutching his temples, his breathing intensified as the memories flooded in. He tried to pretend these newfound feelings did not exist, that he was a completely normal person, and that everything was the same as it had always been, but it was impossible. Even his imagination could not will away this affection.

He heard the voices of Auri and Vesa calling for him. A few moments later, they were crouching next to him, Auri with her arm around his shoulders and Vesa drying his tears. "You disappeared," Vesa remarked. "What is wrong?"

Erathiel glanced around. "Is anyone else here?"

Auri shook her head. "No, it is only us, sweetheart. Please, confide in us."

After a deep breath, he managed to say, "I think I am in love with Auroleus," before bursting into tears.

A smile, half-excitement, half-compassion, spread across their faces. They exchanged a knowing glance, then turned back to Erathiel. "Okay. What would you like to do about it?" Vesa asked.

Erathiel paused. He was unsure. He could push the feelings away, find a wife, have children, and die successful, yet restless and unhappy. Even in the furthest depths of his headspace, he could not conjure a future without me by his side. "I desire to court him...perhaps. But it is impossible. We are two men—this is not to say that there is a problem with that in itself," he added after a pointed glance from Vesa, "but we would be rejected from human society."

"Erathiel," Auri said carefully, "is the company of mortals truly worth forcing yourself into this moral plight? We love you, platonically, and we enjoy your presence."

"Is this true?"

"Yes!" Vesa exclaimed. "And Auroleus does as well."

Erathiel's expression went cold. "What if Auroleus does not love me? He may not feel the same towards men, and besides, I am a mortal, and he is a God."

Auri and Vesa exchanged a look, remembering my two-year-long bout of desperation for Erathiel. "I am not sure that will be an issue," Auri replied.

He nodded, then asked, "How do I tell him?"

Vesa hesitated. "That, dear friend, is up to you. Perhaps you could ask him to dance, let the music guide you, and the rest will fall into place. Regardless, I believe you have a chance, a good chance, at that."

"Go to him," Auri added confidently.

Erathiel nodded, thanked them, and Auri and Vesa embraced him. Auri waved him away, the smiles on their faces the last thing Erathiel saw before he turned away and darted through the crowd to find me.

"Erathiel!" I exclaimed when he reached the table again. "You left. Is everything alright?"

"Would you like to dance with me?" Erathiel blurted. Aestalios dropped his drink and gaped, Haneræs let out an 'awh' noise, and Stilis audibly cheered.

In my state of surprise, I was barely in control as the word left my mouth. "Yes."

Erathiel took my hands and led me onto the dance floor. A slow melody was playing, with a familiar tune that invoked some sort of nostalgia in me. Erathiel and I started to dance, mirroring the couples around us. We had never danced before, but it was impossible to tell. Our bodies moved in perfect sync, gazes locked, souls intertwined. Throughout the dance, he appeared as if he desperately wanted to say something, but the words seemed to fail him.

Suddenly, I felt so small, so insignificant, in the crowd. Everything seemed to be closing in. There was suspense in every step, uncertainty with each motion, and yet, there we were, dancing all the same, our hearts rapidly in sync.

Finally, Erathiel seemed to find the confidence to speak. He moved closer, and his hands slid further up my arms. "You know, Auroleus, that I am not the best with words."

I looked deeply into his eyes. "Are the words truly needed?"

The cosmos stretched out infinitely above us, the stars themselves cowering in Erathiel's presence; they were dull compared to him. I gazed into his eyes, and he gazed into mine, and everything in the world was perfect. The universe was vast, and that was okay. Everything that was beautiful, every moment, every feeling, every urge, every word, every touch, came back to me, and any shadow of a doubt erased itself from me as one thing stood clear above all else:

It is him.

The tension had reached its peak, like two galaxies preparing to collide, like a wave in the height of its crescendo, and the fibres of the universe fell into place when his lips touched mine.

An overwhelming sense of passion flowed through my veins. He clutched the back of my head and pulled me closer. I gasped for air, then returned to his open embrace.

Seconds passed, or it could have been hours, I was unable to tell, and Erathiel pulled away and rested his head upon my shoulder. I gently lifted his chin, and we pressed our foreheads together as we finished the dance.

Adoration for Erathiel filled my mind, and my heart was reborn with every step. I wondered if, once we left the Library, would we be the same? Would he want me, truly want me, or was this just a moment of passion? I took a deep breath and cleared my thoughts. The future was uncertain, but wasn't it always? Erathiel was there, and so was I. In the grand scheme of the universe, we were where we ought to be.

Yes, it is him, yes, yes, yes.

Chapter Seven

AS THE NIGHT STARTED TO WIND DOWN, AURI stood up from the table. She tapped the side of her champagne glass to get the Gods' attention, cleared her throat, and started to speak.

"If I may have your attention." She paused for a moment, her eyes flitting around the now-silent room, then nodded in satisfaction. "On behalf of Esolir, Lunix, and Stilis, I thank you all for attending. This is a momentous day for the trio." Many Gods started to cheer, and Vesa started to speak once the applause died down.

"My partner, Auri, and I have been preparing something for quite some time now, and we have waited until tonight to announce it." She stopped to take a shaky breath. Esolir and Lunix gave her a reassuring look, and she nodded appreciatively. "We are going to Create a God."

The room erupted in cheers and 'congratulations.' Aestalios shouted, "Finally!" Haneræs clapped excitedly, Erathiel and I each embraced the couple, and Stilis looked unsure of what to do.

"Has the child been Created yet?" Anima asked. She and Aques exchanged a bittersweet smile, remembering their first Creation.

"Not yet," Auri replied. "We have decided we will wait...until tonight." She smiled at the crowd. "We wanted to Create the child here."

Many of the Gods clapped excitedly. I sat up in my seat; I had never witnessed the Creation of a God.

Auri and Vesa, hand in hand, walked towards the centre of the ballroom, the crowd parting to make room for them. They stood several paces apart, and the surrounding Gods kept some distance from the pair. Auri and Vesa outstretched their right hands towards each other, and suddenly, their eyes started to glow, a golden light came from each of their hands and created a large spark where the bolts met, and a strong wind erupted from the spark. Illuminated runes, including every Symbol of a God, were scattered around the room. They had passed the first phase of the Creation.

Their stares were locked, their expressions narrowed in concentration. A vine emerged from Vesa's chest and wrapped around the bolt of light she controlled. A rope of flames appeared from Auri's, and its motions mirrored the vine. I recognised this motion. They were combining their base elements (fire, earth, water, stone, or air) to Create the new God.

A gust of wind with purple fibres appeared from Auri's chest; she possessed two base elements. A spurt of water and a wave of stone pebbles emerged from Vesa's; she possessed three.

The elements seemed to successfully combine; they had passed the second and most difficult phase of the Creation process.

From there, all they were required to do was announce the name, sex, and element of their Creation, and the new God would appear before them. A Creation's element had to in some way relate to their Creator's, so I was curious to see what the Goddess of Dawn and the Goddess of Dusk would harness.

The first shock of the evening came when Auri and Vesa's voices boomed in unison, declaring the following words: "We hereby Create and bring into this world Temprysus, the God of Time!"

Let me take this opportunity to tell a story, a legend passed down between Generations. Before the Gods existed, everything was in chaos, left to the whims of nature. In the Mortal Realm, an exceptional human woman named Luxheia was raised in an impoverished village in Lenethaus. The newest threat to the kingdom: the light of the sun was going to consume the world. The light was approaching quickly, and Luxheia's entire village was blinded. The light threatened to destroy the village. Desperate to save her people, Luxheia used her immense courage to harness light.

Although it first seemed as if nothing had changed, the truth was soon clear: Luxheia had become the first Goddess. She, and she alone, could control light itself.

The mortals revered her. They created temples in her honour and began to worship her. However, the jealousy of some drove them into madness. They attempted to steal her power. Terrified, Luxheia created the Immortal Realm, a place where no mortals could enter.

One hundred years after the Immortal Realm was created, Luxheia was almost killed. An arrow pierced the veil of the Realm. Luxheia, intent on seeking justice, relentlessly pursued the person who had aimed at her.

She found Tenedius, a mortal man, whose envy of her power drove him to madness. She was going to kill him, but then saw his face. He was an angry, broken man, and he could not stop sobbing. She began to think of her own family, her former people, and realised how lonely she was, isolated in the Immortal Realm. Thus, she decided to help him become a God. With the aid of Luxheia, Tenedius became the God of Darkness.

As the two aged and their power grew, their figures becoming less and less human, they watched over the Immortal Realm, keeping the balance between light and darkness, between life and death. Soon, they realised that the world was still in chaos, and if the Gods could have more control, the Mortal Realm would gain a stronger sense of peace.

Thus, they Created Aques, then Anima, followed by Ignos, and subsequently Taarin, and finally Laphara. The Gods had more control over the elements. They were worshipped by the mortals, and Luxheia and Tenedius were revered as the rulers and Creators of everything. Soon enough, the Second Generation of Gods decided that the pantheon required more control to ensure stability, and thus, the Third Generation was Created, then the Fourth, and, with the Creation of Temprysus, the Fifth.

The purpose of sharing this legend? To convey the message that when a God is Created, the ability of that God, once under the whims of nature, would be under the pantheon's full control. With the creation of the God of Time, the Gods would have the ability to fully alter and potentially dismantle the fabric of the universe.

Although most people in the ballroom cheered in celebration, there were a few murmurs of confusion.

"The God of...*Time?*" Erathiel whispered beside me.

"Would that be considered overstepping on behalf of the Gods?" a voice (Lacaos, the God of Lakes) asked.

"Nonsense!" Sotis exclaimed. "Such a concept does not exist; the Gods require more power."

Taarin rolled ser eyes. "Sotis, can you manage to restrain your ego just this once?" se spat.

"You are not thinking of the future, Taarin," Sotis responded. "This newfound power will benefit the pantheon greatly."

"Yes, but at what cost?" Gala asked.

"Enough," Aques ordered, his commanding voice silencing the crowd. Although Luxheia and Tenedius held the highest jurisdiction over the Gods, they rarely made a public appearance, considering their lack of physical form. Thus, most public authority was in the hands of Aques, their eldest

Creation, giving him a sense of authority. "Conversations about the morality of this Creation will come in time. For now, we shall celebrate Auri, Vesa, and Temprysus, *not* debate ethics. That is all." With a swish of his cape, he stepped back beside Anima, who offered him a light smile.

There was a long moment of sustained silence, and the tension in the room was high. Finally, Esolir said, "Let us see the child, then!"

There, on the floor, peacefully laid an infant God. His skin was a deep shade of blue, and his entire body was covered in golden markings and runes. A single strand of gold-tinted hair grew from his small head, and his eyes were an icy blue. Particles of light left over from the Creation floated around him. From his appearance alone, it was evident: Temprysus would possess great power.

The crowd of Gods were all attempting to get a glimpse of Temprysus, peering over each other's heads. However, since the Ascended Gods were thrice the height of the Gods still on their first life cycle, they received the best view.

The infant rolled over slightly, revealing his wrist. Anima stared at it for a moment, then let out a shaky gasp. "Is that..."

Laphara, breaking her typical stoic demeanour, rushed over to Temprysus. The crowd jolted in surprise; this was very out of character for her. She grasped the infant's wrist, her gaze confounded, then she looked up and said beseechingly, "The Symbol of the Titans."

Every God in the pantheon had the Symbol of a Second Generation God on their wrist, every God except for Luxheia and Tenedius. They had a distinct Symbol: five circles interlocked. This Symbol was a signifier of their immense power, and no other God was known to possess this marking. After all, the power of Luxheia and Tenedius was immense and highly developed, so refined that they had completed their second life cycle and had become Titans.

The five circles, the Symbol of the Titans, were borne on Temprysus's wrist.

The rulers and Creators of everything, I thought as I took in a shaky breath. The child was incomprehensibly dependent; he was helpless, and he could not comprehend how much power he possessed. Then how, I wondered, could I be so terrified of a child? *His power will be unfathomable.*

Anima walked over to Temprysus, and there was genuine fear in her eyes. "She is not mistaken," Anima muttered, barely loud enough for the other Gods to hear her. "He bears the Symbol of the Titans."

"Impossible!" roared Ignos. "How can the child contain *this* much power?"

"We have not experienced this in millennia," Taarin said; even se did not care enough to snap at Ignos. "This must be cause for alarm, correct, Aques?"

The four other Second Generation Gods stared at Aques expectantly. Aques seemed to be struggling to speak; he had a precarious composure, and a glimpse of fear was present behind his eyes. Even Aques, figurehead of the Gods, was afraid.

He took a shaky breath, then said, "Auri, Vesa, I congratulate you on your Creation. Anima, Ignos, Taarin, Laphara, will the four of you join me in the conventions corridor?" He whisked the aforementioned Gods away.

THE FOLLOWING MORNING, I ARRIVED AT Thyrin Cove at daybreak. Oranges and violets slowly spread across the cloud-laden indigo sky as I perched upon a weathered stone. I toyed around with the wind, shifting it from one direction to the other, changing the speed, watching how the currents of blue light ebbed and flowed.

My thoughts were interrupted when Erathiel silently stood beside the rock, keeping a comfortable distance. "I arrived early to view the breaking dawn," he explained. He could not seem to meet my eyes. "I did not realise you would be here as well."

"I came for the same reason as you," I admitted. I stared at him for a good moment, then asked, "Why have you asked me here, then?"

His complexion grew red as he fidgeted with his hands. "I wish to ask you about...what happened between us yesterday night."

Before he could go on any further, I stood up and gently kissed him. I was worried that I had been too forward, that he was disinterested, and that was the reason he had brought me there, but frankly, I hadn't a care in the world. I had gone on far too long without expressing my love, and I was determined to show it at any given opportunity.

To my great relief, he hung his arms around my shoulders and leaned in. Once he pulled back, Erathiel said with a soft smile, "Well, I suppose that answers my query."

We laughed, then fell silent. I relocated my gaze to the sky and sat back down on the patch of stone. Erathiel sat next to me. I placed my hand on my leg, my last few fingers brushing his knee. He rested my hand upon mine, and I laid my head in the crook of his neck. "You have no idea," I whispered, "how long I have been waiting for this."

He faced me, surprised. "Truly?" I nodded. He chuckled to himself, then buried his head in my hair. "I have been waiting as well, I suppose. I could never seem to admit it to myself. Moreover, I am not a man of words, so I hadn't a clue how to tell you..." He trailed off, then kissed the top of my head. "I cannot describe to you how much this means to me."

I smiled. "Perhaps I can envision it."

Finally, the brewing storm broke, rain gently falling from the sky. Thunder rumbled in the distance, but we felt safe. I closed my eyes and stepped out onto the open beach, spreading out my arms and taking in the feeling of the rain on my skin. I took a deep breath, the scent of rain—petrichor—filling my soul. I was home.

Erathiel walked over to me, wrapping his arms loosely around my shoulders and pulling me into a kiss. I smiled between every small kiss, then placed my arms around his waist and lifted him up. His legs locked around my waist, and I spun around with him.

Finally, I set him down. Our foreheads pressed together, and we smiled. The sound of thunder grew louder, and he pulled away from the gentle embrace.

"Alright, alright, we should probably seek shelter."

We made to run towards the caves, then he stopped and gently caressed the side of my face. "I cannot express how...*elated*   I   am   that   you   are   here."

I began to pull him in for another embrace, then lightning lit a shrub ablaze. "We should be going."

"Yes, yes," he said hastily as we began to run for the caves.

In spite of the storm, I was filled with a sense of glee. Euphoria washed over my fear-ridden face. At last, we were together, and although he was a mortal and I was a God, the world could not break us apart.

"SO THIS IS THE BOY THAT DIVIDED THE pantheon," Erathiel   murmured,   holding   the   infant Temprysus in his arms. Auri and Vesa wanted to properly introduce the child to Erathiel and I, so they brought him to Thyrin Cove.

"He is," Auri replied, undertones of annoyance at the Gods in her voice. "Taarin and Ignos *still* refuse to speak."

"To be fair," Vesa kicked at the sand lazily, "they were never particularly on good terms."

"Ocari told me that they once refused to speak to each other for a century," I added.

"A century?" Erathiel exclaimed. "That cannot be!"

Auri was confused, then chuckled to herself. "I forgot that you humans view time as this massive thing. A century passes in the blink of an eye to an Ascended God; it is really nothing to them."

Erathiel's eyes were wide. "I often forget that Gods cannot die; not of old age, at least. You all seem so...human."

Vesa laughed, gently taking Temprysus out of his arms. "And *that* is why you never hear of humans befriending Ascended Gods...or elderly Gods, for that matter." She gestured to her mind. "The power gets to their heads. Their personality just...fades." She shrugged. "It is nature, I suppose. We younger Gods are far better company, anyway. We actually have souls."

Erathiel laughed anxiously. He turned to me. "That will not happen to you, will it?"

"Well, I—there is plenty of time before that happens, if it does at all, that is, I—"

"Auroleus, you do realise that that is *exactly* what Aques said before his Ascension," Vesa responded dryly. "You cannot tame the inevitable."

"Well, we have all the time in the world until that happens," I huffed.

"Until Erathiel dies," Vesa pointed out.

"Vesa!" Auri exclaimed.

"What? I am simply *pointing out the truth*," Vesa said indignantly.

"Can we move on from my lover's mortality, please?" I half-shouted.

"Lover?" Auri crooned. "So it is official, then?"

Erathiel began to nod, then I slipped into his lap and wrapped my arm around his shoulders. "Is it not obvious that I love this man?"

He turned to me. "You...you really–"

"Is this truly the first time Auroleus has said it?" Auri said, surprised. She and Vesa exchanged a look, then they both burst out laughing. "You may be the last to know, then."

I buried my head in Erathiel's well-sculpted chest in embarrassment. Erathiel ran his fingers through my hair gently and added, "Auroleus was attempting to keep his feelings concealed, you must respect him for–"

"Erathiel, do *not* act as if you had any clue," Auri protested. "If you knew he was in love with you, please explain why, at the Starlight Ball, you–"

"Enough!" Erathiel exclaimed, leaping over Vesa and Ttemprysus to cover Auri's mouth. The infant started wailing, and Auri could not resist the urge to laugh. She carefully took the infant in her arms.

I let out a dramatic sigh. "The Creation of Temprysus renders me ancient, I suppose," I remarked. When everyone else seemed confused, I added, "The older generation of Gods raises the younger ones, right? Temprysus marks the Fifth Generation. I will have to help raise Temprysus." I groaned. "Is this what getting old feels like?"

Auri and Vesa flashed me sceptical glances, but Erathiel let out a small yelp of joy. He explained, "If an older Generation raises a younger Generation, and I am courting you, Auroleus–" I could not help but smile, the fact that we were in a relationship was still very fresh, "–does that mean I can assist in caring for Temprysus? Can you call me his uncle?"

"I must admit, I haven't a clue what an 'uncle' is, but if you insist, sure!" Auri replied, clearly amused by Erathiel's enthusiasm.

There was a moment of silence as Erathiel stared at Temprysus. "He is special," he murmured. "Well, every God must be, I suppose, but he is different." He ran his finger along Temprysus's wrist, tracing the Symbol of the Titans. "You are going to change the world, won't you?"

"That is a nice message," Auri said, wrapping her arm around Erathiel. "Thank you."

"I am proving to be a great uncle, am I not?"

"That, you are, my love," I said, resting my head in the crook of his neck. "That you are."

"I love you," he murmured.

"I love you too. Gods, it feels so good to say. It has been pent up for so long...it is a relief."

"Good." He grasped my hand. "Then let us never cease to say it."

Beside me, Vesa took a deep breath. She gently placed the infant Temprysus into Auri's arms, stood up, then smiled back at us and said, "Dusk calls. Night is awaiting us."

She lifted her hands, a lilac-coloured Symbol of Aques lit up above her palms, and her eyes glowed a vivid shade of violet. She cast her hands towards the sky, and within a few minutes, shades of yellow and orange coated the sky.

Auri, Erathiel, the infant Temprysus, and I sat on the shoreline, hands and hearts connected, as we watched Vesa paint the sky with hues of dusk. A sense of serenity filled the air. I smiled. Everything was alright.

ALLOW ME TO DIVERT THE STORY FOR A moment. Let me paint a mental image, a view into another God's life.

In the Immortal Realm, there is a manor. Its walls of marble and pillars of gold catch the gaze of any God who passes by on the main street. Flowerbeds rest gently in front of the house, and a stone fountain depicting Aques sits above the front courtyard. The building, grand as it may be, is impersonal. Upon first glance, you would not discern it as the house of two of the most powerful Gods; rather, you would think of it as perhaps a town hall, a library, or an academy, somewhere more formal and prestigious than a quaint home.

If you go around the left side of the building and you walk a few paces, you will find that the manor borders a beautiful meadow. The grass, hues of cornflower and wisteria, is illuminated in the sky's lights and glows a shade of turquoise during twilight. Wisps resembling dandelion seeds ride the gentle wind, and trees of muted pinks and reds fleck the open field.

In the field, you may see bits of stone foundation, weathered and worn, once the substructure of a home. Notice the rooms: that one could have been a kitchen, that one might have been a bedroom, perhaps a nursery. The foundation itself was almost haphazard, clearly laid by someone inexperienced. Still, the ruins had heart, and an observer could instantly tell that this was once a hearty home, filled with warmth, pleasant food, and love.

Keep these two buildings in mind. They are not as distinct as they seem.

THE AIR WAS DENSE, MILDEW SPORES GENTLY wafting around. Erathiel stumbled into the manor, weary and sore. He had returned from his swordsmanship training, and his skills were subpar under the extreme heat, so his instructor drilled him vigorously.

He stumbled into the dining room, praying that the maids had cooked instead of Florian. Instead of seeing his family seated at the table, he saw their dishes sitting uneaten upon the wooden surface. Ilyara, a former maid and Florian's wife, was waiting quietly in the corner.

Erathiel took his plate, nodding his thanks to the maid, then, after a moment of uncomfortable silence, he asked, "Where are my parents? They should be here."

Ilyara cocked her head, confused, then gestured to her ears. Erathiel recalled that she was deaf, then signed, "Do you know where my father is?"

"He is outside," Ilyara signed, smiling; Erathiel's signing was rough, but she was grateful he remembered. "Some sort of protest has transpired."

"A protest?" Erathiel exclaimed audibly as he signed. "What—"

He looked out the window, and he saw a small mob of civilians of Chathan's social stature gathering. They were marching eastbound, towards the temple of Ocari.

He dropped his plate in shock. Chathan was never one to participate in protests. His tiredness left his body as he raced towards the assembling crowd. As he approached, he heard shouts of Sotis's name.

What quarrel could these people have with the God of Soil? he wondered.

He found his father in the crowd. "What is going on?" Erathiel asked.

Affronted, Chathan replied, "Have you seen our herb harvests this year? The reaping results of our town's farmers?"

"Sotis is to blame!" Tallis exclaimed. Tallis and his father, Variton, were standing next to Chathan. Erathiel was surprised to see Variton and Chathan together; they typically feuded often, but he supposed they were united over this common plight. "That scoundrel has no respect for us mortals!"

"Then why are we protesting? We should be worshipping Sotis, offering him more gifts," Erathiel responded. He believed Tallis's argument—Sotis was often unfavourable and merciless—but he was sceptical of their route of action.

"Nonsense!" Variton exclaimed. "He must prove himself worthy of worship! He must prove that he has mercy!"

The nearby crowd cheered, waving their weapons towards the sky. They began to chant: "There is no mercy at the hands of God! There is no mercy at the hands of God!"

Erathiel backed away from the crowd, terror tracing itself across his face.

This, he thought, *cannot lead to anything good.*

Chapter Eight

A YEAR HAD PASSED SINCE THEN. AEDIS'S warmth swept through the land, summer bringing new heat and tensions to Lenethaus. Erathiel was sixteen, I was seventeen, and we were closer than ever. Although Erathiel was growing busier, what with the apothecary and his lessons, and I was starting to gain more responsibility myself, we made the most of the time we shared.

Tensions between the mortals and the Gods had begun to escalate. Because of Sotis's refusal to provide decent harvests, many humans worshipped the Gods less and less, some ceasing worship altogether. Riots broke out in the streets, furious mobs making a mockery of the Gods. As a result, many of the higher-up Gods wrought terror upon Lenethaus. Wildfires and tsunamis were becoming more frequent. We Gods dismissed it as a bout of simple rage; after all, we were fully capable of crushing the rebellions if need be. However, certain Gods were growing paranoid. Ignos adamantly suggested that the Gods and mortals should even be separated, and he vowed to take drastic measures to ensure this was upheld. Erathiel and I, along with our friends, did not give much thought to the tension; we had more pleasant matters to concern ourselves with. However, during every interaction with the higher-up Gods, particularly Taarin, Ocari, and Gala, they seemed terrified, as if remembering a nightmare.

I had never seen my Creators afraid before.

I dismissed the notion. Everything was going to be fine. Nothing would go wrong, for how could it, when Erathiel and I were together?

"HELLO! I APOLOGISE FOR MY LATE ARRIVAL!" Aestalios exclaimed as he bumbled through the door. Auri, Stilis, and I had decided to assemble the group from the Starlight Ball again. We met in the Lunar Library observatory, the bookshelves and tables returned to their former locations. He took a seat next to Haneræs, accidentally brushing their arms together. "Sorry," he said. "How are you?"

She smiled and glanced down. "Quite well, thank you."

It was strange to see the two next to each other; they were both very present figures in my childhood, but Aestalios was quite boisterous, and Haneræs was more of a quiescent soul. I suppose they complemented each other, though.

"It is no problem, Aestalios, you are just in time to hear the end of Auroleus's story," Auri said with a smile.

"Oh, Gods," Erathiel mumbled.

"So, I dragged him in from the water, and keep in mind, he was absolutely out of control, he was flailing around like a ragdoll–" I said whilst making emphatic gestures. The group (besides Erathiel, who seemed embarrassed) was entertained; I had become quite the raconteur. "–and finally, he settles down, right, and he rests his head upon my chest for what I think may have been an hour." I shrugged. "As platonic friends do."

"Did you honestly have to tell *that* story?" Erathiel groaned.

I nudged him. "Of course I did."

"I am sorry if I am misinterpreting this," Haneræs began, "but Erathiel, do you honestly mean to tell us that you lived a ten-minute stroll away from Thyrin Cove all your life and yet you *still* have no clue how to swim?"

"Yes, how does that happen?" Auri chided.

"Can I be completely honest?" Erathiel asked. "Even if it means insulting one of you?"

"As long as I am not the God in question, then of course," Vesa replied.

"My father said that the water was dangerous because the tides were...'poorly managed.'" He gestured to Aestalios. "I grew up fearing the water; I worried that I would drown."

"Hey!" Aestalios exclaimed, pounding his fist on the table. "I am a very responsible God, I manage the waters well!"

"Yes, because *this*," Haneræs gestured to Aestalios's dishevelled appearance, "clearly proclaims 'responsibility.'"

Aestalios huffed and nudged Haneræs. "Stop," he groaned.

"In all seriousness," Stilis chirped, finally speaking up, "the two of you are perfect together." Se gestured to Erathiel and I, and he and I glanced at each other and blushed. "In all honesty, I must admit that I am jealous of your dynamic."

"Stilis, you will find a man perfect for you!" Aestalios exclaimed, thumping Stilis on the back. "Or a woman...or perhaps another Tryan, though I do not believe there are many of those in our Generation. Whatever your preference is, you will find someone!" Stilis gave him a grateful nod.

Erathiel wrapped his arm around me, then winced. "Are you okay, love?" I asked, worried.

He nodded. "I am fine; well, sore, but fine nonetheless. My combat instructor was unforgiving with his training yesterday."

"A combat instructor?" Auri inquired. She eyed Erathiel up and down, then said, "You are a swordsman, I presume."

"Yes," he responded, eyes lit up. "Are you interested in combat?"

"Interested in combat...you realise you are speaking with the *most* proficient melee duo in the pantheon?" Auri gestured to herself and Vesa. "We specialise in spears."

"Fascinating," Erathiel mused. "Forgive me if this comes off as ill-mannered, but you seem to lack the traditional build of a fighter."

"Pardon me?" Auri said, affronted. "I am plenty strapped, thank you! Here, let me just–" She gestured to Aestalios to come towards her. He stood up, and was obedient as Auri lifted him with ease. She held Aestalios, who was significantly taller than her and twice her weight, under his legs and around his midsection. Aestalios kicked his leg and flailed his arm out for dramatic effect, which sent Vesa reeling with laughter.

"I was mistaken, then," Erathiel laughed. He nodded to Aestalios. "What about you, then? You are quite the muscular fellow, you must engage in some sort of combat."

Aestalios shrugged. "I prefer to use my Godly abilities. I do pick up a mace now and again, though. I prefer bludgeoning combat, personally." He gestured to Auri. "Word of advice, human. Never underestimate this one. She will make you *beg* for mercy and apologise for doing it." Auri nodded fiercely, then set Aestalios down.

"Now, if you *really* want to challenge a God," Vesa said, gesturing to me, "I would recommend Auroleus."

"Hey!" I exclaimed.

"No, no, Auroleus is well built," Erathiel said, defending me.

Haneræs chuckled. "Compared to a human, perhaps. In the terms of a God, he is about as muscular as a loose twig."

Stilis choked. "Haneræs, that is *brutal*!" se exclaimed.

"Am I mistaken?"

Ser eyes flitted between Haneræs and I, then se shrugged. "Not particularly."

"The lot of you are traitors," I said, shaking my head in false disgust.

"Traitors who could best you in a physical fight easily," Aestalios quipped back. I sneered at him, and a grin lit up his face. "Even Erathiel could *demolish* you, I would wager it."

"All you need is training," Erathiel said, immediately coming to my defence. "You should attend one of my swordfighting practices"

I pictured it for a moment, then vigorously nodded. "I may be interested in swordfighting with you, yes."

He smiled. "Good."

"I would like to try to lift someone," Stilis remarked. "Haneræs, come here."

She looked sceptical for a moment, then shrugged. "If you insist."

Stilis lifted her delicate figure onto ser shoulders with ease, then ran with her around the room. Her excited yelps annoyed the few other Gods who were studying in the Library, but they did not seem to care.

"Erathiel, lift me!" I exclaimed. Erathiel mirrored Stilis's motion, and I yelled at him to 'run faster, run faster!' Aestalios soon lifted both Auri and Vesa onto his shoulders, then chased us around the room. We were all laughing and yelping, tagging each other as we ran.

Suddenly, Turri, the Goddess of Cyclones, and Fulir, the God of Lightning, entered the observatory and witnessed the chaos we had caused. Fulir burst out laughing, while Turri's face flushed a deep shade of crimson. Stilis turned around, noticed the pair, then, in shock, dropped Haneræs. Haneræs shouted expletives from the ground (quite out of character for her, if I may presume).

"Aestalios? What are you–" Turri pointed towards the door. "*Out.*"

Although the pair was hardly older than any of us, they were intimidating, and we obliged. Quickly, we raced outside the observatory, Auri and Vesa still on Aestalios's shoulders.

Laughing, we stumbled down the steps of the Lunar Library, delirious and struggling to get our footing.

Stilis, visibly lightheaded, stumbled and half-fell, half-sat on the stairs. The rest of us joined sem, and we clustered in a circle.

"I will not exaggerate," Aestalios said, still beaming with ecstasy, "this is the most enjoyable day I have had since the Starlight Ball."

"Agreed," Vesa added. "The Starlight Ball coterie is truly something to behold."

"The Starlight coterie...I do enjoy the sound of that," Haneræs said with a soft smile. "We really should meet up more often."

"Terrorising the poor scholars...I, frankly, am not opposed." Auri cracked a smile. She grasped Vesa's hand, and their fingers intertwined. Vesa hung an arm around Aestalios's shoulders, and he linked arms with Haneræs. I slid down and laid my head in Erathiel's lap, my elbow brushing Haneræs's. Stilis leaned ser back against Erathiel's side, and rested ser hand atop Auri's spare one.

I closed my eyes and breathed in, taking in the scent of nature and the people whom I cared for most. Something great was to come of that group, I could tell.

I WALKED AROUND ERATHIEL'S BEDROOM, examining every corner. It was rather cluttered, heaps of crumpled paper scattered across the wooden floor, but it felt lived-in, as if it was the studio of a great inventor who had only gone a *tad* bit insane.

The scent of tea drifted through the air; his brother, Florian, had prepared some before leaving to work at the apothecary. I had not yet had the pleasure of meeting Florian, as he had to leave quickly, but I hoped that I would be able to make his acquaintance soon enough.

I stumbled upon Erathiel's desk, and noticed drawings: some blueprints for mechanical animals he had yet to create, but most were drawings of people, places, some I even recognised as from Thyrin Cove. I was surprised at how skilful the sketches were; shading in all the right places, accurate linework.

"I did not know you were an artist," I remarked.

Erathiel was startled at my sudden speech (we had been silent for the last few minutes), but responded, "Yes, Florian taught me some time ago. I have been practising ever since."

"You should attempt to draw me sometime." I put on a pretentious face that highlighted my jawline. "Make me your muse."

"Oh, I could not think of it," he said immediately. "I would try to draw you, but the world's greatest artists could not capture your beauty."

It took every last bit of self-control to fight off an intense blush. I cleared my throat. "Even still, this is impressive," I said, gesturing towards his work. I took a seat, sitting backwards on the chair and hanging one leg over the backrest. "A craftsman *and* an artist. You are quite talented, you know."

He blushed and cracked a smile. "T-thank you."

I shot him a sly glance. "You must be good with your hands, then."

His face grew tomato red. Finally, he managed to stutter, "I—er —well—cannot say I have much experience with-"

I took a sip of tea. "It is never too late to try, now is it?"

He managed to croak, "I suppose not."

"Good." I continued to sip my tea.

After we finished our tea, we made our way down to the training grounds. Erathiel paused, then said, "One moment. Let me change into something more practical."

He stepped inside, and after a moment had passed, he re-emerged. He wore sun-worn taupe trousers more suitable for combat that were held up by leather brown suspenders. I had forgotten what he looked like without a shirt, and I have to give Erathiel credit, he was rather muscular, even when compared to a God.

"Alright," Erathiel said, approaching me. I tried to pay attention, but alas, my eyes had a difficult time remaining focused on his. "I will demonstrate a few basic motions first, then I will allow you to use a blade afterwards. I would rather you watch me perform the motions first before you start swinging around a sharp weapon." This elicited a nervous laugh from yours truly. He nodded, a small smile spread across his rose-tinted lips. "Watch me carefully; I will walk you through this again, but I would like you to try and retain as much of this as you can."

I stepped back, and he approached the sword rack. He securely clutched his blade of choice, then began to practise his footwork.

His blows were precise and calculated, yet impactful and loaded with force. There was a certain flight to his step, his advances and retreats airy yet effective, almost as if he was taunting this invisible enemy, and why would he not, when he could so clearly champion any foe? You could not convince me, I thought, that this man was not a God, from how his abilities were so refined.

Finally, after a successful lunge, he returned to his base position. He wiped his forehead and sighed, satisfied. Beads of sweat rolled down his back, and his hair was tousled. There was a certain gleam to his eyes that captivated me, fierce determination surging through his irises.

I could no longer resist. I approached him, avoiding going towards the sword rack entirely. "What are you—" His words were cut off as I grasped the back of his head, wrapped my arm around his upper back, and pulled him into a passionate kiss.

He could not seem to render what was happening for a moment, then he tossed aside the blade and pulled me closer to him. After moments of fervour and intensity passed, we could no longer do with simply standing there, could we? Still intertwined in a kiss, we found our way back inside the manor and slammed the door closed behind us.

As for what happened next...well, use your imagination.

TALLIS SLAMMED HIS FIST DOWN ON THE table. "A God of Time?" he exclaimed. "This is preposterous!"

"How could the Gods have the audacity to harness time?" Variton asked. "This is an overstep of power!"

Erathiel and Florian sat next to each other at the other end of the table. Their eyes flitted back and forth between Tallis, Variton, and Chathan, too anxious to speak. Neither of them were particularly fond of conflict.

"To be fair," Florian chirped, finally joining in, "the Gods always had the capacity to eradicate the human race. Ignos could start a wildfire, Turri could unleash a massive cyclone—"

"Do you not realise how different this is, you impotent child!" Chathan berated. "With control over time itself, the Gods can have the potential to take us down without a fighting chance—nay, eliminate humans from existence entirely!" Florian shrank back in his seat timidly.

"Consider this," Variton said after a moment. "We are only just discovering Temprysus's existence; he has been alive for two years. We have no idea what he has changed!"

Tallis's face went pale. He took a long sip of mead, then belched and proclaimed, "We will not stand for this!"

"Rebellions against the Gods have been rising throughout Lenethaus," Variton offered. "Perhaps we should consider joining."

"You do realise that the Gods have full capability of wiping out Lenethaus if they please?" Florian snapped. "I urge you *not* to give them a reason!"

"Do you stand for this, boy?" Tallis sneered.

"Of course not; not in any sense of the word! This is a breach of trust on behalf of the Gods; they have forgotten where they came from. I would simply implore you to be more calculated with this."

Variton nodded understandingly, but Chathan appeared angry. "Are you threatening to support the Gods in this?"

"No, I am not. *You* are simply too much of a dimwit to understand." Florian stood up as he spoke succinctly. "I am done having this conversation. Keep shouting, nothing will come of this other than the very outcome which *you* wish to avoid." He flourished his coat, turned on his heel, and left the room.

Tallis spat. "Forget him, then!" He gestured to Erathiel. "You have been awfully quiet, boy."

"I just cannot say I am surprised, that is all." Erathiel instantly regretted the words he spoke. Suspicion arose in Variton's eyes. Erathiel's cover was blown.

"Do you mean to say," Variton hissed, "that you somehow *knew* about Temprysus's Creation, and you did not tell us?"

"*What?*" Tallis bellowed.

Erathiel's silence answered the question. He tried to speak, tried to justify himself, but he was overwhelmed by nerves, and the words did not come.

"Listen," Variton snarled, standing up and pointing a finger at Erathiel, "I haven't a clue how you acquired this information, but–"

"You are a traitor to humanity!" Chathan bellowed. "Out!"

"But–"

Erathiel was cut off. "Out! Get out of this house, traitor scum!"

Erathiel, terrified, ran out of the house and into the crisp autumn air as fast as he could.

AURI AND VESA'S QUIET EVENING IN THE bakery was interrupted when Auri received a plea for help from Erathiel. Auri stood up suddenly and started to pace the room. "Are you alright? You are not in danger, are you?"

"What is happening?" Vesa asked. Prayers of any sort could only be heard by the God they were directed to, so she hadn't a clue as to what was going on.

"It is Erathiel," Auri whispered to Vesa before her attention reverted to Erathiel. "Okay, okay, we will be right there, do *not* panic!"

"Oh, Erathiel, is that the mortal boy?" Arberra, the Goddess of Trees and owner of the bakery, mused. She frowned. "Is something wrong?"

"His father evicted him from his home," Auri explained. "His cousin is trying to hunt him down, we need to get him to a safe place!"

"Take him to the Lunar Library," Haneræs suggested from another table. "Actually—wait, no, Erathiel is my friend, I will not leave him in danger! May I come with you?"

"Of course!" Vesa said. She threw coins down on the table to pay for their pastries, then stepped outside the bakery to create a rift, for ease of transport for the whole group. After the initial explosion of light and runes, a rift was created, the light around it slightly erratic.

Arberra dropped the tray of pastries she was carrying. "What is going on?" she exclaimed.

Without dawdling to respond, Auri, Vesa, and Haneræs leapt into the rift.

WITHIN A FEW MOMENTS, THE GODDESSES had brought Erathiel to the Lunar Library. They had figured that since it was inaccessible to mortals without the assistance of a rift, he would be safe from Tallis.

Erathiel thanked the trio profusely as they led him up the stairs. Lunix was positioned at the front desk and smiled warmly when she saw Erathiel.

"Erathiel! It is wonderful to see you!" Lunix chimed. As he got closer and she saw his dishevelled appearance, she frowned and appeared concerned. "You look terrible, is everything alright?"

Erathiel shook his head, but could not muster the words to explain. Haneræs helpfully said, "His father forced him out of his home."

"Oh..." Lunix trailed off, sympathetic. "Please, stay here! We can get you set up in a private study room, the sofa should be comfortable enough." She gestured towards the trio of Goddesses. "Will the three of you show Erathiel to the nearest available study?"

Vesa nodded, then led Erathiel down the second hallway to the right.

The hallway, trimmed with gold, had no comprehensible end. Rather than doors, the boundless hall was lined with rectangular veils of unpassable silvery mist with a similar texture to cobwebs, teal and violet lights pulsating underneath. Auri approached the first door on the left, lifted her hand to it, and a chime rang through the air as the Symbol of Anima illuminated and fizzled away. The veil faded, and behind it was a comfortable study.

The trio of Goddesses let Erathiel get comfortable and process his shock, and they fetched him a plate of freshly baked pastries (courtesy of Arberra, who sent her best wishes), a set of new clothes (tailored by Gala; they were intended for me, but it hardly mattered), and a warm quilt with careful floral stitchwork (quilted by Lunix, who personally delivered it to ensure Erathiel was alright).

Erathiel mumbled a 'thank you' to the trio for the gifts, but he was still quite reserved. Vesa and Haneræs, who were standing in the corner of the room, looked confused, but Auri, who leaned against the doorway, nodded her head in understanding. She took a few steps over to Erathiel, pulled him into a loose embrace, and Haneræs joined her. He took a deep breath, then smiled, and the pair let go. Vesa grasped his shoulder for a moment, gave him a sympathetic nod, and then the Goddesses left Erathiel alone.

Soon enough, Erathiel was wrapped in the quilt that was just a bit too scratchy, wearing clothes that were just a bit too oversized, eating pastries that had gone just a bit too cold. Once he could not will himself to eat any more, he laid down on the sofa that was just a bit too small to sprawl across comfortably, stared into the veil that was just a bit too strange for comfort, and breathed in the unfamiliar scent of the place that felt just a bit too different from his home.

Well, he supposed, *I never particularly considered it home.* But it was the place he slept every night for seventeen years, the place he trained without fail, the place his mind longed for when he was away for too long, the place where he had grown up, and that had to have meant something. It felt strangely material, mourning a house that was hardly home, but still, he mourned all the same. A sense of adomania filled his veins; he craved the simpler days, when he was only a child weaving crowns of flowers, wishing he could sleep in the stardust. And yet, now that he slept amongst the stars, he found himself yearning for land.

Even still, was this an improvement? Erathiel found himself waiting for the shouts of his parents, for the bickering of his siblings, for the drunken raving of his cousins, for a pounding on the door, a hand forcing him back, but it did not come. Instead, there was silence, which felt off-putting, but Erathiel figured that he would grow into it with time.

This is better, Erathiel gleaned. *It is not home, but this is progress towards it.*

So, Erathiel curled up, and as his mind willed himself to sleep, the lights in the room faded, and he drifted off in the place that was just a bit too alien to be home.

But it was closer.

Chapter Nine

FISYN PAINTED THE GENTLE WARMTH OF spring across the kingdom of Lenethaus. This year, the creatures of the forest were hesitant to leave their dens, almost as if they could sense something was wrong in the human world.

The protests had failed to cease. Even the noblemen, the people who were least affected by Sotis's wrath, were starting to riot. Worship for the Gods drastically declined, and a temple of Sotis was destroyed after the autumn harvest; Sotis failed to provide a good reaping. Taarin, Ocari, and Gala were no longer alone in their worries; all of the Second-Generation Gods had begun to fret.

Throughout all of this, though, the Starlight coterie had never failed to stay neutral, and we intended to keep it that way. Throughout autumn and winter, our main support was, of course, directed towards Erathiel, who was still residing in the Lunar Library and unable to return to his childhood manor. My deepest sympathies extended to him, but I must admit my selfishness: part of me was quite glad to be able to visit him more frequently.

Even still, most conversations with Erathiel felt almost stunted, as if there was something unspoken between us that we were both too cowardly to mention.

"HURRY!" ERATHIEL CALLED AFTER ME. I matched my pace to meet his. He smiled, then took off faster.

"Unfair!" I exclaimed, chest heaving as I tried to keep up.

Erathiel and I ran at full speed, trying to reach Thyrin Cove. The weather was finally growing warm, and Erathiel figured that Tallis had stopped searching for him, so we decided to visit Thyrin Cove.

We raced down the road, clouds of dust kicked up after us. The pathway to Thyrin Cove was in view, and we saw it—

Out of nowhere, our view was obstructed.

A protest marched up the street, shouting at the sky, at the Gods. Peasants and nobles alike joined together in defiance of their overlords.

One protester, likely a peasant, turned their head to face me. Their face grew pale upon comprehending my Godly status, then they exclaimed, "It is Auroleus!"

"What is a God doing in the Mortal Realm?" a burly peasant said threateningly.

"Is the Immortal Realm not enough for you?"

"We should rid this Godly scum from our plane," a nobleman, evidently the leader of the group, proclaimed. He turned to me, pointed a trembling finger, and exclaimed, "After him!"

Erathiel's hand slipped into mine, and we ran as fast as our legs would carry us. We slipped into the pathway to Thyrin Cove, gnarled branches scraping our sides as we ran. I turned to look behind; the mob still pursued us.

Finally, we emerged from the forest, and we were running along the coastline. Erathiel's limbs started to quiver, and I was growing weary. The mob shouted obscenities, cursed the Gods, but one taunt stood out to me above all:

"Is this human boy infatuated with him? Revolting! Kill the homosexual *along* with the God!"

I stopped in my tracks, a delirious smile spreading across my face. I gently pushed Erathiel behind me and slowly raised my gaze to meet theirs. Insatiable rage coursed through me. As soon as their eyes locked onto mine, the Symbol of Aques appeared before me and let out a chime. I seemed to grow slightly in size as a wind coursed through my hair. The veins in my body lit up with a golden hue, and my eyes glowed a solid blue. I began to levitate, the air in the vicinity growing heavier.

"You can curse my name," I spoke in a deep, broken register. "You can taunt my presence. You can disrespect the Gods themselves. But you will never, *never!*, speak a *single* ill word of my love." I raised my hands, the Symbol of Aques swelling and trembling between them, and unleashed a mighty gust of wind that sent the mob into the ocean, further than the horizon line could reach.

My feet reached the ground once more, the effects of the rage fading. Erathiel's mouth gaped in shock. "What was that?"

"Godly Wrath," I explained. "When a God reaches an intense point of anger, they enter a powered state–"

"Yes, yes, what I mean to say is, what have you done? You cannot let them die!"

"But–"

His voice lowered as he gripped my arm. "If we let them die, what separates their cruelty from ours?"

I let out a wavering sigh, then closed my eyes, the Symbol of Aques appearing between my hands once more. I concentrated on their presence, pinpointed their location, and summoned a strong wind to carry them to the nearest island. "There," I said once I was sure they had reached land. "They are alive. They will have to fend for themselves, but they are breathing."

"Good," Erathiel sighed. He took a few deep breaths.

After a sustained moment of silence, I asked, "Are you angry with me?"

He rested his head on my shoulder and pulled me into a side-embrace. "No," he whispered. "You were only defending us."

I smiled, then crumpled into his arms. "I am exhausted," I managed to groan. "May we sit somewhere?"

"Of course," he murmured. He took a step back and extended his arm. I intertwined my arm with his, and he led me towards the forest.

He sat and leaned against a tree, and I collapsed into his lap. I moved my legs into a seating position, then flung my arms around his neck and leaned against his chest. "I feel terrible," I groaned.

He tilted my chin up. "Why?"

"If you hadn't intervened, I would have killed those people."

Erathiel shrugged. "Maybe...regardless, you were defending me, defending *us,* and that must be worth it."

"Could you hold me closer?"

Before the words finished leaving my mouth, I already felt his warmth.

I WOULD LIKE TO SPEAK OF THOSE BUILDINGS again, the manor and the ruins.

Let me take you back to five thousand years ago, when Luxheia and Tenedius's Creations were still in their developmental years.

Aques, the eldest Creation and the God of Water, was a rather cautious child. He always watched his step as he traversed the forest, checked the balance of a bridge before he crossed it, and made sure to wear clothes suitable for the day's weather.

Anima, second-eldest after Aques and the Goddess of Air, was an adventurous soul. She was never afraid to take a risk, whether it be swinging between trees, swimming in rapids, or climbing so-called insurmountable towers. She was scraped and bruised many a time as a child, but she always had a keen proficiency for healing herself in these trying instances.

Growing up, Aques and Anima were especially close. Normally, Aques had difficulty feeling anything other than fear and nerves, but around Anima, there was a sort of spark, something that pushed him to dare defiance and to take a chance. Conversely, being around Aques made Anima more grounded, in a sense. Above her Creators, above the mortals, even above herself, Aques was the only person she ever seemed to worry about.

Throughout most of their formative years, they had this sort of unspoken fondness for each other. Their love, at the time, had an innocence and pureness that would make even the coldest heart melt.

Finally, when they turned eighteen and came of age, they began courting. Their relationship was timid and carefree simultaneously; neither of them had experience with a relationship, so they had no semblance of a clue as to what they were doing, but they loved each other, and that was all that mattered.

I would implore you to keep in mind that at this point in history, the only Gods in existence were Luxheia, Tenedius, and their Creations. Seeing as Luxheia was too concerned with the affairs of mortals, being not only the Goddess of Light, but of Life, and that Tenedius had a very reclusive nature, being not only the God of Darkness, but of Death, their five Creations typically spent most of their time around humans.

Naturally, Aques and Anima began to look forward to the milestones that were expected of a human relationship, seeing as they were so exposed to mortals.

Because of this, their wedding ceremony was grand, and all of Lenethaus was in attendance. Just after the ceremony had ended, Aques and Anima began to build their home from the ground up. Now, they knew next to nothing about architecture, so the building was arbitrary and disorganised, but it was their home.

Aques always seemed to be keen on a clear and consistent plan; thus, he and Anima had their life planned out. They were going to Create multiple Gods, and unlike how Luxheia and Tenedius treated Aques and Anima, they were going to care for the Creations as if they were the couple's children. They were going to be a family. They were going to grow old together.

Aques and Anima were thrilled; they could not wait.

AFTER CHECKING TO ENSURE THE STREET was devoid of protesters, Erathiel and I walked down the street towards Thyrin Cove. Erathiel paused in his tracks and inhaled. "Do you smell smoke?" he asked.

I sniffed. There was the faint scent of smoke, but we were near a village around suppertime, so there was bound to be someone cooking. "It is nothing, I am sure of it," I answered. "Come, now. Let us keep going."

There was a sinking feeling in my stomach as we approached the cove. The scent of smoke was growing stronger.

As we arrived at the pathway, our worst fear was brought to reality.

The entire forest was reduced to ash.

We walked through the forest. What had once been a forest of plenty was now a smouldering flame. The cherry trees had been charred, the remaining stumps a charcoal colour. Dust and ash tainted the grass, and the incinerated corpses of small animals littered the decrepit field of view. A sense of poignancy filled Erathiel's soul as he gazed upon the banjaxed scene.

"No," I muttered as I picked up a handful of ash. "No, no...who could have–" I looked up, clenching my fist. "Ignos."

I stood up and immediately went into Godly Wrath. I recalled a meeting among the Gods, where Ignos made the statement that humans and Gods were not to intermingle. Was this his way of punishing me? Although he was a mortal, and I was a God, Erathiel was my beloved, and nothing could separate me from him.

The memories flooded back. A day at the beach, ice skating, fireside nights, a mechanical bird, two ships floating in the water, curiosity turning to friendship turning to love that stood in defiance of all odds.

The memories were reduced to ash.

"I am going to kill him," I hissed.

Erathiel ran after me and grasped my arm. "Auroleus–"

"Do not touch me!" I shouted, swinging him off me. He stared after me for a moment as if I were a stranger, then I could not bear to meet his gaze any longer. I distilled into light and reached the Immortal Realm.

I appeared outside Ignos's cave. The rage in my veins was only growing stronger, and I was more than prepared to kill him.

Once I reached the entrance, though, my legs could not support me any longer. I trembled, then collapsed against the cave walls and began to sob uncontrollably.

Why must our place of safety have failed itself?

ERATHIEL PUSHED OPEN THE HEAVY DOOR OF the dining hall. He had returned to his childhood manor to visit Florian. Of course, he had to ensure that Variton, Chathan, Tallis, and Tallis's brothers were absent, but he was pleased to see his brother.

"Erathiel! Please, take a seat! I've cooked supper," Florian said, ushering Erathiel into a chair. The dinner served was a concoction that vaguely resembled stew, but Erathiel was not quite sure. He took a bite, forced it down his throat, and gave Florian a wavering smile.

"Erathiel, I must inquire, where have you been staying?" Florian asked, taking a seat across from Erathiel. "Tallis must have searched everywhere."

Erathiel was hesitant to reveal his location, but he trusted that Florian would not reveal it to his family. "I have taken up residence in the Lunar Library."

Florian's eyes widened. "I recall you mentioned you were close with a God—Auroleus, was it?—but I did not realise he would allow you to live in the Immortal Realm!"

"The Lunar Library is easier for mortals to access," Erathiel explained. "All a God needs to do is create a rift, and a mortal can enter. Esolir and Lunix specifically constructed it to be a space for both mortals and Gods."

"So it is impossible for a mortal to enter the Immortal Realm?"

"Not necessarily," Erathiel admitted, "but it is difficult. Have you ever seen a God distil into light to transport to the Realm?" Florian nodded. "A mortal holding onto the God can travel to the Immortal Realm, but the God must be willing and able to transport them."

"I see." There was a moment of silence between them, then Florian gently said, "I have missed you in your absence."

Erathiel sighed. "I have missed you, but only you. I am not safe here."

Florian walked around the table to where Erathiel was sitting, and he wrapped his arms protectively around Erathiel. "You do realise," he spoke softly, "that I will fend off every demon and beast for you?"

Erathiel eyed Florian skeptically. "The only 'demons' I need to fear are in our family."

Florian shrugged. "Perhaps the worst demon of all is the human soul."

Erathiel hugged his legs, and Florian cradled him closer. "Why must the world fall apart as soon as I get myself together?"

Erathiel started to cry, and Florian gently stroked his hair. "Fate is cruel, I know, I know."

"Does...everything work out, Florian?"

Florian paused, a bitter expression creasing his face. Erathiel did not need to know about the stab wound below Florian's belt, nor would he ever learn. "Maybe. No matter where you end up, though, please understand that I will always be here to support you." Florian was beginning to cry himself, but he masked it so that Erathiel would not learn. "I am not going anywhere."

"Thank you." Erathiel wiped his nose. "Genuinely. I am lucky to have you as a brother."

Florian winced, then held Erathiel tighter. "Of course."

A TRANQUIL AURA DRIFTED OVER THE LUNAR Library. The Starlight coterie gathered around a table, making light chatter. Stilis was reading a scroll, Haneræs cradled Temprysus, and Erathiel and I sat in uncomfortable silence. In another corner of the Library, Fulir sat atop a table, and Turri sat in a chair directly next to him. They spoke in a low register, their faces pressed together. Sitting cross-legged on a window seat, Lunix stitched a cream-and-rose quilt while Esolir talked her ear off about a book he had recently read. At the centre table, the group of Gods that controlled the seasons (Fisyn, Aedis, Auxra, and Hithar) made pleasant, almost flirtatious, banter. The group appeared rather close.

An awkward silence hung between Erathiel and I. We had not spoken since I threatened to kill Ignos.

Finally, I turned to him. Erathiel spoke, his expression unreadable. "So, you have finally decided to speak to me?"

I sighed. "I apologise...for everything. I was upset. I should not have caused such an outburst." My gaze met his hopefully. "Will you forgive me?"

He paused, then smiled. "Of course." His fingers twined with mine. "After all, we don't have eternity."

I grinned back. As I was about to say something, Auri interrupted me. "If you two would have the goodness to *stop* acting so depressed, that would be wonderful, thank you!"

"Besides, Stilis was about to tell us something," Aestalios added. He turned to sem expectantly. "Well?"

Stilis gave Aestalios a long glance, then shook ser head. "Never mind."

Aestalios shot Erathiel and I a pointed look. "Well, you just ruined the moment, didn't you?"

Erathiel blushed sheepishly. "I apologise," he muttered.

There was a long moment of silence, then Vesa said, "Quite honestly? I am in the mood to disparage someone."

Auri hit her partner's arm. "Vesa! We cannot start a tirade, not in front of Temprysus. What kind of person will he grow up to be?"

Vesa shrugged. "What?" she responded innocently.

"If you would like to speak of scandal," Aestalios began in a hushed tone. He gestured to Turri and Fulir.

I widened my eyes. "Turri? Truly?"

"You had a sort of childhood rivalry with Turri, did you not?" Stilis asked me.

"Oh, I would like to hear about this!" Erathiel exclaimed.

"It was simple. She was the eldest Creation of Gala, and I was Created soon after her. We each had a lot to live up to in our own right. She was strong-willed; she bested every trial that came her way, filled her title well, and I...well, clearly I did not. There is a reason that I have very few temples in my name."

The frivolities of the Gods went far over Erathiel's head, but he gave me a look of pity all the same.

"Unfortunate. I must admit, I never spoke to her much, and for good reason, too. She is far too ostentatious to sustain a conversation with," Haneræs complained. She glanced at Aestalios. "So? What scandal surrounds her?"

"Well, first, I want to start this off by clarifying something to our friend who may be less *well versed* in terms of more unspoken Godly matters," Aestalios began. "Gods cannot...necessarily...force marriage upon anyone. You mortals often arrange marriages, which makes sense, since your time is limited, but when you are a God, you might as well marry for love." He shrugged. "Even still, seeing as Turri is the eldest Creation of Gala and I am the eldest Creation of Ocari, *every* Creation of Aques or Anima has been trying to push us into getting married."

"Really?" Auri asked, shocked. "How have I not heard of this?"

"Esolir never particularly pushed it, I suppose," Aestalios replied.

"Even still, how long has this been going on?" Haneræs asked.

Aestalios let out a melodramatic groan. "Since we were *infants*, I tell you! All my life, there was never a proposed future without Turri."

"Is that a future you would desire?" Stilis asked.

Aestalios vigorously shook his head. "Absolutely not! Turri is far too tasteless to earn my hand. Even still, she is possessive of me to no end. The fact is simple: she needs me to sustain her respect, I have earned that right on my own."

"So you would desire a paramour, then?" Haneræs inquired.

Aestalios leaned closer to her so that Turri would not hear from where she sat at the other side of the Library, then he muttered, "Absolutely. Preferably a paramour with personality, thanks."

Stilis nudged Aestalios. "Do you have anyone in mind, then?"

Aestalios shrugged and grinned at sem. "Perhaps."

"Would Turri be angry if you took up a paramour?" Erathiel asked.

"I believe she would be resentful, but only because she is so damned possessive over me." He cast a glance at Turri across the room. "If she were to be angry, she would be a hypocrite. Turri and Fulir have been courting for ages." He eyed Fulir up and down as he chattered away at Turri. "Truthfully, I feel sorry for him. He is unafraid to be vocal about their relationship. She, however..." Turri pulled on Fulir's collar, insisting that he 'quiet down.' Aestalios cocked his head. "That about represents their dynamic."

"Tragic," Vesa whispered, shaking her head.

As if on cue, Turri marched over to Aestalios, a warm smile plastered across her face. "Aestalios, come with me, will you, my dear?"

Aestalios stared at her skeptically for a moment, then decided to make a mockery of her. "Of course, my friend. Let me just..." He kissed Stilis on the cheek, causing sem to blush a crimson red (very significant, seeing as Stilis had deep purple skin). Turri was furious, but took Aestalios's arm all the same and walked with him outside the Library.

Erathiel glanced at Fulir. He looked abandoned, almost like a lost child. He seemed not to have noticed Aestalios's exchange with Stilis, for he was very downcast. After a deep breath, Fulir regained his composure and walked over to a bookshelf as if nothing had happened.

A few moments later, Aestalios rushed into the library, hair windswept and face panic-stricken. "Auri...Vesa..." he panted. He pointed outside the library. "Luxheia...bring Temprysus."

"What—"

Auri's speech was interrupted as the group turned their heads to face the windows.

A blinding golden light emanated from a swirling vortex of substance and particles, a shape and form too complex to fully comprehend. Resting above the shape, there was one singular gigantic eye, which had two silky golden cloths bandaging it.

Luxheia, the Goddess of Light, Life herself.

Auri, in a fear-stricken state, ran with Temprysus outside the Library. Vesa stood up, exclaiming, "What does she want with Temprysus?" She soon ran after her partner.

Erathiel stood up. "Stay here," he commanded, as if he would fare any better against Luxheia than any of us. I obeyed, as did Haneræs and Stilis, as Erathiel ran outside the library.

The mass force around Luxheia surged, nearly causing Erathiel to lose balance completely. He managed to make his way over to where Auri and Vesa stood. "What do you want with our Creation?" Vesa bellowed.

In a booming voice that sounded feminine and so calm to the point of boredom, Luxheia said succinctly, "Because of the escalation with the humans and the potential that your Creation possesses, Tenedius and I have decided that we shall be the ones to raise the God of Time. We will train him properly to benefit the Gods as we see fit."

"We cannot let this happen!" Auri demanded. "He is our Creation, and he shall be raised by the Fourth Generation, as he was always intended to be!"

Vesa gripped Auri's arm as the swirling around Luxheia intensified. "We should not resist," Vesa uttered. She glanced up at Luxheia. "Lest this lead to our demise." Auri looked at her partner and sighed. Vesa held Auri's shoulder and nodded. "It is worth it; I cannot lose you."

With a shaky voice, Auri held Temprysus up to Luxheia. "We offer you our Creation, Temprysus, the God of Time."

A spiralling golden light swept down to the couple, wrapped around Temprysus, and pulled him towards Luxheia. Once he was inside Luxheia's vortex, Auri managed to breathe, "Take care of him...please..."

Luxheia nodded. Her voice grew sympathetic, almost sorry for the couple. "Of course. I sincerely apologise that it came to this."

With that, she dissipated into golden light.

Auri could no longer stand. She collapsed to the ground, sobbing uncontrollably. Vesa and Erathiel immediately wrapped their arms around the Goddess of Dawn. Vesa tried to console her lover, but she was rendered speechless herself, so she merely clutched her tighter.

Erathiel managed to say, "He will be alright. The Titans will take good care of him, I am sure of it."

Auri gave him a bittersweet smile. "Thank you, Uncle Erathiel." She burst into sobs and could speak no further.

As Erathiel held Auri, staring off at the space where Luxheia had just been, a dark expression creased his face.

The conflict with the humans was escalating to the point that the God of Time needed to be trained by the Titans.

This, he deduced, *cannot end in peace.*

Chapter Ten

ERATHIEL, VESA, AND I CROUCHED OUTSIDE the Library window. "How long is this going to take?" I groaned, sitting up a bit.

"Hush, they might notice you!" Vesa chastised, pulling me down.

It had taken months, but Erathiel, Vesa, and I had finally convinced Aestalios to confess his attraction towards the person he desired to be his paramour. We still had no idea who the person was (Aestalios was very reluctant to tell us), but we knew they were in the Starlight coterie.

"Will this change things?" Erathiel whispered. "In our group." If Aestalios was rejected, then a cumbersome lull would hang over the coterie. If Aestalios was successful, then that would leave one member of our group single.

"No, no, I would imagine not," I said reassuringly, although I was having the same doubts myself. I perked up. "There he is!"

Aestalios entered the library with another person. Unfortunately, we could not see who they were; our view was obstructed. The library was fairly empty; only Anima, Lunix, Aestalios, and his secretly beloved.

"Who is he with?" Vesa asked.

"I cannot see!" I complained. Aestalios started to talk. "Gods, why are we unable to hear him?"

"Because the glass is denser than you," Erathiel said, hitting me gently in the back of the head.

"Hey!" I exclaimed.

Erathiel gave me an affectionate stare. "Do not worry, love. I have enough brains for both of us."

"Will you two stop flirting?" Vesa asked indignantly. "I am trying to focus!"

Erathiel muttered an apology and watched Aestalios. Aestalios, who was doing a splendid job of masking his anxiousness, spoke for a few moments, then met the other person's eyes hopefully. Based on Aestalios's demeanour, his tone was a perfect balance of emotional and succinct; Erathiel assumed it had gone well.

To the eavesdropping trio's delight, they saw Aestalios's face light up. "Yes!" I exclaimed. Aestalios pulled his partner into a kiss, and even Erathiel appeared surprised at the person's identity.

Haneræs?

In a sense, he was surprised, but in another sense, he was not. The two had very opposing personalities, but he supposed that they were each other's contingent. Erathiel softly smiled. They would be a wonderful couple, he could tell.

"Good for them!" I exclaimed.

Vesa looked confused. "To be frank, I honestly expected—you know what? Never mind. I am happy for them."

After a few moments, Erathiel, Vesa, and I entered the Library and took a seat at a table nearby. "Finally!" I exclaimed. "It took you long enough!"

"At least I attempted to be discreet," Haneræs teased. She nudged Aestalios. "In retrospect, I am *clueless* as to how I did not realise your affections."

Aestalios gasped, fake-offended. "How *dare* you?"

Vesa eyed the pair, then asked, "You two won't be 'unable to keep your hands off each other' like these queer folk, right?" She gestured to Erathiel and I.

"Rude!" Erathiel exclaimed.

"Well, I mean..." I trailed off. I was fully draped around him, sitting on his lap with my legs tangled around his, and my arm hung on his shoulders. "She may be correct."

Erathiel shrugged. "Perhaps." He and I chucked lightly.

Vesa gestured to us. "Do you see what I have to put up with? This is the paragon model of what *not* to be."

Erathiel gave an obscene gesture to Vesa, who smiled. He turned to Aestalios and Haneræs, then said, "I am happy for   you   two,   you   know?"

Aestalios let genuine emotion slip through his confident demeanour. "Thank you," he said earnestly. "You know, we should get Auri and Stilis here, gather the coterie again–"

Just as Aestalios prepared to summon Auri and Stilis, footsteps sounded at the door.

"Anima! Help!" a voice exclaimed. It was Turri, who ran through the door holding Fulir. "Fulir has been attacked!"

Erathiel had never seen ichor, the blood of the Gods. It was a golden substance with a thick, milky texture, with a sheen that made it appear as if it was glowing. It was entrancing, mesmerising its onlookers. Fulir hung pathetically in Turri's arms, and as Erathiel gazed upon the ichor, he had to wonder who could have been so cruel as to spill something so pure, so illustrious.

This can mean nothing good.

"He was assaulted by the humans," Turri spat, giving Erathiel a vengeful look, as if he had personally spilt the ichor. Her expression slipped into hysteria once more, and she cried, "Anima!"

Anima   instantly   appeared   at   Turri's   side, simultaneously soothing the Goddess of Cyclones and examining Fulir's wounds.

"He will be okay," Anima said as she began to stitch up Fulir's wounds. "It is just a few gashes, I promise–"

"This is not normal!" Turri exclaimed, Fulir's blood tainting her hands. "The humans have not spilt ichor since–"

"Hush, let me concentrate." Anima finished stitching Fulir's wounds, then said, "I am nearly done, I–"

A message transmitted to the Gods cut across Anima's speech. In a calm, unwavering voice that I recognised as Aques, the message communicated:

"This is Aques, the God of Water. The ichor of a God has been spilt. The Immortal Realm has entered a state of emergency. Until the state of emergency is lifted, no being will be admitted entry to either the Immortal or Mortal Realms. I will be in conference with Luxheia and Tenedius to discuss further action. Up until then, the Immortal Realm is on strict lockdown."

A TENSE MOOD HUNG OVER THE LUNAR Library. I hyperventilated in Erathiel's arms as he asked Anima what seemed like a million questions. "What is going on? When will the lockdown be lifted? Can we communicate with Aques?" Anima hovered with her Symbol between her hands as she tried to reach Aques, but there was only a low, nearly melodic, hum.

Fulir, who was slumped against the wall, reached out pathetically for Turri, but she acted as if she did not notice him. "Aestalios," she muttered, approaching him. She twined his arm with his. "You are–"

"Stop," Aestalios said, pulling away from Turri. She gave him a pained look, and he stared back at her with cold eyes. "Simply stop." Aestalios walked over to Haneræs and twined his fingers round hers. Turri took great care to ensure that Fulir did not notice the exchange, then sat near Lunix and

Vesa, who were making nervous conversation. The pair edged away from Turri.

There was a long moment of bitter silence after Anima ceased her attempts to reach Aques.

"So," Erathiel finally began, nodding to Fulir. "What happened?"

It was only then that I realised what a terrible state Fulir was in. His skin looked drained and pale, the light pulsating in his hair significantly slower. The aura of static around him was severely diminished, and his expression was dazed, almost delirious. His speech was slurred and hoarse, his demeanour exhausted and drained. Although not much of his ichor was spilt, ichor was the life force of the Gods. Even a few drops spilt, especially from a God on their first life cycle, were capable of weakening the deity.

"A human riot assaulted me," Fulir managed to utter. "I failed to pay attention—I was in a temple, I thought I was safe—"

"Stop talking," Anima said, hushing the feeble God. "You are hysterical; keep moving, and you are bound to tear something." Fulir slumped against the wall again.

Erathiel and I exchanged a horrified look. He and I had the same thought, I could tell: what would this mean for us?

If these riots continued and the Gods escalated, would Gods and mortals be cut off from seeing each other? Would the veil of the Immortal Realm be thickened so that no one could cross? Would Erathiel and I be prohibited from meeting up?

As the future we had together seemed to slip through my fingertips, I clutched onto any semblance of hope I could. Aques was a fair, reasonable man, and Luxheia would ensure the most honourable solution to this plight. Even if Tenedius fought for genocide, chaos, and partition, Aques and Luxheia's rationale would outweigh his haywire mentality.

Nothing could separate Erathiel and me, and I was sure of it.

So, imagine my shock when a message was transmitted to the Gods, a sentence that would seal eternity:

"After careful consideration, the Gods have decided to invoke warfare on humanity."

It had come to the worst.

THE WORDS FAILED ERATHIEL.

His headspace was vast, his imagination boundless, but in all the corners of his psyche, he could not possibly conjure the thought that war between humans and Gods was possible, let alone probable.

I managed to let out a few sputtering noises, then held Erathiel tightly, as if I were grasping the precipice of a cliff as I dangled off its edge.

The only person in the Library who managed to speak was Anima, who, just after the initial shock, demanded that Aques 'come to the Lunar Library this instant, the confusion you have caused is immeasurable, and we deserve answers.'

As if on cue, Aques appeared before Anima. "I apologise for the confusion, truly, I do—"

"Save it," his wife snapped. "So. Is this something they have initiated, or are we invoking war on the species we vowed to protect?"

"I—"

"Will we be assuming a defensive position, or is this some poorly disguised attempt at genocide?"

"It is—"

"You realise that if we attack, they will be annihilated, the species itself eviscerated!"

"Will you let me speak for one moment?" Aques

bellowed. Anima was silent. Aques took a deep breath, his calm yet wavering tone continuing. "Thank you. We *will*, in fact, be assuming a defensive position. The intent of this war is not to exterminate the race, but to get them under control."

"And what, pray tell, is the cause of this?"

"Many things," Aques admitted. "This is all fueled by Sotis's ignorance of the humans' pleas for a decent harvest." Erathiel and I exchanged a grim look. "Their tensions with the Gods picked up, of course, when Temprysus was Created." Vesa looked at the ground, a bitter look—not quite guilt, something else—creased her brow. "This all reached its peak yesterday, when the king issued a statement, saying that if we are to have no mercy on them, neither will they upon us."

"They will lose immediately if we attack them."

"I know," Aques blurted instantly. He and his wife exchanged a look of mutual remorse. "But we cannot go on like this forever. These mutinies, the uprisings, now attacks? This is too much for us to handle."

"We will only attack once provoked, yes?"

"Of course," Aques said darkly, "but do not expect the mortals to come quietly. They are cleverer than they seem, and their blades are sharp with vengeance. They will not relent."

I began to hyperventilate. Everything was just starting to go right, all for it to collapse once more. For the first time in my life, I comprehended my mortality.

I looked at my lover. "We don't have eternity."

"We never did."

"Our days are numbered."

"They always were."

"Why must there be an end?"

"Can you just kiss me?"

"Alright."

He pulled me into a kiss, and Aques's debriefing ceased for a moment. Aques gave Erathiel a sympathetic look, then said, "You had best be getting back to the Mortal Realm. It may be in your best interest to stay there."

I gently pulled away from Erathiel, then slowly turned my head to Aques. I looked at the God—who was much larger and more capable than I—directly, which was difficult seeing as he had numerous eyes. Even still, I maintained equanimity and said, "No. Erathiel shall stay by my side, as he always has before. This war, which is madness, I will tell you that, will *not* put a divide between us, nor will anything else."

Erathiel, wide-eyed, appeared nervous; clearly, he did not expect me to have the gall to speak to Aques in such a disrespectful manner.

Even still, Aques gave Erathiel a courteous nod. "Erathiel, was it?" Aques inquired. Erathiel nodded in response. "I believe I have seen you around; you live here, in the Library. You have earned the trust of the Gods by now." He gestured to me and smirked. "You may continue to take up residence here, but do *not* tamper with our trust."

"Thank you, sir," Erathiel said. He half-expected that Aques would insist that Erathiel simply call him 'Aques,' as Esolir had done, but Aques simply whisked his coat tail and strode away.

After the preliminary shock had settled, I could once more think of something other than my mortality. My thoughts slipped away to daydreams of mine and Erathiel's future, as the prospect usually gave me comfort.

In my reverie, rather than the usual scenes of a forestside home, dancing by candlelight, and days wasted away at the coastline, I saw us fleeing from mobs, patching each other's wounds, small moments of passion before battle, a love stifled by warfare, confined by secrecy.

I shuddered, took a deep breath, glanced into his eyes, and everything was worth it.

Until death do us part, I decided, *and forevermore thereafter.*

ERATHIEL AWOKE, TAKING A FEW BREATHS. Nothing in the air had changed, the room had not rearranged itself, and the veil was the same as before.

And yet, everything was different.

He stood up from the sofa, his back aching. He ran a silver comb through his hair, then changed into a set of leather armour. He had but one goal for the day: to obtain his jade longsword again. His practice was growing soft, and he determined that, because of the war, he would need a way to defend himself.

"Good morning, Lunix," Erathiel called after he exited the study room, left the hallway with no determinable end, and entered the main chamber. Esolir was operating the front desk, and Lunix was dusting off a table (the dust itself was iridescent and let out a small tinkling noise when it hit the ground, almost glass-like). Erathiel nodded to the God of the Sun. "And to you, Esolir."

"Would you care to resume our lessons?" Lunix asked. About a week before this day, Lunix had been teaching Erathiel how to quilt. Erathiel's measly attempt at a quilt had ended in a pile of string that somehow entangled his arms.

Erathiel laughed and shook his head. "Not today, Lunix, not today. I must be going, after all."

"Departing so soon?" Esolir asked. "What, may I ask, is the occasion?"

"I am a swordfighter, I am not sure if you knew–"

"Oh, we have heard," Esolir chuckled. "I recall Auroleus describing your skill to his friends. He was...very detailed."

"*Very* detailed," Lunix added.

"He mentioned you had a jade longsword, yes?"

119

"Precisely," Erathiel affirmed, confused. "I want to be able to defend myself, and all the Gods' blades are far too large for me to brandish properly. I will return, briefly, of course, to my childhood manor, and obtain the sword–"

"Wait," Lunix said, gripping Erathiel's arm just before he left. "Let me ensure you are safe before you leave." She cupped her hands, and the Symbol of Laphara briefly appeared before it transmorphed into an orb-like shape, which levitated above her palms. Erathiel peered into the orb, and he saw a mob defacing a temple of Ocari. The God of Oceans himself was fending off attacks, trying to harness the power of the ocean, as the building was defaced and demolished.

"The temple is far from the manor," Erathiel asserted.

"You realise the mob will not be confined to one place, correct?" Lunix implored.

Erathiel paused, then said, "It is far enough; I will be safe."

Esolir and Lunix exchanged a nervous glance, then nodded. "Be careful," Esolir called after Erathiel.

Finally, Erathiel emerged from the building, and he saw me waiting in the courtyard. I was wearing a flowing blue garb with golden accents, as well as a gold-accented white satchel hung around my shoulder. He eyed me up and down. "You are truly wearing that?"

"Yes, why?" I retorted.

He shrugged. "It highlights your features. It is conspicuous, perhaps, but you will be fine."

I grinned and offered him my arm. "Shall we?"

He took it. "Of course."

I created a rift, and we travelled to the Mortal Realm.

Once we arrived in front of Erathiel's manor, we heard the clamouring of a nearby cavalry, distinguishable by the *clip-clop* of horse hooves against well-trodden dirt paths.

I turned to Erathiel with a fearful expression, but he seemed insistent on acquiring the blade. "I will make haste," he promised. "In and out. I swear."

I nodded, masking my doubt. Erathiel turned and made his way towards the training grounds.

To his great delight, the blade was just as he positioned it on the rack, almost as if nothing had changed since his last training session. Erathiel grinned, carefully lifted the blade, and realised that it had been continuously polished and was rather well-cared for. It was as if someone had been caring for it while he was away, perhaps because they expected him to return.

When Erathiel turned around, he saw an unwelcome sight:

Tallis.

"Been staying with the Gods, have you?" Tallis asked, speech slurred. As he stumbled towards Erathiel, Erathiel noted Tallis's delirious state. His breath reeked of alcohol. Once Tallis was a fairly close distance from Erathiel, he shook his head. "I always knew there was something wrong with you, boy."

He made the motion to reach for his sword, and Erathiel entered a proper stance in preparation, but rather than using his sword, Tallis pulled out a battle horn made from bronze, adorned with curled silver embellishments. Tallis blew into the horn, which let out a deep booming cry, and a few seconds later, there was an identical distant noise, as well as the sound of approaching clip-clops.

A signal.

Tallis reached to hold Erathiel down, then Erathiel hit him round the head. Tallis looked almost surprised, then struck Erathiel in the eye. Erathiel staggered back, adrenaline masking the pain, then regained proper posture and stabbed Tallis cleanly in the stomach. Tallis groaned, stumbling. Erathiel stabbed him once more, but only managed to graze his arm. Tallis slashed Erathiel just below his cheek and threw Erathiel off him. Erathiel slid across the courtyard and, in a fit of blind rage and determination to win, charged at Tallis with all his speed and might.

Although Tallis was taller and much heavier than Erathiel, Erathiel successfully managed to knock the larger man off his feet. Tallis laid on the ground, his tunic failing to soak up his blood. Erathiel pinned Tallis's chest down with his foot, then bashed his head in with his sword's pommel.

Erathiel struck and struck, then, after a few minutes, he finally comprehended what he was doing.

His first thought:

I must admit, I am rather surprised Tallis even has brains.

His second thought:

I have slaughtered my cousin, and there is an army approaching.

Erathiel tried to flee the scene, but the cavalry had already arrived.

At least forty men on horseback were in a line in front of Erathiel. He glanced down at Tallis's corpse, which still twitched and budged. There was a certain shock on Erathiel's face, so strong that one might have thought that Erathiel had just noticed the body there. He looked back up at the cavalry, then said, "It is not what it looks like."

The shouts came all at once.

"He has killed another man!"

"He has slaughtered Tallis!"

"Is that the boy who lives among the Gods?"

"He must be a worshipper!"

"Kill him!"

The cavalry charged.

Erathiel did not bother to run, there was no point. His demise was imminent. Erathiel only made one motion: not protecting his face, nor brandishing his blade, no. He opened his mouth and prepared to speak, for in his mind, he was ready to hear my name on his last breath.

Before he could cry my name, however, he realised that the cavalry had stopped approaching. There was a large forcefield of wind surrounding him. Instantly, he thought I was his saviour, then he realised that we were too far from the ocean for my abilities to have effect.

Instead, he turned his head and saw the towering form of Gala, the Goddess of Wind, standing beside him.

Chapter Eleven

GALA WAS A TOWERING FIGURE, HER STATURE twice the height of Erathiel's. She, like Esolir and Lunix, was beginning to Ascend, but she and her husband, Ocari, were further along in the process of Ascension. Her skin was a violet-red, her hair shades of plum and wine wound into a loose bun. She wore a lilac dress that was tied above the knee; this allowed it to be more practical for motion. Her gold-flecked fig-coloured eyes were narrowed, and her expression was determined.

"Gala," Erathiel managed to breathe. He bowed his head. "Thank you."

She nodded, her eyes examining Erathiel. She sized him up, then remarked, "You appear to be a fighter."

"I am a swordsman, yes."

"And a proficient one at that." She gestured to Tallis's corpse, which Erathiel had forgotten about for a moment. Then, as more of a statement than a question, she said, "You are going to assist me."

"I—well, I am not sure how much aid I will be capable of providing, but you have saved my life, so I will—"

"You will assist me in saving my husband."

Erathiel was taken aback. "Ocari is in danger?"

"No, well...yes. His temple is being ravaged by a mob, and he is attempting to defend it. He will die before he sees one of his temples destroyed." She let out a light laugh, then her expression grew solemn. She repeated in a more serious tone, "He will die before he sees one of his temples destroyed."

"He can easily overpower a human mob, can he not? He is a God, after all."

"The ocean is too far for more calculated attacks, and too large of an assault could destroy the temple along with the humans inside it. If he were to ambush them physically, well...let us just say that his fighting days are well past him." She let out a sigh. "And yet, he refuses to relent."

"Forgive me, but what could I possibly do to help?"

"You, and Auroleus, if he is still here," she nodded to the place where Auroleus waited for me, "will occupy the mob. Once I reach Ocari and ensure his safety, I will rid the temple of the humans, and we shall return to the Immortal Realm."

"How do you know you can trust me?"

She gave him a light smile. "Erathiel, you might as well be an honorary God at this point."

A sentiment had never felt so right, yet so wrong.

WITHIN MOMENTS, WE APPEARED OUTSIDE the temple of Ocari. Gala handed me a large dagger, gave us a nod, then rushed off to find Ocari.

Erathiel immediately started to strategise. "I will flank left, you flank right. Remember, our goal is to distract, not to provoke or assault. I would rather harm as few as possible—what?" He noticed my nervous expression. This was far from my typical scene of comfort; I looked very out of place. "Are you okay?"

"Yes, yes, simply nerves, that is all."

He gave me a sympathetic pat on the shoulder, then it seemed as if an idea had dawned upon him. "Shout to the sky."

"What?"

"Shout, as loud as you can. It will clear your nerves, I swear it. Here, I will do it too."

He gave me a reassuring nod, then I grinned. As we raised our blades together, crossing them mid-air, we each let out a shout as loud as our lungs would allow. Erathiel flashed me a grin, then darted around the left side of the mob. I mirrored his motions, and the distraction had begun.

"Is   that   a   God?"

"After him!"

My goal was simple: draw the mob away from the temple. As it turned out, all the races I had with Erathiel as a child had paid off; I could outrun the horde easily. Erathiel seemed to be succeeding as well. We had essentially split the mob in two.

After enough running, however, they had given up and retreated to the temple. Erathiel and I exchanged a nod, then we ran after them. I prepared to enter Godly Wrath to prevent them from breaking down the temple's doors, which were sealed by a metal bar on the interior. However, the rage could not reach me. So, Erathiel, in a fit of desperation, threw himself in front of the doors. He only sustained a few gashes, but I let out a low scream. "Erathiel!"

I pulled him away from the doors and stabbed one of his attackers in the chest. The attacker coughed, blood and mucus pouring from his mouth, then collapsed. I withdrew my dagger, and then the swarm of angry mortals charged at me.

Just before their blades could penetrate my skin, there was an overwhelmingly strong gust of wind. Being the God of Ocean Winds, I was able to resist its effects, and I held onto Erathiel to support him. However, the army was blown off their feet, and as Gala descended from the sky, they scrambled up and ran away.

Gala's voice rang: "I have convinced Ocari to abandon the temple. Let us go."

Erathiel and I each held onto her hands, and we distilled into a pale lavender light as we drifted off to the Immortal Realm.

TO BE FRANK, ERATHIEL DID NOT EXPECT Ocari to appear so withered. Gala, Esolir, and Lunix, although they were quite elderly, all had a very formidable appearance. Ocari looked as if he were once a powerful man, but those days had passed long ago. His skin, hair, and beard had begun to grey, giving him a wilting appearance. He required a staff (gnarled wood with a blue gemstone levitating at its tip) for support walking. Erathiel was confused at his appearance, seeing as Gods did not typically demonstrate the typical human deterioration that came with old age. However, the golden scars running along Ocari's sides and arms explained it.

"Decades ago, far before my Creation, Ocari was attacked by humans," I explained in a hushed whisper when I noticed Erathiel's confounded expression. "He was defending Gala and a temple of hers."

"There were human uprisings?"

"Every Generation has experienced a revolt from the mortals at some point or another," I responded. My expression darkened. "None have escalated this far, though."

We were seated in the Hall of Ocari, the main ballroom in Ocari's manor. It was Erathiel's first glimpse of the real Immortal Realm, and the view did not disappoint. The room was the epitome of elegance, with silver sconces illuminated with blue flames lining the walls, curtains made of whispering tendrils that, when one put their hand through them, gave the feel of plunging oneself underwater, and a floor suspended above what appeared to be a large body of iridescent water. Yes, many things in the room, as with the rest of the Immortal Realm, defied the laws of physics and reality that humans were accustomed to, but that made the view all the more spectacular.

Erathiel and I sat on the same sofa, and Ocari sat in an armchair across us. Finally, Gala entered the room, carrying with her a bottle of wine that appeared to be an offering from a human. She poured the wine into four chalices, then gave Erathiel and I each one. Erathiel examined the chalice; it was encrusted with purple garnets.

"You two must be close friends," Gala remarked as she took a seat and handed Ocari a chalice.

"We are courting," I said, correcting Gala. I took Erathiel's hand in mine. It took him a moment, but he clasped mine back. "It has been over two years now, I believe."

Gala looked between us, then asked, "Is this why you have failed to complete your lessons for the past decade?"

Erathiel glanced at me, surprised. "You had lessons in the first place?"

"There is an Academy, where the Gods are taught to harness their power. I *may* have missed a lesson or two–"

"Ten years of lessons," Ocari croaked. He shook his head, then laughed. "You children."

"When Pluvia was growing up, she was permitted to skip lessons–"

"Pluvia was a deranged madwoman who was treated too softly as a child. *That*," here she paused to take a sip of wine, "is exactly why you should never raise your Creations like children."

"I will drink to that," Ocari grunted before taking a large sip.

Erathiel's eyes darted between the two Gods as I clenched my fists. He could sense my rage. "I would treat my Creations as if they were my children–" Gala's jaw clenched, "–if I am to Create a God at all."

Gala's lips pulled into a tight smile. "This has always been a point of contention between us, has it not?"

"Perhaps it should continue to be so, seeing as you refuse to acknowledge my side of this."

"Auroleus, I understand your acrimony, but it simply could not work! A God raising their Creations has been tried, and it has failed miserably. Do you not remember what happened to Aques and Anima?"

"I remember, but I will learn from their mistakes and be more careful."

Gala let out a long sigh. "You impotent child...you truly think you could do better than Aques?"

I was silent as I glared at her.

Ocari grunted. "You two had best be leaving, I think."

"Right away, right away," Erathiel said as he stood up. I still glared at Gala as he pulled me up from the sofa and dragged me out the door.

Once we were outside the manor, he said, "I do not believe I am fond of your Creators."

I let out a bitter laugh. "Sometimes, I doubt whether I am fond of them either."

"Shall we go?"

"Please."

HER NAME WAS PLUVIA.

She was the Goddess of Rain and the first Creation of Aques and Anima.

Pluvia was the perfect blend of Aques's perfectionism and Anima's lust for adventure. A calm, well-rounded child, Pluvia enjoyed reading, deciphering runes left by the Ancients, and evening strolls. She had dazzling periwinkle eyes, silvery hair that was (much like Anima's) always tied into a braid using blue bows, pale blue skin with purple splotches, and a lopsided smile that could illuminate the darkest soul.

Seeing as she was the Goddess of Rain, she had an affinity for the outdoors. Some evenings, she enjoyed standing in the meadow (always barefoot, so she could feel the grass brushing her ankles). She would lift her hands to the sky, and she would create rain. She sang as she made the rain fall, dancing in the raindrops until the scent of petrichor consumed her and healed her once more.

Then, she would walk inside the cottage that her Creators built, and she would be immediately greeted by the aroma of freshly cooked meals and the warmth of the fireplace, which glowed a colour beyond what language can describe. Pluvia could never think of living in a place as cold and impersonal as the first building, the manor with Aques's statue, which at the time had not been constructed. How could she even think of it when she was raised in an imperfect but wonderful house that her Creators made feel like home?

Anima would welcome her with a hug and instantly start chattering away about her day and the happenings of the Gods. Aques was more soft-spoken, but he would laugh along at his wife's jokes and quips, even if he failed to find them amusing.

Aques, Anima, and Pluvia, water, air, and rain, were very tight-knit, especially compared to Luxheia and Tenedius's relationship with their Creations. The Titans were uncaring and distant, setting their Creations up for prosperity and power rather than happiness and love. Aques and Anima were determined not to make the same mistake, and they raised Pluvia with love.

When you think about it, they were the closest thing the Gods ever got to being a true family.

When Pluvia laid in bed, she dreamt of the sky, and how it would one day consume them all. She envisioned herself with a body a mixture of blues, purples, and an unmistakable gold. She saw herself distilling into fractals and nonexistence, creating one last rain as the scent of petrichor consumed her very soul. It was an intimidating future, but it was one she did not think she would resist.

Then, she would drift off to sleep, wake the next morning, and the cycle would repeat itself.

Sometimes, she was under the care of Ignos, Taarin, or Laphara. Seeing as she was the only Third-Generation God that was in existence at the time, they took an interest in her future. However, she spent most of her time under the careful care of Aques and Anima.

She was a rather solitary person, which made Aques worry, but then again, Aques worried about everything. Secretly, Anima worried as well, but she would never admit it.

Rather than spend her time with mortals, or the Gods in her Generation once they came along, she would do something that never fails to remind me of Erathiel: drift off into the expanses of her headspace, conjuring up daydreams and reveries too vast for many to comprehend.

She, too, was a dreamer.

IT WAS THE MIDST OF TWILIGHT, AND THE pantheon had begun to wind down for the night. I laid Erathiel down in the grass in front of Ocari's manor, and I had begun to mend his wounds.

"My wounds are truly not that deep; they will heal on their own," Erathiel protested.

"You are scarred enough, my love," I muttered, examining the wounds further. "Let me take care of you."

"Are you certain you know what you are doing?"

"Positive," I reassured him. "I am a descendant of Anima, after all." I pulled out a small jar filled with a mint green pulp from my satchel, then grinned at Erathiel. "I came prepared."

"This truly is not necessary," Erathiel complained as I began to apply the ointment to his wounds.

"I promise you, it is," I said. I lightly pressed down on one of his wounds. "Does that hurt?" Erathiel shook his head, but I felt his muscles tensing. He was visibly resisting the urge to wince. "Exactly. Swallow this." I pulled a pinch of crushed herbs out of a different jar. "This should ease your pain."

"Thank you," he grumbled as he swallowed the herbs. He gagged. "This tastes worse than my brother's cooking—do not tell him I said that," he said as his expression grew nervous.

I chuckled. "I will not." I smiled, then said, "Oh, I must inform you, this substance can make you a tad bit drowsy."

Erathiel shrugged. I finished applying the ointment to his slash marks, then nodded. "Done."

Erathiel leaned against me and groaned. "Will the duration of this war cause nothing but pain?"

"No...no, there will still be pockets of joy. We may just have to search harder for them."

"I need more than 'pockets of joy,' though."

"Then let us create it." I shrugged. "Our coterie always agreed to stay neutral, right? No one can force our involvement in this frivolous war. The only ones who can dictate our standing on this matter are ourselves."

Erathiel slumped against me, all of his muscles fully limp. "I love you," he murmured as he leaned on my shoulder.

"You are delirious," I chuckled as I stared at the sky. I saw a pair of neighbouring stars, and recognised them as the stars Erathiel and I had named after ourselves. I kissed my lover on his forehead. "I love you too."

The wind began to pick up, and I held Erathiel tighter. He soon fell asleep in my arms. I rested my head against his, staring off into the night sky until I closed my eyes and, at last, managed to rest.

ERATHIEL PUSHED OPEN THE APOTHECARY door, and a small chime rang out from the bell attached to the moss-green frame.

"Hello, faithful customer! I apologise, we have just closed," Florian's voice called out. Florian walked around a shelf full of different types of berries and herbs, cleaning a jar as he walked. His face lit up when he saw Erathiel. "Erathiel! Come in, come in!"

Erathiel smiled sheepishly as Florian escorted him into the store. "I apologise for not arriving sooner," Erathiel said, narrowly avoiding crates full of candles that had just begun to cure. "I wanted to wait until after closing, you know—"

"Oh, I understand." Florian nodded knowingly. He eyed Erathiel up and down.

Erathiel sighed. "You have heard about Tallis, then?"

Florian smirked. "Everyone has." Erathiel started to justify himself, then Florian said, "I must say, I am quite impressed. I always knew you were quite the swordsman, but I never saw your abilities put into action."

"You do not seem upset."

Florian seemed genuinely confused. "Why would I be? You chose the best possible target. I am only upset that you did not let me strike him first." Erathiel smiled coyly. Then, Florian led him towards the back of the shop, where Ilyara (Florian's wife) sat on a turquoise loveseat. She gave Erathiel a warm smile, which he gladly returned. "Erathiel, this is my wife, Ilyara," Florian said and signed simultaneously.

"I believe I have made your acquaintance before," Erathiel signed slowly. "It has been quite some time."

"It has," Ilyara signed in response. "Would you like some tea, Erathiel?"

"Her tea is simply the best," Florian added.

Erathiel was surprised at this. "Better than our mother's?" Myrinai, Florian and Erathiel's mother, was known for her excellent tea-making skills. It was, perhaps, her only talent.

Florian nodded wisely. "Infinitely."

"Then I must try some," Erathiel laughed.

Ilyara stood up, nodded, then asked, "What type?"

"Surprise me." Ilyara smiled, grabbed a few herbs off the back counter, and went into the back room of the shop, where Erathiel knew the stove and kettle were. He used to play there as a child; he and Florian would pretend they were talented pastry chefs. Myrinai would chastise them for spilling spices on the floor.

Erathiel glanced around the shop. The shelves, full of candles, jars of herbs, beauty products, and tea leaves, were falling into disrepair. The paint on the walls had begun to chip, and one of the windows was cracked. "Has Father failed to keep up with repairs?" Erathiel inquired.

Florian sighed. "To be frank, we simply have not sold enough to keep up with repairs. Because of Sotis, our plant supply has diminished," he gestured to the shelves of herbs and tea leaves, which were sparsely stocked, "so we had to raise prices. The locals, who are mostly farmers, mind you, were affected by Sotis as well, and they simply could not keep up."

"Shame," Erathiel mused. "I remember when this place was filled with customers."

Florian nodded slowly. He glanced at Erathiel as if he was about to say something, then Ilyara came through the door, holding three cups of tea.

Erathiel thanked Ilyara, then took a small sip of the tea; it was still quite hot. Erathiel's eyes widened. "This is the best tea I have ever tasted," he said and signed.

"Thank you—I advise you not to drink too fast!" Ilyara signed as Erathiel poured the entire cup of tea into his mouth. "You will burn your throat!"

"I apologise if I gave the impression that I cared," Erathiel muttered and signed as he finished off the tea.

Ilyara giggled. "Would you like seconds?" Erathiel nodded furiously, and Ilyara went to fetch him another cup.

"Oh! That reminds me," Florian exclaimed. "I cooked something for Ilyara and I earlier today," He ran to the back and fetched a plate of homemade bread (?), adorned with what smelled like garlic butter. Erathiel took a bite, and it was surprisingly edible, but not much beyond that.

"Florian and I plan to open a tavern once the war ends," Ilyara signed. "I will make beverages, and he will cook for   everyone."

"I can assure you I will be a faithful customer," Erathiel said, only a half-lie. He could only imagine the quality of Ilyara's craft brews, and he was excited to taste them.

"Hopefully it will please Father," Florian said, undertones of worry in his voice. "He was rather upset when we told him that we did not plan to have children."

Erathiel was surprised. "No children?"

Florian shrugged. "Neither of us are particularly interested in intimate matters," he explained after taking a bite of the garlic-flavoured bread.

"And what of you, Erathiel?" Ilyara asked. "Have you found a partner?"

Erathiel froze, then turned to Florian. "It is not...unheard of, for a God to take a human lover, is it?"

Florian shook his head. "Not by any means, it is quite common; during a god's formative years, that is."

"Good," Erathiel breathed. He instantly tensed. He had not intended to speak that thought aloud.

Florian cocked his head. "Why do you ask?"

"I–"

Florian read the expression on Erathiel's face. "Are you courting a Goddess?"

Erathiel exhaled slowly. He could no longer keep the truth concealed. "No, no, actually, I am courting...a God. Auroleus."

Ilyara gasped and clapped, and Florian's expression narrowed in surprise. "Hm." Erathiel was silent, his anxiousness tumultuous. "Does he make you happy?"

"Yes."

"Do you love him?"

"With all my heart."

Florian laughed. "Then why are you telling me as if it is something shameful? I see no problem with it. You are in love, and that fact alone is what matters. Perhaps...do not inform Father about this; he may have an unfavourable opinion."

Erathiel sighed in relief. "Thank you."

"You have nothing to thank me for!" Florian pulled Erathiel into a hug, then stepped away for a moment. "How long have you two been courting?"

Erathiel pondered it. "Over two years now, but I had feelings for him long before–"

Florian guffawed in fake offence. "Then you should apologise to me! For *years,* you deprived me of gossip about your beloved, how *dare* you, sir?"

Erathiel snickered and laughed. "Unlike him, I am discreet about my affections."

"You two seem adorable. I simply must meet him someday."

"Florian, I have no idea how you failed to figure this out," Ilyara remarked. "He spent more time at Thyrin Cove than at home; who do you think he was meeting up with?"

"Shame about Thyrin Cove," Florian mused, bringing a pang of sadness in Erathiel's chest. "I knew you were friends with Auroleus as a child, but, again, I had no idea you were this close." He chuckled. "I must be oblivious."

Ilyara nudged Florian playfully, which elicited a laugh and a gentle kiss. Erathiel smiled, suddenly wishing I were there with him.

For the rest of the evening, Erathiel, Florian, and Ilyara sat in the apothecary, drinking tea and talking of happier days. Erathiel always longed for more moments like this: quiet, peaceful time spent with his few family members that felt like just that: family.

Chapter Twelve

ERATHIEL AND I WAITED OUTSIDE A LARGE wooden door with ornate floral engravings. Taarin was hosting a dinner, and to my surprise, Erathiel's presence was requested as well.

"How long is this going to take?" I muttered. As if on cue, the door opened.

A forest sprite, a half-humanoid creature with antlers, flowers growing from its moss-textured skin, the Symbol of Taarin borne on its chest, and hair made from vines, was waiting at the door. All of the Second-Generation Gods created sprites to aid them. I did not interact with the sprites much, seeing as they typically resided in the region their host God did.

The forest sprite, disgruntled as it looked, ushered us through the door.

We were greeted with a wonderful view: a vast garden, with pockets of flowers growing between a few sparse trees, paths made of multicoloured dirt branching in every direction, veil creatures resembling birds flitting between trees in a nearby forest, and rolling hills of aquamarine grass stretching to the horizon line. Smaller forest sprites, perhaps children, played in the garden and wove flower crowns. One rushed up to Erathiel and offered him one, and he accepted it as if it were the greatest gift he had ever received. Larger forest sprites, perhaps more mature, were strolling along the paths, making conversation in a language neither of us could understand, nor could we hear. After all, the sprites spoke the language of the forest; thus, only Taarin was able to communicate with them.

"Is there anything I should know about Taarin?" Erathiel asked. His first interactions with Aques, Ocari, and Gala had been subpar, to say the least, and he was determined to be on the Goden of Earth's good side.

"You will not have to worry about offending sem, if that is what you mean," I assured him. "Taarin is quite the charlatan; everyone loves Taarin, and Taarin loves everyone. Se plays the lute, enjoys exploring the Mortal Plane, well, when there is not a war going on, that is, and–" My face went pale as I recalled a memory about Taarin's past. I took a step away from Erathiel. "We must pretend as if we are not together while we are here."

Erathiel looked surprised, almost hurt. "I thought the Gods were open-minded."

"No, no, this is not because we are two men. You are a mortal, and I am a God."

Erathiel's expression eased, but only slightly. "Why?"

I looked wistfully out at the cerulean forest, which we were approaching. "Centuries ago, Taarin took a lover," I explained. "Adia was her name, I believe."

"Correct me if I am wrong, but is Adia not a human name?"

"It is. Adia was a human."

Erathiel was silent for a moment. "Oh. Did they have a bitter relationship?"

"Quite the contrary. This was before Aques and Anima had fallen in love, so amongst the Gods, they were the symbols and icons of love. I never spoke about it to Taarin personally, no one has; se refuses to talk to it. From what Aques and Anima have told me, they were passionate, yet they were tranquil around each other in a way that could not be replicated."

"If their relationship was so perfect, then why should we keep ours concealed for the night?"

"Adia passed away, Erathiel."

He gave me an incredulous expression. "Yes...of course she did, all humans die."

I looked at Erathiel with a pained countenance, then said, "She died in Taarin's arms."

Erathiel was rendered speechless. "Oh." He looked up at me. "How did she die?"

"There was a human uprising. She and Taarin stayed neutral, but she was caught in the crossfire." A flash of—what, recountance? Fear?—flashed in his eyes. "Now, of course, Taarin has moved on from the crushing grief, but you must understand the crushing effect the loss had on sem. Se isolated semself for *decades*. Se cut everyone out of ser life. Ser grief was all-consuming."

"Se seems to be better now, is se not?"

I gave Erathiel a crushing look. "Yes, se is speaking to the other Gods again. But even still, the aftermath of Adia's death lingers. Taarin has not been able to fall in love since. After all, how could she place semself in something so fleeting?" I looked at the ground, my mannerisms growing angry. "It is unfair. Se had so, *so* much love for the world, se still does, but ser past left sem loveless." I solemnly gestured around to all the forest sprites. "Taarin has made a home for so many, but since Adia's passing, se has never been able to feel at home semself."

Erathiel nodded. "We keep this—us— quiet, then."

"It is only for tonight. Taarin deserves as much."

"Se does."

We continued the rest of the walk in silence. Once we were led through the cerulean woods, a patch of forested land with too much rustling in the undergrowth for comfort, we emerged from a clearing. I gaped as I beheld the sight ahead.

There was a tree, the largest tree I had ever laid eyes upon, with a canopy of turquoise leaves stretching as far as I could see. A wooden spiral staircase ran alongside the tree, and it led to a large house that appeared almost cabin-like.

The house of Taarin was truly a sight to behold.

Erathiel and I nodded our thanks to the forest sprite, then ascended the stairs with many other Gods. We noticed Auri and Vesa, who waved at us, and Gala, who shot me an angry look; we had not spoken since the unfortunate confrontation in the Hall of Ocari.

Finally, we reached the top of the stairs, and we were greeted by a booming 'Welcome!' from the Goden of Earth semself. Erathiel and I were led to a large, rustic dining hall, where we were seated towards one end of the table.

Food was shortly served; a meal entirely composed of mushrooms and plants, yet it was quite decadent.

As Erathiel ate, he barely spoke to me, so as not to draw attention to us. Instead, he looked around the room. It was filled with paintings, trinkets, hanging plants, and memorabilia, all relating to nature or the Gods. There was nothing to show that Taarin had suffered such an immense loss. The only thing that stood out in the room was a shelf hanging above the head of the table. The shelf held a lute in a glass display case, which was marked with a plaque he could not read from where he sat.

Bored of looking around the room, his attention shifted to the Gods at the head of the table, all Second-Generation Gods. He noticed the way that Ignos talked in a boisterous, almost overpowering, tone, how Taarin made comedic remarks and laughed, yet there was a glint in ser eyes that made them appear lost, how Aques was only just as talkative as he needed to be, how Anima tried to encourage her husband to speak more but then ultimately gave up and grew quiet herself, and, perhaps most significant of all, how Laphara, whose body was completely covered in a modest dress, did not speak at all, and avoided eye contact with her husband, Ignos.

After a few hours of light chatter, the party had begun to wind down, and some of the Gods had started to filter out. Erathiel and I were about to leave, then he heard the voice of Taarin behind him.

"Excuse me, are you Erathiel?" se asked. Erathiel turned around. Taarin was a towering figure; expected, seeing as se was Ascended. Se wore a simplistic robe, but se adorned it with strands of ivy woven around it. The ivy ran up the robe, around ser shoulders, and down ser emerald arms, which were covered in tattoos. Ser hair, a shade of green slightly darker than ser skin, was long and interwoven with flowers. Se had many eyes with black scleras and amber-brown irises, and every eye stared at Erathiel with a warm, welcoming expression.

"Yes, I am," Erathiel answered.

"May I speak to you for a moment?" Without waiting for an answer, Taarin led Erathiel to the back of the room, escorted him through a door, and closed it behind them.

Taarin sat down on a sofa in the small room; well, small compared to Taarin. Erathiel stood near the doorway.

Taarin took a few moments before se spoke, but finally asked, "You and Auroleus?"

Se locked eyes with Erathiel, and a thousand unspoken words went between them. Erathiel felt the weight of ser history in the single, sorrowful glance, and Taarin felt all of Erathiel's hope and fear in his reciprocation. "Yes," Erathiel finally managed to respond.

Taarin nodded slowly, fidgeting with ser ring finger. Se spoke the next two words clearly before motioning for Erathiel to leave. "Be careful."

Erathiel left the room, passing the lute in the glass case.

He noticed that dust had collected on the lute; it had not been played in years. The lute's fourth string was broken, and the porcelain plaque labelling the case read:

"An Ode to Adia: may I never love another soul; my heart is eternally yours."

"I DID NOT KNOW IT COULD RAIN IN THE Immortal Realm," Erathiel remarked as he joined me on the roof of the Lunar Library. The Library had a rooftop garden, with flora coloured hues of teal, magenta, and violet. Wispy creatures resembling butterflies flew between the flowers, leaving behind a trail of stardust. Benches dyed with a charcoal tone were scattered across the neatly organised garden beds. The rooftop garden provided a wonderful view of the top of the observatory's glass dome, and, of course, the celestial pillars above.

Erathiel sat down next to me on a bench and stared up at the sky, which was void of clouds. "Where is the rain coming from?"

I glanced at Erathiel briefly. "You learn to stop questioning these types of things when you live in the Immortal Realm. I have no idea what Luxheia had in mind when she created this place. All you can do is enjoy the strangeness and beauty of it all," I leaned against his shoulder, "and take in the petrichor."

"Since when were you so poetic?"

"You can be the genius and the artist, let me have this."

"I am by no means a genius."

"Spare me the facade. Your mechanical animals are talk of the town," I remarked. I held out one of his newest creations, a mechanical grasshopper. It was still at first, then I sent a gust of wind through the machine, and it began to hop around, eventually finding its way atop Erathiel's head.

Erathiel chuckled. "They would be functionless without your wind, though."

"Perhaps our abilities complement. Perhaps we were *fated* to be together."

Erathiel stared up at the sky. "Perhaps we were written in the stars." He noticed the neighbouring stars we had named seemingly a lifetime ago, and smiled. The person he was back then and the person he was now were completely different, but at their core, they were the same.

"Do you remember when you made your first mechanical animal?" I asked.

"How could I forget?" he responded jovially. "Does that bird still work?"

"It does. It still flies around the clock tower, without fail."

"I may be a genius, then, as you say."

"Okay, now you are simply acting arrogant." I nudged Erathiel mirthfully, then asked, "Do you remember the day we first met?"

Erathiel groaned. "I called you down from the Immortal Realm–"

"Just so I could help your toy boat to sail," I laughed.

"Then I had you help me build a second one," he recounted.

"To be frank, I thought you were rather bossy." This earned me a shove from Erathiel.

"Rude," he gasped.

I smiled. "No, no, I am simply teasing. I believe I loved you from day one. What can I say, those gorgeous amber eyes drew me in..."

I trailed off, and Erathiel and I were silent for a moment. His expression grew more solemn. Finally, he asked,

"Do you remember that day, by the fire, when you asked me if you could be my family?"

My throat tightened. "As clearly as if it were yesterday."

"I have...another one of my questions about the Gods, you could call it. Has a God ever had a Creation with a mortal? Is that physically possible?"

I pondered the question. "It has never been done before, but I do not believe it would be impossible to create a Demigod, if you will. Why do you ask?"

His face was flushed, his expression flustered. "Well, I was pondering the concept of time, and what we perceive as the future. It is never truly 'here,' is it, the future? It is simply this entity that we can foresee but never predict, and we always assume that something, anything, will come next, because that is what the universe was built on, was it not? I mean, we have to assume that this *something*, this *everything*, came from what once was nothing, right? Was it fate that brought us where we are, or is it really just luck? Were we, 'we' being humanity, that is, destined to be as we are? Were *we*, 'we' being you and I in this case, fated to end up here? Perhaps all of this was just luck. But perhaps," here he smiled, "the stars lined up at the exact right place, a fire was dull enough to allow us to move closer, the ocean fought against the tide, causing a boat to remain still, an arrow managed to pierce the veil, a mortal somehow harnessed life itself and became something greater, enough chaos and nature was bound into order, and, perhaps... perhaps all of this has a reason. So, what I am trying to say is–" his face grew even redder and his speech sped up– "considering time and the universe, and, you know, fate in itself, I was thinking that, maybe, when this war ceases, when all is said and done, that perhaps we could," he took my hand, "start a family together."

I was speechless. Immediately, he blubbered, "I am well aware that Gods do not typically have...*families*...I know that it has been tried and failed, and it would have to be temporary, wouldn't it, considering that *we don't have eternity,* and you do not desire a Creation, which is—"

"You are right about one thing," I finally managed to say. "I do not want a Creation. I would not want to treat them as simply a concept that was made to serve a purpose and nothing else." I met Erathiel's gaze. "I want a child."

Tears started to brim in Erathiel's eyes. He was beginning to choke up, I could tell. He murmured, "Imagine a daughter."

Those three words broke me, and I instantly began to sob against Erathiel's shoulder. These were not tears of grief, not tears of sorrow, but not necessarily tears of joy either. They were tears of acceptance, of an overwhelming sense of *being* and acknowledgement of reality.

For the first time, there was a future, a future that would require defiance of all tradition, but a future nonetheless. I half-expected this future never to play out, for why would I, when fate had failed us so often before?

And yet, I could picture this future so clearly.

A few years would pass, and the war would end on peaceful terms. Erathiel and I would build a home together, perhaps in a meadow painted hues of cornflower and wisteria. By some miracle, we would find a way to Create a child. We would watch her grow up. She, like Erathiel, would be a dreamer. She would run around in the grass, playing pretend with Temprysus and other children her age. I would watch Erathiel tinker with his inventions while listening to our daughter's cheerful yelps.

There would be peace.

Loving.

We would grow old together.

Erathiel would live a long time, smile lines creasing his face as he gracefully ages. We would make sure to watch every sunset and dance in every rainshower. I begin to Ascend, and Erathiel grows quite old, and then...then...

Then, I am not sure what happens next.

How can I be?

But, then again, I do not need to have that part of the story figured out quite yet.

I pulled Erathiel into the tightest embrace, and I silently vowed never to let him go. "You would make a wonderful father," Erathiel mused.

"So would you," I whispered in return.

For the first time since the war began, I saw our future, clear as day, and I could not wait.

"WHERE ARE THE EXTRA PLATES?" ESOLIR shrieked. "Where are the salad spoons? And where are—"

"Esolir, calm down," Lunix sighed, patting her husband on the shoulder. "Everything will be fine—"

"Simply 'fine' will not suffice!" Esolir screeched, clenching his fists, shattering the glass in his hand. In a calmer tone, he muttered, "This is the first time this library has hosted a wedding. Everything must be perfect."

"You are being irrational," Lunix said, helping Esolir pick up the shards. "Erathiel, tell Esolir he is being irrational."

"You are irrational, Esolir," Erathiel called as he exited his study room. While Esolir and Lunix were in a cleaning frenzy, ensuring that the Library was in perfect condition for the wedding, Erathiel's only job was to assist Stilis in fetching the wedding couple.

"Erathiel, I thought you would be on my side of this," Esolir said, shaking his head. "You are quite close with the couple, are you not?"

"I am, but I am not an obsessive perfectionist," Erathiel smirked.

"Exactly!" Lunix exclaimed. Esolir huffed, then glanced out the window.

"You had best be going now, my boy. Stilis is waiting for you outside."

Erathiel nodded, said his goodbyes, then left and saw Stilis waiting for him in the courtyard. "Stilis!" Erathiel exclaimed, firmly shaking ser hand. This caused sem to jolt slightly, but se leaned into the gesture after a moment.

"It is good to see you, Erathiel!" Stilis smiled, then sighed. "I cannot believe the people I have grown up with all my life are getting married."

"They have been together for quite some time now."

"I know...the change will take some time to adjust to, though."

"Understandable." Erathiel eyed Stilis's ensemble: a billowing cloak, the interior of which reflected cosmic entities, and a large scythe, the blade of which was a blue and magenta chrominance. "Interesting outfit for a wedding."

"Oh, I have another outfit prepared." Se sighed. "Death never ceases, even on the morning before a wedding."

"You work for Tenedius?"

Stilis shook ser head vigorously. "I would never; quite the opposite, actually. If Tenedius had his way, mortal souls would be sent straight to the Realm of the Dead, immediately plunged into the darkness of the universe. I advocated for change, and change was given, so long as I actively serve the role, mind you. I am considered the Reaper, if you will. My role is to guide the souls to the Realm of the Dead, ensure they are ready to depart, you know?"

Erathiel nodded. "So every time there is a death, do you guide the soul to the Realm of the Dead? That seems tedious."

"No, no. I collect groups of souls. Oftentimes, the people are strangers, but they find camaraderie in each other and become like a family, of sorts, before passing on. Until I collect them, the souls sort of float in nonexistence, if that makes sense."

"So you have seen the Realm of the Dead?"

Stilis shook ser head. "Not the Realm itself." Se smiled. "Only the gateway." Se glanced at the sky, then said, "They will be waiting on us. Let us go."

Erathiel took Stilis's hand, and they distilled into purple light.

They arrived outside a set of silver gates, leading to Aques and Anima's manor. Erathiel heard the roaring of a nearby sea, and he pulled his dress robes tighter around him to prevent the cold of the sea breeze.

"Vesa should be getting ready here," Stilis shouted over the wind. "I will fetch Auri; she is in Ignos's cave."

Erathiel nodded, and Stilis dissipated.

He called out for help, and a water sprite appeared, opening the gates for him.

The sprite tried to speak in the language of water, but Erathiel shook his head; he was unable to decipher what it was saying. The sprite appeared upset with itself, giving a few frustrated chirps, then finally managed to ask, "Vesa?"

Erathiel nodded, grinning. The sprite let out an excited yip, and Erathiel cheered; he was happy for the giddy sprite. It then led Erathiel through the gates, inside the manor (which, he realised, hardly looked like a house at all; it was far too formal), through the entrance hall, and down a narrow staircase to the left.

As Erathiel descended the stairs, he realised that the waves he had heard did not come from a nearby sea; rather, they came from inside the manor. He kept descending, and the walls became transparent. It was only then that he noticed that the staircase was surrounded by water.

They were, of course, protected by the walls, but it was still rather unsettling, especially considering Erathiel's inability to swim. The staircase seemed to go on forever. They kept descending, and they were soon so deep that sunlight could not reach. Rather, the water was only illuminated by mysterious glowing orbs of light of every colour imaginable (and unimaginable, for that matter) suspended in the water.

Finally, Erathiel and the water sprite reached flat ground. There was a hallway ahead of them. The expanse was pitch-black; there were no discernible objects in the vicinity.

The sprite led Erathiel down the hallway, orbs in the water illuminating as he walked past them. Towards the end of the hallway, there was a door, which Erathiel opened to find a room with at least twenty or so different doorways.

To his relief, Vesa emerged from one of the doorways, and Erathiel's mouth dropped open upon seeing her.

She wore a form-fitting black ball gown that ruffled at the bottom, and intricate gloves that ran up to her elbows. Her hair, still tied up, ran down her back in coils. She wore an elaborate, feathered escoffion, which was draped with pearl-adorned lace. Dramatic midnight blue eyeliner winged her eyes, which were filled with self-assuredness. She was stunning, and she knew it.

"You are beautiful," Erathiel gasped.

Vesa smiled lightly. "Thank you."

"I cannot believe you and Auri are finally getting married; I am very happy for you!" Vesa simply smiled and nodded. Erathiel narrowed his eyes in half-concern, then bluntly stated, "You do not seem particularly enthused. Lighten up, Vesa, it is your wedding day!"

Vesa shrugged. "Well, I suppose that after this, Auri and I will live in our cottage permanently, but other than that, not much will change, will it?"

Erathiel paused, twitched his head in disbelief at Vesa's relative passiveness about the day, then Vesa created a rift, and they soon appeared at the Lunar Library.

The crowd was vast, with sprites of every element and Gods, many of whom Erathiel hardly recognised, flooding through the doors. Erathiel led Vesa under many archways topped with gold-and-galactic veils, then raced with her through the main hallway and to a large room that had been cleared out for the wedding. He positioned her at the front of the room, then darted off to find Stilis.

He found sem near the back of the room, where se seemed to be looking for Erathiel. "Stilis!" Erathiel exclaimed. "How did things go with Auri?"

"Well, I had to redo her makeup after she started sobbing," se began. Erathiel looked concerned, then se clarified, "Tears of joy, of course. She is ecstatic. I assume it went about the same with Vesa?"

Erathiel did not have the heart to tell sem that Vesa had barely given an emotional reaction. "About the same, yes."

"Good!" Stilis sighed, grinning. "I am so happy for them. This is a wonderful day, you have no idea."

Erathiel looked around. The room was decorated beautifully, the guests were chattering excitedly. It was, indeed, a lovely day. "It is."

Stilis looked down at the ground for a moment. "I never thought any of this would happen, you know? I never thought I would be here, with this group, I—I used to spend time with a different crowd, and yes, they allowed me to be intellectual, but it was never truly *real,* you know?" Se eyed Erathiel up and down quickly. "Yes, yes, of course you of all people understand." Se considered it for a moment, then pulled Erathiel into a tight embrace, which Erathiel returned.

Finally, Esolir's voice rang throughout the room, and Stilis said, "We must get to the front of the room!"

Erathiel and Stilis raced to the front of the room, where they positioned themselves behind Vesa. Aestalios was already standing there, and he widely grinned at the pair. Erathiel nodded at Aestalios, and Stilis gave the God of Tides a bashful smile.

At last, the doors to the room opened, and a hush fell over the room. Music started to drift from some seemingly unknown source; then, Erathiel looked up and saw several sprites levitating mid-air playing harps. The sprites grinned at Erathiel, who smiled back.

Aques, Anima, Ignos, Taarin, and Laphara emerged from the doors. The latter four Gods took a seat in the front row, whilst Aques walked to the front of the room and stood in the centre of the podium. Esolir and Lunix came next. Esolir was sobbing loudly, while Lunix comforted him.

Finally, Haneræs and I emerged, stopped at the doorways, then each took one of Auri's hands as they guided her to the podium.

Auri was stunning. She wore an elaborate cream gown, the layered skirt of which was thrice her size. A wispy headdress adorned her hair, which was neatly tied up, and flowers traced the neckline. Stars were painted along her arms, mirroring the starry freckles on her face. Erathiel heard Vesa lightly gasp when she saw her bride.

Once they reached the podium, Haneræs and I squeezed in next to Aestalios and Stilis. Erathiel smiled at me. "You are dazzling," he whispered.

"Hush, this is not *our* wedding," I responded.

Erathiel raised his eyebrows. "It could be someday," he responded coyly, which caused me to blush profusely.

Finally, Aques cleared his throat and began to speak. "Thank you all for gathering here today. We are here to witness the wedding of Auri, the Goddess of Dawn, and Vesa, the Goddess of Dusk. First, I would like to thank Life and Death, Luxheia and Tenedius, the rulers and Creators of everything." Aques's teeth were gritted during this part of the ceremony; he seemed uneasy. "Without them, none of this would have happened." While everyone in the room gave their thanks, he exchanged a glance with Anima, then his eyes darted to the ground. "None of this would have happened," Erathiel heard him mumble.

Aques's forlorn expression cleared, then he continued, "Now, because of them, because of every action that has led us to this moment, we are here, all of us, to witness the eternal bonding of these two souls."

He looked at Auri. "Auri, Goddess of Dawn, do you take Vesa to be your wife, your lives intertwined in the eyes of the universe, your souls connected for eternity and evermore?"

"I do," Auri said, voice giddy with excitement. Suddenly, runes of golden light scattered around the room.

Aques turned to Vesa. "Vesa, Goddess of Dusk, do you take Auri to be your wife, your lives intertwined in the eyes of the universe, your souls connected for eternity and evermore?"

"I do," Vesa said with a tone of clairvoyance and assuredness. The runes around the room started to swell, letting out a humming noise.

"Then, in the eyes of the Gods and fate itself, I pronounce you wife and wife. You may kiss each other!"

Auri pulled Vesa into a kiss, and the runes around the room burst into multicoloured light. The room erupted in cheers, and when Vesa finally pulled away, they gave each other a smile, one that reflected hardships and struggle, yet closeness and new beginnings. They looked, in a sense, at home.

This, Erathiel thought, *must be love in its purest form.*

Chapter Thirteen

AND TIME WENT ON.

The war had continued, human lives claimed and ichor shed. The madness of it all had not yet ceased, and the Starlight coterie was anxiously awaiting a peace contract, along with many humans who were either neutral on the issue or were still loyal to the Gods. However, a peace treaty seemed unlikely at this point in the war, seeing as the humans had assembled a full army and had not relented. Many temples and icons of the Gods had been ravaged and destroyed, and the Gods, although still maintaining a defensive position, hardly visited the Mortal Realm. After all, they were sure to be attacked if they did so. The war was confusing, and I hoped for an end soon.

However, there was also joy to be found in daily life. Erathiel and I, both of us newly eighteen, had been discussing our future, and we thought that it might soon be time to build a home together. As much as Erathiel adored Esolir and Lunix, sleeping on a sofa (which was just, mind you, a chair that could fit an Ascended God) was not the most comfortable arrangement. Haneræs and Aestalios were still going strong, Stilis found solace in ser reaping duties, and Auri and Vesa had constructed a house together.

Speaking of Auri and Vesa, they typically were permitted to visit Temprysus, the God of Time and their Creation, once every full moon. However, Luxheia and Tenedius now forbade these visits. Now, as to why, Auri and Vesa hadn't an inkling of a clue. Perhaps it had to do with the ongoing war.

Regardless, the world was in a heavy, difficult place, but we were all trying our best to make it another day, romanticise the mundane, and find comfort in small moments of joy.

SHADES OF MORNING WERE PAINTED ACROSS the humid summer sky. I rubbed my eyes, emerging from the Hall of Ocari. I managed to avoid any interaction with Gala. She had refused to honour me with a coming-of-age celebration, seeing as we were still bitter from previous quarrels.

I cleared my head. It was going to be a wonderful day, I had decided that already. After all, I was taking Erathiel out on a date. I planned to take him to Arberra's pastry shop, then we would enter Taarin's garden and watch the sprites play.

Before I arrived at the Lunar Library to pick up Erathiel, I decided to check the state of the Mortal Realm. I cupped my hands, and the Symbol of Aques appeared. The Symbol transmogrified into an orb.

I focused on the presence of mortals, and I could sense that a large number of them were gathered outside the ruins of a former temple. I could almost hear their screaming; rather than screams of defiance, however, they were screams of terror.

I narrowed in on the humans, and the orb displayed the scene.

Temoris, the God of Earthquakes, descended upon the earth. He levitated over the splintered ruins of the desecrated temple. "You mortals chose the wrong foe," he said in his deep, booming voice. Light spread in a cracking pattern up his arms. He was entering Godly Wrath. He raised his hands, and the human army slowly began to retreat. "But you are right about one thing. There is no mercy at the hands of a God."

With that, Temoris unleashed a mighty earthquake.

The ground rumbled violently, the army was knocked off their feet. The crumbling steeples collapsed on the army, whose flailing and crawling could not save them from the massive structures. Some humans managed to fight the quake, rolling away from the falling temple. These were far and few between, though. Many were crushed by the falling structures. Some humans let out a noise through their battle horns, a warning cry. A few people grovelled, begging for mercy. They cried for their families, they said they would relent, they even mentioned that they would ensure the war would end, 'just spare us, spare us, please,' but Temoris only smiled.

As I watched the onslaught, a sickening revelation dawned upon me. The temple was already destroyed when the humans arrived at it. They were protesting, they did not intend any violence.

I stared at Temoris's wicked smile, and I grew queasy.
This is no defence. This is a massacre.

I clenched my fists, and the orb dissipated. I collapsed against a wall, exhausted and nauseous. Was this destruction not only something the Gods were capable of, but willing to commit?

Something was terribly wrong with this.

What, then, were the implications of this? What did the wrath of the Gods say about me? About Erathiel and I? I began to doubt the basis of our relationship. There was a clear imbalance. How could a mortal, the embodiment of humanity, love a God, a being destined to become monstrous and soulless?

I appeared at the Lunar Library.

Erathiel waited outside, holding a pocket watch in his hand. He closed the watch and smiled when he saw me. "Auroleus!" he exclaimed.

"I apologise for being late," I mumbled, keeping my distance from Erathiel. I had a dazed expression, and my insides felt completely numb.

Erathiel cocked his head, concerned. "It is alright...are you unwell?"

He was so innocent. Weak. I could not bear it any longer. "I will have to cancel our outing."

A flicker of disappointment ran across Erathiel's face. "Okay, just get some rest, alright? I love you–"

I snapped. "How could you, how could—how *dare* you love me, you should be *terrified* of me! I–"

We stopped for a moment. I breathed heavily, tears stinging my eyes. Erathiel's expression grew dull. "Should I have a reason to fear you?" he asked in an apathetic tone.

He walked away.

EYES OF BLACK.

A sight that terrified Aques as he looked in the mirror one fateful day.

Aques and Anima, in love as they were, were more than ready to grow old together. Their Creation, Pluvia, was nearly of age. They had built their home together, made their dreams come true, and it was time for them to move on, to see what was next.

So they waited.

And waited.

And waited.

Aques was growing tired of waiting.

He and Anima were beginning to Ascend, just as Luxheia and Tenedius had millennia ago. Anima had no semblance of a clue as to why she expected any other fate, but she was crushed by the reality.

They became shells of their former selves. Aques still led with a just jurisdiction, yet he absorbed himself in his work. Anima still healed people with a gentle manner, yet she was very methodical, almost mechanical, in her work. It was strange—nothing had *really* changed, but then again, hadn't everything? Something had changed in them, something that no one could quite define, but it was altered.

Aques and Anima, in an attempt to continue the next Generation, Created several Gods. The new Gods were sometimes Created by Aques and Anima, but sometimes, they were only Created by one of the Gods, and oftentimes, by a completely new pair. Creation did not necessarily have to be a romantic act, it often was purely for the sake of harnessing more specialised elements of nature. After all, it was difficult, for example, for Aques to properly control every aspect of water, so he created Ocari to control the ocean. However, abandoning Creation as a romantic act, although Aques and Anima themselves were not Created as a result of romance, abandoned all hope of the concept of 'family' amongst the Gods.

Pluvia was starting to worry. Her Creators left for work early and arrived back late. They barely acknowledged her, except when she made a mistake. Her home had become a house, her past had become a faint memory, and her semblance of a family had become simply the people who raised her.

One day, after a particularly rough patch, she had decided that these were not the people who raised her. These strangers in her house were too distant, and the tension had reached a boiling point.

So, Pluvia left, never to reappear.

ALTHOUGH THE BURDEN OF FATE SEEMED all-consuming, it could not destroy everything. Elsewhere, there was tranquillity. Perhaps, there was even blossoming love.

On a stretching coast in the Silver Isles, a small archipelago of floating islands suspended above an inlet in the Immortal Realm, Aestalios and Haneræs walked and stared out at the swirling waters below. Aestalios was waving his hands, making the ocean dance for Haneræs.

They came to a river, and seeing as no Gods had made their residence on the Isles, there was no bridge. A few stones jutted out of the water, their surfaces thick with moss.

"I will bet that I can make it across in less than a minute," Aestalios said, grinning.

"I'll bet you get pulled into the water," Haneræs quipped.

"Five coins."

"Deal."

Haneræs climbed up into a yellow tree, and Aestalios approached the river. He jumped onto the first stone with ease. His foot caught on the edge of the second stone, but he was still stable. Aestalios crouched, preparing to jump for the third stone, but just as soon as he kicked off, a ball of sand materialised from nowhere, pelting Aestalios in the face.

Aestalios fell into the river with a thud, then scoffed at Haneræs and swam to the shore.

"Over one minute," Haneræs called, glancing down at the pocket watch that Erathiel made her. She dissipated into light, then materialised on the other side of the river.

"How dare you?" Aestalios grunted playfully as he cleaned the sand off his face. "This sand will linger for days!"

Haneræs shrugged. "My five coins, please?" she asked, holding out her hand.

"When we return," Aestalios assured her. "So, why have you brought me to the Isles?"

Haneræs took Aestalios's arm in hers, then said, "You will see in time." Haneræs then pulled away from him and asked, "Why do you feel slimy?"

"I–" Haneræs already started to walk away. "Wait!"

Haneræs led Aestalios through a yellow forest, birds resembling finches flying between branches. Along the way, Aestalios tried to convince her that Taarin was, objectively, the greatest Second-Generation God, and Haneræs called him ridiculous and said that Anima was objectively superior.

Finally, when they reached the other edge of the island, Haneræs stopped. Aestalios looked around. A few trees and dandelion wisps were scattered near the dropoff point, a coast of silvery sand, and he heard the sounds of a waterfall nearby. Below the floating archipelago, Aestalios saw a purple mountain range stretching out to the setting sun.

"What did you take me to see?" Aestalios asked.

"The view," Haneræs said simply. A soft smile appeared on her face. "I used to play here as a child. Beautiful view, is it not?"

Aestalios looked at Haneræs. "She is."

Haneræs stepped closer to Aestalios and chuckled. "Flirt."

Aestalios mirrored her. "You enjoy it."

Haneræs wrapped her arms around his neck, then shrugged. "I may."

Aestalios and Haneræs smiled bashfully at each other. They were at peace in their pocket of the universe. Elsewhere, a newly married couple placed the finishing touches on their new home. A Reaper formed a connection with wandering souls, knowing fully well that they, nor the world, would not remember sem for this action, but it did not really matter. A couple made up after a fight; not as eagerly as they had before, but it meant something. Two people stared out at a rainstorm, thinking of someone they cared for dearly, although the care was difficult to express. They wondered where she was, but knew she was safe.

Everything was fine. Not nearly perfect, but fine.

Chapter Fourteen

STARING AT MY REFLECTION, I NEARLY FAILED to recognise myself.

I wore a dramatic, silver coloured metal headpiece, resembling a burst of light, the middle prong of which was an arrow. A long, collared dress cloak, muted blue with accents of silver, draped down to my ankles. The cloak had sleeves so ostentatiously large that it was difficult to grab anything. Heavy, thick rings weighed down my hands, and a rather uncomfortably tight form-fitting garb underneath caused me to itch at random intervals. The Symbols of Aques and Anima were drawn upon my forehead, as was tradition. The only signs of customisation in my ensemble were heavily winged eyeliner and, of course, the grass anklet that Erathiel had woven me ages ago.

Do not mistake my words; I do very much enjoy formalwear. However, seeing myself in traditional garb, it made me feel almost like an impostor, a different person, rather, a caricature that people could tolerate.

Without warning, Gala entered the room. "Would it kill you to knock first?" I asked indignantly.

"Our guests will be arriving soon. You had best be ready." Gala looked me up and down, then noticed my anklet. Her eyes narrowed. "What is that?"

Cursing myself under my breath, I swept the hem of the cloak over the anklet. "Trick of the light."

She closed her eyes and sighed. "So help me...take it off."

"No."

"What was that?"

"Am I not allowed to have the slightest bit of autonomy in this? Will wearing an anklet *really* offend the Titans? If so, then we should reconsider why they are the ones in power."

"There is a very strict set of traditions for a coming-of-age ceremony that must be adhered to–"

"Really? Because, unless we experienced a group hallucination, Stilis's coming-of-age ceremony was, firstly, private between sem and ser Creators, and secondly, se did not have to wear this *ridiculous–*"

"Esolir and Lunix are rather... unconventional...when it comes to their Creations. Let them be, they will all end up like Pluvia. I will make it my job to raise the rest of your Generation correctly."

I was affronted. "You did not *dare–*" here I looked back up at her–" speak ill of Pluvia's name." She returned my stare callously. I bit my lip. "And if Esolir and Lunix are so 'unconventional,' as you say, then tell me why they have more respect than you?"

Gala was silent for a moment, but I saw her trembling. She opened her mouth to say something, then heard chatter behind the door. She held it slightly ajar and saw the hall filled with Gods. "You are lucky that the Gods have already arrived," she hissed. "Otherwise, I would have cancelled this *whole* ordeal."

As she walked away, I feigned sadness and called, "Oh, what a tragedy! It is not as if you have already postponed it for *months,* of course!"

"Well, we are here now, are we not?" Gala called behind her. "Because, finally, my Creation has decided to stop complaining!"

"No, you are mistaken, darling! You have simply stopped listening to him!" I shouted back. Gala did not acknowledge me. I slumped against a table in the room. "Pathetic, is she not?" I asked the shadows in a corner.

Out from the shadows stepped Erathiel. "She is." He nodded, then remarked, "You did not inform her of my presence."

"I intended to ease her into the fact, but, seeing as she had such a meltdown over an anklet..." I shrugged. "Perhaps it will be best for her to learn the hard way."

Erathiel smiled. "She will be furious."

"Let her be." I let out a yawn. "Is it possible to be exhausted by an event that has not happened yet?"

"I suppose...but please, be serious for a moment. What happens when she finds out?"

"I highly doubt she will say anything until after the fact, because Gods forbid she cause a scene, do you know how terrible that would look for her?" I said, mocking Gala's voice. I laughed. "It is all fun and games, is it not? Welcome to Godly high society, where every action is a competition for influence. Gala is perhaps the worst of them all; this is all a show, really, she simply craves attention. I swear on Luxheia's name, I would wager all my fortune that she *enjoyed* the attention she garnered from Ocari's injury."

"Alright...even still, I think the other Gods will notice my presence," Erathiel pointed out.

"Erathiel, my love, you live in a subsect of the Immortal Realm, you have not visited the Mortal Realm in a year—to be quite frank, I believe the Gods would be quicker to point out your absence in this sort of event rather than your presence."

He shrugged. "I must be an honorary God, then." He gave me a light kiss, then there was a knock at the door.

"Are you coming, Auroleus?" Auri's voice asked. "The room is waiting for you!"

I pulled away from Erathiel's embrace, then stood at the door and linked my arm with his. "Showtime."

I pushed the door open, walking with Erathiel to the front of the hall. Tables and chairs filled a good portion of the room, a God or sprite at every seat. Gala and Ocari stood at the front of the room, and I saw Gala's lips pursed at the sight of Erathiel. I walked slowly up the hall, taking great care not to tread on the train of my cloak. I felt the eyes of the room on me. I took a steady breath. It was going to be alright.

I positioned myself at the very centre of the podium, and Erathiel walked to sit near Stilis. "No," I said, clear enough for the room to hear. "Stand with me."

"Auroleus, is this really–"

I cut across Gala. "Auri stood with Vesa for both of their ceremonies. Aques stood with Anima for hers. How is this different?"

Gala clenched her jaw and stiffly nodded. Erathiel slowly walked onto the podium, staring at Gala as if she was going to bite him, then stood a few steps away from me. I looked around the room, an uncomfortable silence hanging over everyone, then back at my Creators. "Well?" I asked expectantly.

Ocari cleared his throat, then croaked, "We are gathered today to witness the coming-of-age of Auroleus, the God of Ocean Winds. Auroleus, for the last eighteen years–" *and a few months, give or take–* "you were raised under the careful care of the Third Generation. Now, you become a man, and your future will be of your own volition." *As long as it conforms to your expectations of me, of course.* "We hope you will use your Godly abilities to their full potential, and that you may someday achieve Mastery in order to Ascend." Ocari looked up at the sky. "Auroleus, as one of your Creators, I grant you the freedom to pursue Mastery. In the eyes of Luxheia and Tenedius, rulers and Creators of everything, may you prove your worth as a God."

Scattered runes appeared around the room; this time, they were a vibrant blue rather than the typical gold.

Gala repeated, "Auroleus, as one of your Creators, I grant you the freedom to pursue Mastery. In the eyes of Luxheia and Tenedius, rulers and Creators of everything, may you prove your worth as a God."

Half the runes shifted to a shade of violet. A swelling noise came from the runes as I lifted my hands towards the sky, the Symbol of Aques appearing between them. "I am Auroleus, the God of Ocean Winds!" I proclaimed as I felt power surging through my body. For once, I felt my full potential, as if I was worth every drop of ichor in my veins. "And I will champion my fate!"

With that final proclamation, one that I have had to recite hundreds of times but had never resonated with as much as I did in that moment, a sweeping gust of wind surged from my hands, carrying tendrils of blue light. I heard the sounds of the wind on the nearby ocean, and I could not help but smile.

The room erupted in cheers, and even Gala gave me a light nod. Soon enough, the cheering subsided into chatter, champagne glasses were brought out, and the festivities of the night began.

As Erathiel took in the scene, an overwhelming notion was clear in his mind: he was a mortal, and I was a God. This formality, this excellence, this perfection, this inhuman nature...it was not him. It was clear to him when he saw me in such a place of greatness, greatness he would never be capable of achieving himself.

A lump rose in his throat. No matter how much time he spent around the Gods, he could never compare to them. There was a reason he was stared at everywhere he went; there was a reason he could never quite consider the Immortal Realm home, and it was all because of a tragic fact that he refused to acknowledge: he simply did not belong, and he needed to stop pretending that he could.

So, the moment I turned away, Erathiel left out the back door of the house, ready to return to the Mortal Realm.

"WHERE ARE YOU GOING?" I BELLOWED OVER the wind. Erathiel and I stood atop the cobblestone courtyard overlooking an ocean. The wind I had created was starting to pick up because of my heightened concern for Erathiel, and it had started to rain. The scent of petrichor was especially strong that day, as it seemed to be as of late.

"I do not know. Not here, that is certain. I cannot bear to be a bystander to this preeminence any longer!"

"Erathiel, stay with us! This party will be over before long anyway–"

"It is not simply about the party, though, is it? It is not the party, nor the balls, nor the weddings, nor the rituals or politics or anything else, it is the simple fact that you will always be greater than I, and that my presence is weighing you down!"

The wind intensified. "Erathiel, that is preposterous, I–"

"Love you, yes, yes, you have said it countless times, but do you—*can* you—really, when I am so much lesser? Compared to you, I am *nothing,* I have done nothing to deserve your love!"

I paused for a moment. He could not have been genuine; it was impossible, but the droplets in his eyes spoke the message for him. He turned away, and I felt the need to say something, anything, lest he turn away for the final time.

"Erathiel, please believe me when I say that I love you. I will love you through our lives—as they were, are, and will be—in our deaths, and forevermore thereafter. In every timeline, every reality, my heart is eternally yours," here my voice started to break, "you are the *only* good thing that has *ever* happened to me, Erathiel, and I need you to believe that. I do not know how many more times I must proclaim it for you to believe me, but I will. I will scream it to the mountaintops, to the edges of space, to the confines of our universe, whatever it takes for you to hear it and believe it's true, I *love you*, Erathiel, I love you, I love you..." I broke into sobs. "I love you." I shakily outstretched my hand. "So?"

His sobs mirrored mine as he, with a trembling arm, placed his hand in mine. "I love you too. I do not know what I did to des—"

"Stop." I sighed. "Simply an 'I love you' will suffice, thank you."

I led him to the half-wall bordering the ocean, and we climbed atop it, sitting close enough that our legs brushed. Within a few moments, Erathiel began to sob into my shoulder, and I let silent tears roll down my face as my hand found his.

After my clothes were thoroughly soaked, both from the rain and Erathiel's tears, Erathiel pulled his face away slowly. "I have no idea how you can tolerate me when I am like this," he sniffed.

"It does not happen frequently, I promise. I am usually the one in your arms."

He let out an empty laugh (he clearly did not believe me), then gestured to the tears running down his face. "Do you see these tears? They are a show of my weakness."

"Erathiel, you are simply having emotions. The tears mean you are alive." I sighed. "How can I tolerate you? I can tolerate you because you make me feel what no one else has. You give me a stronger sense of home than any material place. Your moments of humanity...they are necessary lows to our moments of joy." I intertwined my fingers with his. "We do not have the time nor the patience to obsess over perfection. After all..."

I stared out into the horizon line, and Erathiel finished my sentence for me.

"We don't have eternity."

"COULD WE GO SOMEWHERE?" HE ASKED lightly. Erathiel turned his head on my shoulder so that he could meet my gaze. "I do not feel like re-entering after causing such a scene."

I nodded. "Understandable. Would you like to return to the Library?"

"Can we go back to Thyrin Cove?"

I paused, surprise creasing my brow. "Are you sure you want to return there?"

"Positive. I think I need to see it right now."

I nodded, took my hand in his, and we dissolved into light.

We appeared in Thyrin Cove, and it was nearly unrecognisable.

Rather than the charred forest or even regrowing cherry trees, the former woods had become a breeding ground for Taarin's monstrous plants. Thick vines and gnarled undergrowth filled the grove, giving it a nearly jungle-like appearance. Mounds of twisted plants curled and stretched above our heads. Erathiel drew out a dagger and started hacking away at the plants, leading us towards the caves.

"The caves should be left untouched," Erathiel figured. "Taarin would not destroy ruins from the Ancients."

He was right, the Ancients were revered in Godly history. They were the first humans to walk the planet, the people that Luxheia and Tenedius lived amongst, before they became Gods.

"True," I admitted. "Let us keep going."

Erathiel continued slashing apart the knotted overgrowth, advancing towards the caverns. A massive mound of twisted vines and roots stood in front of the entrance. Erathiel slashed across a mossy, nearly rotting piece of growth that appeared to be the core, then a pair of glowing eyes slowly opened.

We staggered back, and out from the growth stepped one of Taarin's sprites, but it couldn't have looked more altered.

The flowers and vines growing around it were wilted and crumbling, and mould spread up its mossy skin. The area around its eyes was rough and knotted. Its fingers were long and gnarled, and the roots where its legs should have been spread quickly along the ground, rapidly advancing the creature towards us.

"Run."

We ran through the growth as fast as we could, my cloak growing tattered and stained by mud. The creature caught up to us, and Erathiel used his dagger to attack the creature while it lashed out at him. Erathiel recoiled back after a nasty scrape to the neck, then kept hacking away at the creature.

I bashed the seemingly corrupted sprite in the back of the head with my silver headpiece. After enough blows, the corrupted sprite let out an unbridled hiss, then its sinews detached from its body. The structure of the creature dissolved, and it was nothing more than a pile of leaves and petals.

Erathiel stared at it for a moment. "We should get inside the cave."

"What if there are more of them?"

He paused. "It needed earth to travel upon. It could not traverse the caverns."

Without waiting for my protests, he continued, and I followed after him.

After a few minutes, we reached the entrance to the caverns, which was packed with vines. Erathiel, after several failed attempts, managed to slice the vines in two, and we entered.

We stepped into the cave, and Erathiel pulled a mechanical insect from his pocket. "It will send out a signal if it detects motion, assuming your wind can give it some sort of autonomy, as it did with the bird." I sent a gust of wind through the machine, and it flew off into a branching tunnel of the cave network.

We waited for some time. "Either this cave is very, *very* long," Erathiel deduced, "or we should be safe."

I nodded, and we started to walk down the cave. My wind did not seem to work as we got deeper into the cave— we were too far from the ocean—so it would have been impossible to see without the bioluminescent lichens and toadstools.

We reached an ending point in the tunnel, and I heard the sounds of the ocean outside the cave walls. I used my wind to illuminate the cave, and gasped when I saw the wall.

There were murals, left by the Ancients.

"What does it mean?" Erathiel asked as he examined the runes and caricatures.

I tried to remember my lessons in the language of the Ancients, but alas, I spent more time in this very cove with Erathiel than paying attention. However, I was able to determine the meaning of the pictures.

An injured and diseased person, covered in lacerations, was lying on a table. A woman in a blindfold stood over him, holding a chalice of turquoise water. In the next panel, the man drank the water, and in the next, he was cured of his ailments.

"A blinded woman..." A small gasp escaped my mouth as I recalled my history lessons. The image was referring to the village of blind healers that Luxheia came from. They had long since been abandoned and forgotten, but these murals depicted some sort of water that could cure any ailment, and that deserved further research.

"A healing water," I explained to Erathiel.

"We have no idea if this is true."

"If it is...this could save countless lives." I looked up at the mural once more. "We have to inform Anima."

This war had caused too much loss and injury. Perhaps it was time to do some good.

Chapter Fifteen

THE AIR WAS WARM AND LIGHT AS WE traversed the mountainside trail. Anima, Erathiel, and I walked along a tan path alongside a rolling green mountain range. Trees of white and pink blossoms were scattered in the area, and wild rabbits hopped around, staring at us curiously and twitching their ears.

"You truly believe the healing water is real?" Erathiel asked Anima.

"I am nearly certain." About a week before this, Erathiel and I informed Anima about the murals. Once she investigated them for herself, she managed to deduce the location of the Village of the Blinded, the village where Luxheia was raised. It was believed to be abandoned, but Anima, intent on finding the healing water, desired to see for herself. Erathiel and I, out of curiosity (and perhaps out of wanting to get the credit for discovering the water), joined her.

After we walked in silence for quite some time, a particular daydream was gnawing at my mind as I looked out at the beautiful scenery. It was completely uninhabited, save some deer and rabbits, and there was no sign of human nor Godly civilisation.

A thought stood clearly in my mind: *This would be a perfect place to build a home.*

I glanced at Erathiel, then I pictured a young girl: with freckles, blue skin and hair, amber eyes, short ears, and a playful smile.

Our daughter.

"Anima," I suddenly inquired. "Is it possible for a Demigod to exist?"

Anima appeared confused. "So, a Creation between a human and a God, then?" I nodded. She looked between the two of us. "Are you...actually, that is not my place to ask. Regardless, it has never been done before, but I would assume it would be possible."

Erathiel perked up. "How so?" he asked.

"Creation works by a God transforming their base elements into another being. A God's base elements make up the essence of their ichor, so I can only assume that if you add blood to a Creation process, the result will be something of a Demigod."

Erathiel and I exchanged a grin. "Would the result resemble both of us?" Erathiel asked. "I want her to have your hair," he added to me.

"I hope she has your eyes," I responded.

"Yes," Anima answered. She looked between the two of us, amused at first, then almost worried. "I do have to warn you...this Creation would be half-human, so they would most likely be unable to Ascend, nor would they have great power. Chances are, the most a Demigod would be able to control would be something small and relatively insignificant."

"That is fine," Erathiel said immediately. "I could not care less; as long as we could provide her a good life."

Anima bit her lip and sighed. "May I be blunt?" she asked. I nodded slowly, and she sighed. "Erathiel, I would advise you especially to look at this from a realistic standpoint. Your Creation, although not fully a God, will certainly outlive you." She turned to me. "Auroleus, please consider that someday, you will have to raise your child alone. I-"

"Alright," I said, cutting her off. "Thank you for the information, we will make up our minds after the war. And if you could refrain from speaking of my lover's death, that would be wonderful."

She nodded stiffly. "I apologise." I blinked in return, then fell back to walk with Erathiel alone.

He could see that I was visibly glum, then said, "Cheer up. It is possible, we can have a daughter."

My hand found its way into his, as it usually seemed to do. "Can we build a home together, like Aques and Anima before..." I trailed off; the fate of Aques and Anima was well known.

"Of course," he said softly. He looked around. "Somewhere near the ocean, that is for certain."

"In a forest, perhaps..."

"May I have a workshop?"

"Only if I can have a parlour."

For the next hour, we spoke of our future home. We could never really seem to settle on much, but it was an entertaining conversation nonetheless.

Our banter was stopped, however, when we came up on the top of a hill, and we saw a village nestled between two mountains.

Plumes of smoke came from the chimneys of the quaint village, whose houses of pale stone and straw were neatly clustered. They could hear the faint chattering of civilians and the rushing of a nearby spring.

Anima was in awe. "The Village of the Blinded," she said, mouth agape. "It is like staring back into time, I—I thought it was lost to history!" She took a deep breath, letting out a low humming sound. "The birthplace of the Gods. It is truly here."

WE ENTERED THE VILLAGE, WALKING ALONG a stony path. There was a quaint marketplace with stalls selling remedies and medicine. In the centre of the marketplace was a great marble statue of Luxheia's human form, a young blindfolded woman, who was reaching towards the sky.

Erathiel immediately observed that every person in the marketplace was an ash blonde-haired woman, all of whom wore cream or golden robes and a cloth blindfold.

Anima approached the first person she saw. "Excuse me," she began, "do you have a head doctor? I would like to speak to her."

The woman blinked at Anima slowly. "Yes," she said, confused. "She is in the head doctor's office." The woman pointed to a building directly behind her, which was clearly labelled 'Head Doctor.'

"Thank you," Anima said dumbly. The woman shook her head, walking off. Anima told Erathiel and I, "I am going to speak to the head doctor. Explore the town, will you? I visited here once as a child, it is a lovely little place."

Erathiel nodded, and we were off.

We passed by several stands selling colourful potions; some still and clear, some violently bubbling and opaque. "I have the urge to drink one," I muttered to Erathiel.

"Well, I suppose you are immortal," he responded, "but I will most certainly not be joining you on this endeavour. I value my life, thank you."

I laughed. "More for me." I handed a few coins to the saleswoman, who looked as if I had personally offended her, then took a red, fizzing potion off the rack.

"I do not even want to watch this. Find me when you are finished being a fool."

"You are missing out!" I called after him. "This tastes amazing—wait, no, eugh, this is awful, wait–"

Erathiel wandered around the small yet crowded market, observing the stalls and gardens. Erathiel observed the complete lack of men, but the close nature between the women in the group. Many of them reminded him of Auri and Vesa.

After a while, he decided he should try to find Auroleus, but he was nowhere to be seen. More and more people flooded into the market, and Erathiel grew flustered. Eventually, the area was so packed that Erathiel struggled to move at all.

"Is the marketplace always this crowded?" Erathiel asked a young woman standing near him. She appeared around Erathiel's age, most likely no more than nineteen. Her straight ash-blonde hair ran down her back gently, and she wore a set of casual cream robes.

"Unfortunately," she groaned. "If you would like, I have a room in one of these buildings." She gestured to the building behind her. "It could help to get rid of all this noise."

Erathiel nodded frantically, then realised she could not see him. "Please."

She took his hand and led him towards a building. The woman felt a notch on the doorknob, indicating which building it was, then opened it and led Erathiel to a small room.

The room had a curtain of beaded strings rather than a door. The space inside could only fit a small sofa and an armchair, but it was much better than the noise outside, which was starting to overwhelm Erathiel.

"Thank you," he said earnestly.

She nodded. "It is no bother. We hardly ever get visitors around here; I wanted to make your acquaintance as soon as I heard of your arrival."

"Word gets around fast, I suppose," Erathiel laughed. "How could you tell I was a visitor?"

"You are a man," she said simply. "Or, in better terms, you sound masculine, I do not mean to presume–"

"I am a man," Erathiel said simply, a tone of amusement behind his voice. "My name is Erathiel. Erathiel Karalor."

"That is a wonderful name, Erathiel." The woman outstretched her hand for him to shake. "I am Priya, Priya Faye."

Erathiel smiled and shook her hand. "Wonderful to meet you, Priya."

"It is my pleasure." She laughed. "You know, it is strange; I am not used to having visitors in here. Typically, this room is reserved for patients."

"Are you a healer?"

"A practitioner," she answered. "I am still in training, but I do perform some healing." She thought about it for a moment, then added jokingly, "So, Erathiel Karalor, has anything been ailing you as of late?"

"Well, Priya Faye..." He started off the sentence jokingly, then trailed off, and his tone grew serious. "Yes, actually."

She cocked her head. "Tell me more."

"It is...I do not know how to put it into words, really. It is sort of this cloud, this omnipresent doubt, no, more like a looming sense of failure, as if my existence constitutes that I have done something wrong. It may be because I spend most of my time around the Gods, but I almost see myself as inferior, if that makes sense? I–" He stopped, frustrated that the words could not come faster. "It is almost like...no matter what I do, or what I say, or how great I aspire to be, I will never come close to anything that will be remembered. I escape into my headspace from time to time, I imagine myself as a great inventor, or a fighter, or a poet, and I work towards those dreams, but when all is said and done, are those dreams really worth anything? Am I?"

He was worried that he spoke too much, that he would scare off Priya, but she simply met him with a knowing grimace. So, he continued. "I am not sure if it is some sort of illness, some disease that clouds my mind, but I often find myself unable to focus, unable to handle the noise and the crowds and the gatherings associated with the Gods, I–"

"I think, from a medical standpoint, I have reached my conclusion," Priya said simply.

Erathiel perked up. "Really?"

She nodded. "I fear you're simply human. I diagnose you with the notion of being alive. My prognosis is unpredictability, and my prescription? Good luck. You may need it."

Erathiel deflated slightly. "This is something everyone feels, then?"

"To some degree, yes. After all, how can you fail to feel inferior when a woman who came from *your* village harnessed life itself and transcended physical form?"

Erathiel and Priya were silent, a moment of solidarity shared between them. Although they were strangers, that they had never met before and most likely would never meet again, the bond forged between them was unbreakable on the account of one thing: they were both so undeniably, unmistakably human, and that meant something in the eyes of the universe.

"Your village seems fascinated by Luxheia," he stated after a moment of silence. "Why?"

"She grew up here," Priya answered matter-of-factly. "See that statue, just outside?" Erathiel nodded, glancing at the statue in the centre of the marketplace. "That is the exact spot where she stood when she became the first Goddess. In fact," she chuckled, "it is because of her, and only her, that we are blinded."

"I know that your entire village was blinded when light threatened to consume you, but I assumed that it would not be passed down."

"It was not," she admitted. "This will sound strange, but...whenever a daughter is born into our village, her eyes are slashed and blinded." Erathiel gasped, horrified. *How could a society centred around peacefulness and healing inflict such violence on an infant?* he wondered. "I know what you are thinking," she quickly said, "and the practise sounds terrible, I know. But, think about it for a moment: a woman, raised in your village, nearly sacrificed everything to save her people and the generations to come, and the rest of the world refuses to see her as anything more than a half of a pair, when the pair only existed in the first place because of a horrible act of violence from a jealous man." She huffed. "So, that is why we blind ourselves, to show unanimity with Luxheia."

"You really seem to despise Tenedius."

Priya laughed. "The whole village does. Consider it from our perspective: a madman shot at the sky, pierced the veil, and nearly killed Luxheia. Luxheia spares him because of her generous nature, and transforms him into a God. Right?"

"Yes."

"Then, the rest of the Mortal Realm reveres him as an equal to Luxheia, as one of the...?"

"Rulers and Creators of everything," Erathiel finished.

"Exactly!" she exclaimed. She calmed down. "And I suppose, in a sense, that he is. After all, he did Create the rest of the Gods along with Luxheia. That," she chuckled, "is *exactly* why we only worship Luxheia: because every other God's existence can be traced back to Tenedius."

"Understandable." Then, after a moment, he asked, "This may be a reach, but is Tenedius the reason why there are no men here?"

"Precisely!" Priya exclaimed. "You are quite sharp, you know. This town needs more people like you; everyone here is a scholar, yet they fail to think."

"I do not intend to sound rude, of course, but I must ask...how can your population continue without men?"

"The population dwindles with each generation, I must admit that," she confessed, "seeing as most of us are attracted to women. Some of us, however, are attracted to men as well, or men exclusively, for that matter, so they travel outside the village, find a man, and if they produce a daughter, bring her back here."

"It   sounds   tedious,   I   must   admit."

"It is. That is why most of us settle down with other women. It is a shame for those of us who are attracted to men as well, though," she said, the statement sounding a bit personal. "It is like, there is something, *someone,* waiting on the other side of the village's confines—"

"—a stranger, yet an idea which you are enamoured by—" Erathiel added, thinking of me and our early days.

She stood up. "—you can leave to find him if you wish, but doing so will pull you away from the only people you   have   ever   known—"

"—and you doubt that he will love you for *you* anyway, you see yourself as broken, so why would he view anything differently—"

She moved closer. "—and even if you did leave, found him, you would either have to leave him—"

"—or you would abandon your people, to whom you feel a sense of belonging towards, but you never really belonged *to*...regardless, it all falls apart in the end—"

"—because the fact is simple—"

"—fate and history—"

"—they fail us all." Priya was especially close to Erathiel; I was the only other person who had come as close to him. "I admire your mind, Erathiel Karalor."

He knew what was coming next, but for her sake, he complied. "And I admire yours, Priya Faye."

She carefully leaned in and kissed him; not particularly filled with emotion, but lightly, carefully, more curious than anything. She seemed sorrowful, yet content, as if she had found her place. He did not lean into the embrace, but did not resist either. He felt quite the opposite; he seemed almost distorted, lost.

She pulled away slowly, and after a moment of tension and suspense, Erathiel said, as if answering a question, "Priya, I am flattered, I truly am...but I have a lover, whom I care for dearly."

Her face fell. She looked horrified. "Oh! I—I am so sorry, I deeply apologise—"

"It is alright, you had no idea." Erathiel stood up, feeling the strong desire to leave. The moment had passed. "I should go find him, he is probably concerned as to where I am."

"'Him...' Oh, Gods, I feel worse now, er—I have some medical records to sort, I believe..." She trailed off as she stood up. They accidentally ran into each other as they attempted to leave simultaneously, and both of their faces were flushed with embarrassment. "It was a pleasure to meet you," she mumbled as she nodded her head briskly.

"You as well," he muttered in response before leaving the building as fast as he could.

As Erathiel walked in search of me, a sense of dread filled his stomach. He felt nauseated. A simple conversation had turned abhorrent, and yet...

There was a part of him, a tiny fraction, that, when Priya leaned in, hoped, perhaps even prayed, that he would feel something, because if he felt a connection, it would prove that he contained some semblance of normalcy.

But he felt nothing.

THE SENTIMENT WAS CLEAR AS DAY.

There was not, nor would there ever be, a 'family' amongst the Gods. They would live together, yes, they would care for each other, perhaps even find love, but they would fail to hold the capacity for the closeness of family.

This was, of course, indicated by Pluvia's disappearance. Pluvia had known for a while, and so did the rest of the Gods, and perhaps even Aques and Anima could tell deep down, that the family was destined to fall apart. After all, it was happening before their eyes.

After Pluvia left, there was a strange disconnect in the home of Aques and Anima. They each mourned the mysterious loss of their eldest Creation, but they mourned in very different ways.

Aques absorbed himself in his work. After his Ascension, he took his role as figurehead of the Gods very seriously. He had a strictly diplomatic relationship with mortals and a distant approach to the other Gods. When he was not putting all his energy into manipulating water, he attempted to solve the political and militant affairs of both the mortals and the Gods. Aques, the caring family man, had faded, and Aques, the leader, was born.

To everyone's surprise, he even regained contact with Luxheia and Tenedius, the pair of whom he had previously refused to speak to. He had originally held grievances with the way they raised him—distant, only trained to serve a purpose—but when Taarin, who held similar issues with ser Creators, asked Aques for clarity, he responded by saying that 'perhaps they had some things right.'

Anima, on the contrary, dedicated herself to healing people. Although she was never quite the same as she was before her Ascension, she tried as hard as she could to regain the side of her that truly, unconditionally, cared for every living soul. Whether it be a mortal or a God, peace or war, physical or mental, Anima was determined to heal any wound. After all, maybe, just maybe, if she could cure her distant side, then she would be worthy of finding a family again. Deep down, she knew it was impossible, but the joy that Pluvia gave her was unlike any other, and finding that feeling again was worth the world a thousand times over.

The conflict was simple. Anima tore away her barriers, and Aques put more up. They clashed, they fought, they made up, yet never truly felt resolution. Nothing would ever be the same as it once was, and they both knew that. It was clear in the few times that they spent hours screaming, blaming the other for Pluvia's disappearance, when internally, they believed it was their fault. It was clear in the frequent bouts of silence, the days spent in solitude, only a pained look ever exchanged between the two. It was even clear in the light moments, the happy, the joyous, when even as they smiled and laughed and spoke for hours, they found themselves wondering when it would all fall apart.

Why, then, did they not separate?

No one really knows.

My theory? They only ever knew each other. Their relationship was strained, but it was familiar, and they desperately needed any sort of stability they could get.

Despite their moral differences, they seemed to agree on one thing, something so sick and corrupt that everyone who heard the tale could not help but wonder why, why...

Why did they attempt to replace Pluvia?

They Created a man named Prucaris, the God of Storms. He was intended to be a sort of version of Pluvia, but better, an improved model, someone who would be raised for success and a purpose, like Aques and Anima were themselves. Prucaris, much to his Creators' surprise (although

184

it was entirely their fault), was a furious, coldhearted man who was callous and unfeeling in his mannerisms. He performed his job, and he performed it well, but he held a sort of resentment for life, as if he knew that he was only a replacement, even though he was never explicitly told. Thus, he felt the urge to ravage and destroy. So, he sent out a wave of terrible storms. Aques spent much of his energy trying to restrain Prucaris from tearing apart humanity itself. Eventually, Prucaris relented, yet his rage still shows from time to time.

Aques and Anima had a similar relationship, to some degree, with the rest of their Creations. They were mentors, not parents, with the purpose of assisting, but never quite connecting. In a sense, it mirrored the very mistake that they tried to avoid: ending up like Luxheia and Tenedius.

As more and more Gods had the same outcome, the vast majority never even wishing for a family in the first place, it sank in: there was nothing they could do to change this fate. They could only regret their flaws and apathy.

Then, a year after all was said and done, something small, barely noticeable, fell from the sky, yet it would change everything.

Calm, gentle droplets descended from a sea of clouds. It started to rain.

Now, at this time, keep in mind that Aques and Anima were in a particularly nasty fight. Aques stepped outside for a moment, needing fresh air and a moment to breathe, then he noticed the gentle rainfall.

Pluvia was alive.

Aques rushed inside and pulled Anima into the meadow to watch the rainfall. She was confused and reluctant, of course, but when she noticed the rainfall, she faintly gasped and fell, her figure caught by Aques.

They embraced tighter than they had in years, their argument completely forgotten, at least for a time. And they sobbed, oh, how they sobbed! They sobbed for the love that was lost. They sobbed for a family that was broken, and for the piece of it that was out there, somewhere. Most of all, they sobbed for the words that were unspoken in that moment but that both of them desperately needed to hear:

"I miss you."

"I'm sorry."

"I still love you."

"I want our family back."

As Aques gained self-control, he could not bring himself to say any of this to his wife, who was still crying in his arms, even though he held these feelings. He thought of their childhood, their growing affection, their wedding, building a home together, their first Creation, and trying with utmost vigour to prevail over fate and time, even if they failed in the end. All he could manage to say was:

"For what it's worth, it's always been you."

Time passed.

They would fight, they would recover, they would crumble and heal and destroy all at once, but there was one constant. Without fail, every time there was a gentle rain, Aques and Anima would find each other and watch.

They would sit in silence, hold each other but stay at arm's length, and know that somewhere in the universe, their Creation—no, their daughter—was alive, maybe even loved by someone braver than they could be. They would picture her, wherever she was, happy.

Perhaps she was singing, dancing, basking in the rain, like she did when she was a child.

Aques and Anima could never seem to speak; perhaps their sentiments were better left unsaid. So, instead, they would simply watch the rain, let themselves be overwhelmed by petrichor, and mourn for the family that was never meant to be.

ERATHIEL AND I WADED IN THE WATER AS WE filled up a stoneware jug with the Symbol of the Titans engraved on it. "I am surprised," I remarked. "I, quite honestly, did not expect the head doctor to permit Anima to take some of the water."

"To be fair..." Erathiel replied, keeping any sign of discomfort concealed. He had not yet told me about the kiss he shared with Priya, nor did he intend to. "They are hardly giving us any, if you think about it." He gestured around at the cerulean spring. "These waters are vast, and they are only giving us *this*." He motioned towards the jug.

"Consider it: if a single sip can heal a person completely, this should be substantial."

"I suppose." Erathiel spun around in the water, his arms spread out. Because he was submerged in the healing water, he felt its effects. "I feel so rejuvenated! I could run to the edge of Lenethaus and back."

"Interesting," I remarked. The water made me feel rejuvenated, in a sense, but it brought me a sense of calmness. "I feel more tranquil than anything, really. I feel as if I could just melt into the water. Or your arms. Whichever you would prefer."

Erathiel, smiling, took my hands in his and led me to a rocky nook at the edge of the spring. Once we sat down, taking in the heat of the water, he appeared much more relaxed. After all, he had never quite gotten over his fear of swimming, and though we were only waving, he may have been afraid of a dropoff.

"I nearly forgot what you look like without a shirt," I said as I ran my hand slowly up and down his arm. "Remind me more often, alright?"

Erathiel blushed. "Noted."

"This may be a controversial opinion, but I am under the belief that clothes are overrated. Specifically yours, that is."

His face was red as a beet. "If we ever become fathers, Auroleus, you would be a horrible influence."

"No, no, I would be an amazing father."

"You would," he said earnestly.

"That reminds me, I was thinking about our daughter," I began. "Like Anima said, she would only be able to control something small and insignificant, correct?" Erathiel nodded. "I believe that she should be able to control a tiny beauty of nature, something that we take for granted but would miss dearly if it left us."

"I agree," Erathiel said, nodding vigorously. "That would be...beautiful."

"It would." I took a shaky breath, then leaned against Erathiel's shoulder. "I have come to realise something: nearly every pivotal moment in our relationship has happened in the rain. Think about it: the day after we embraced for the first time—"

"—that night in the courtyard outside your coming of age ceremony, even the day I asked you if you wanted to start a family in the first place."

"Exactly."

"Rain feels too large-scale for a Demigoddess to control. Also, there is already a Goddess of Rain, unless I am mistaken."

"No," I said, a sigh escaping my nose. "Pluvia. She is...well. She is missed, wherever she is."

"Is she dead?"

"No. She is lost, or, rather, not lost, but searching." Erathiel nodded slowly; he did not understand, but he got the sense that he did not need to. "Regardless, yes, rain would be far too large-scale for a Demigoddess to control."

"What do you propose, then?"

"Well, perhaps our daughter could be," my arms slipped around Erathiel's shoulders, "the Goddess of Petrichor."

He smiled. "I would like that."

I gazed up at the sunrise. Somewhere in the Immortal Realm, Auri was creating a masterpiece. "We will be a wonderful family."

"Indeed," Erathiel agreed.

"Simply the best of the best."

"The best of the..." Erathiel trailed off, hesitating for a moment. His voice was empty, almost fear-ridden, when he asked, "Will the world remember us?"

I laughed, pulling him closer to me. "Of course it will."

Chapter Sixteen

A YEAR HAD PASSED SINCE THEN.

The war continued to rage on. The humans managed to spill Vesa's ichor. Anima quickly recovered her with the healing water, but the mental damage had already been dealt. It was clearer than ever: the humans would not relent.

So, each Second-Generation God released an army of corrupted sprites. The existence of these sprites was once more experimental than anything, but now, the Gods were ready to take an offensive position without attacking the mortals directly. The corrupted sprites could only travel in or around their core element, but they were formidable foes. After all, their sole purpose? To ravage and destroy.

Confrontations between the human and corrupted sprite armies were growing increasingly common, many ending in a massacre to one side or the other. The effects were devastating. Because of the risk of corrupted water sprites, mills were shut down throughout Lenethaus, slowly depleting the food supply. People froze to death in the winter because they were unable to start fires, not wanting to accidentally spawn a fire sprite. Many heretics locked themselves in their homes, purely afraid of what may lie outside. Neutralists and loyalists to the Gods begged for an end to this madness, as did most of the Starlight coterie and a few other Gods, including Esolir and Lunix.

Finally, the King of Lenethaus heard his people's pleas, and he scheduled a meeting with Aques. Every God, except for the Titans, of course, was to be in attendance, as well as a large entourage of humans.

Talk of this fated day filled both the Mortal and Immortal Realms, and an overwhelming rush of excitement kept the population going. This day had gained the moniker 'Peace Day,' seeing as, at last, there was bound to be a ceasefire.

The war was brutal and a difficult burden to bear, but within days, it would be over.

THE STARLIGHT COTERIE STRODE TOWARDS A grand palace, where the meeting would take place. The structure was vast, with black turrets and earth-toned walls displaying wealth and privilege. However, as we approached the entrance to the east wing, I noticed that the walls were beginning to crumble. Perhaps it was deterioration over time, perhaps it was due to the war, but something felt almost broken about the royal family's wealth.

Auri, Vesa, and Aestalios walked in front. "Temprysus will be here," Auri said with a smile. "This will be the first time we meet him in years!"

"I must admit, I am excited," Vesa remarked.

"Look at you two, getting sentimental," Aestalios teased. Auri jabbed him in the arm. "Okay, okay, I am simply poking fun!"

"I hope there is champagne," Vesa said.

"This is a peace ceremony, I highly doubt there will be alcohol," Auri replied skeptically.

Aestalios shrugged. "One can only dream."

After a moment, Vesa complained, "My legs are exhausted."

A sly grin spread across Auri's face. "Yes, yes, me too. If only there were someone who could carry us..."

Aestalios huffed. "I am honestly starting to doubt that your legs get tired this often. I think you just want me to carry you."

"Does it really matter?" Auri asked.

He shrugged. "Not particularly." He crouched down, and Auri and Vesa got on his back. Once he stood up, the couple kept demanding that he go faster.

Erathiel and Stilis walked fairly close behind. "King Reluraun Karalor," Stilis mused. "Karalor...quite honestly, I often forget you are related to royalty."

Erathiel shrugged. "Barely. No noble titles were passed down to my father, only to his brother, Variton. Besides, I have only met the king on a few occasions."

"Do you recall anything about him?" se asked.

Erathiel slowly smiled. "Yes. Luscious hair; the women love him for it."

Stilis and Erathiel burst out laughing; it was common knowledge that the king was bald.

Haneræs and I brought up the rear. "I am ecstatic to see Sotis brought to justice," she remarked, visibly giddy.

I perked up. "Is that part of the plan for the peace terms?"

"I believe so."

"Wait, I must know, what is your gripe with Sotis? I mean, no one particularly likes him, but..." I trailed off. "Is there something personal?"

Haneræs's expression dulled, eyes distant with recountance. "Years ago, when I was just a child, he and I were present at a gathering. He was delirious, drunk, you get the gist."

"He often is."

"Precisely. He..." Her throat tightened. "He grasped me by the wrists, pulled me out of the house, then he, well—he a-"

"Haneræs," I interjected, giving her a knowing look. She paused for a moment, catching her breath. "You need not continue."

"He did the same with you?" I nodded. She was shocked. "Truly?"

"Yes." I sighed. "It was impossibly difficult to cope with at first. But I am in a stable relationship now. I try not to think of such cruelty."

She nodded in agreement. "Exactly. Things have also improved greatly since my gender confirmation ceremony."

"I nearly forgot you went through the ceremony." Haneræs exhibited many signs of womanhood since early childhood, and she underwent the ceremony when she was fourteen. Her feelings were always present, but she decided to undergo the ceremony sooner rather than later after Sotis's cruelty.

"I did. It helped me...so much." She smiled, then frowned again. "My body is now as I wish it to be. Sotis, however, never fails to remind me of everything wrong with who I used to be."

I nodded. "I have avoided him, but in the few times I talk to him, he makes me feel disgusting and vile for my actions, even though he was the one who forced–"

"Precisely." A wicked grin spread across her face. "This justice, then, will be all the more satisfying."

I took her hand. "I am sorry for what we went through."

She glanced at me and nodded sadly. "As am I."

"I think our pasts will always be there to haunt us," I said tentatively. "But I think we can manage to change from them."

Haneræs smiled. "I think the same. So, rather than viewing ourselves as tarnished, we shall transform our bodies into works of art. Perhaps we could be masterpieces someday."

We walked in silence the rest of the way. Soon enough, we arrived in a grand hall, lined with golden sconces and sculptures of heroic mortals, the ones who were remembered, at least for a time.

The Gods stood on one side of the hall, and the humans on the other. Auri noticed Temprysus from across the hall, then smiled at him. He looked as he should have, like a small boy, but something was off about his appearance. Temprysus did not return Auri's gesture.

Erathiel looked conflicted as he glanced between the mortals and the Gods, then I took his hand and led our group to the middle of the hall. He nodded at me with a smile. The humans and Gods looked to each other, some with an air of hostility or coldness, but most simply appeared hopeful.

King Reluraun and Aques stepped to the front of the room, greeting each other with a cordial nod. The King cleared his throat and opened a scroll. "We, the people of Lenethaus, have been engaged in this war for far too long. My peasants are starving, our resources are being depleted, and many are too fear-stricken to leave their homes. We need change."

"On behalf of the Gods, I agree," Aques replied. "Our sprites are dying, and we cannot risk a death amongst the Gods."

"However, if we are to accept peace, there must be great reform. Our first term of peace: you will, immediately, destroy every corrupted sprite in existence, and you are never to create any more."

Aques nodded. "I agree." No one protested.

"Our second term: You will punish Sotis for his cruelty against our farmers. We have provided him with ample offerings, and yet he has still refused to provide us with a decent harvest for years. Taarin, seeing as se is his Creator, will oversee him in all future harvest seasons, ensuring that Sotis will grace us with a fair reaping."

"This is blasphemy!" Sotis exclaimed, his speech slurred.

"It is only fair," Aques said, glaring at Sotis. Taarin hit Sotis in his side, and Aques nodded. "I agree." There were disgruntled grunts from Sotis, but no one dared protest.

"Finally, our third and last term of peace," King Reluraun grunted. He closed the scroll. "You will kill Temprysus, the God of Time."

Roars and protests erupted around the hall. Auri looked distraught. "This cannot be!" she exclaimed. "You will not slaughter my Creation!'

Even Aques looked shocked. "Do you realise how much you are asking?" he asked, horrified. "To kill a God? It has never been done!"

"How do you expect us to place our trust in you if you have the ability to manipulate time itself?" King Reluraun asked. "We mortals and our offerings make you Gods who you are, we *shape* you, and this is an overstep of power. We cannot in good faith allow this to happen. At its core, Temprysus is what started this war."

"What if we swear never to use Temprysus's abilities?" Aques suggested. "That way, he can stay alive, and you will not have to worry about an abuse of power."

The King shook his head and smiled sadly. "Do you honestly expect us to believe that you will not use his abilities? I apologise, but you will need to gain back our trust. Either Temprysus dies, or this war continues."

"Please," Vesa blurted out. She looked to Aques with a desperate expression. "Spare Temprysus."

Aques stared at Vesa with an unreadable gaze, then turned back to King Reluraun. "We will not slaughter one of our kind. We reject your third term of peace. If we can find a compromise–"

"We are unwilling," the King said bluntly. "These are our conditions for peace, exactly as stated."

"Then let there be war," Aques said sadly.

The King nodded. "Unfortunate." Many mortals in the room started to shift in place, revealing that each one held a sword. "Invoke the alternative plan."

The mortals charged the Gods, swinging their blades wildly. Many of the Gods immediately dissipated. Auri and Vesa grasped Temprysus, and the trio dissolved into light, evaporating from the room.

Once the humans reached us, it was too late to dissolve. We were engaged in intense combat, trying to dodge the blades. I kicked a human man's legs, knocking him off balance, then Erathiel clocked him around the head as the man swung for me. Erathiel handed me a dagger as he drew another from out of his belt.

"You brought weapons?" I asked.

Erathiel eyed me skeptically. "Do you think I believe in peace anymore?"

Erathiel did not linger long. He jumped in front of a blade that threatened to hit Stilis. Monsais, the God of Mountains, unleashed a torrent of rubble towards the person attacking Stilis. A human woman with brass knuckles charged towards Erathiel, but Esolir lifted her, held her by the throat, and threw her across the room. A man, who appeared as if he had not slept in days, managed to shed the ichor of Lunix, but Anima immediately healed her wound and sent out a corrupted air sprite towards the man in question.

The room had devolved into chaos and senseless fighting. It was clear: there would be no end to this war.

Erathiel had just finished helping Aestalios finish off five of his attackers. Across the hall, he saw a group of three mortals approaching Haneræs. She backed into a wall, weaponless and unable to fend off three people at once. Erathiel charged towards her in an attempt to take the hits for her, but he was too late.

The soldiers ravaged Haneræs.

It was all a blur: Aestalios, Erathiel, and I trying desperately to pull the people away from Haneræs, Aestalios grabbing the dagger from my hands and stabbing Haneræs's attackers until they were almost unrecognisable, Stilis begging Anima to give Haneræs healing water.

Anima shook her head as she examined the body.

"It is too late. She is gone."

Aestalios, wide-eyed, stood up slowly. His hands were tainted with ichor and blood. His figure nearly doubled in size as light ran up his arms, his legs levitating above the ground. Godly Wrath and unbridled rage surged through his bulging veins, and he approached the King, who hid in the corner of the room, face stained with apathy and cowardice. Aestalios slit King Reluraun's throat, then slaughtered every human in his path, save Erathiel and the ones who managed to flee.

Stilis, Aestalios, Erathiel, and I were alone in the room with Haneræs's limp body.

After blood and carnage littered the room, every member of the human party either dead or escaped, Aestalios found his way over to Haneræs's body. He looked at it curiously, almost in a childlike manner.

Stilis and I broke down sobbing, clutching her ichor-tainted wrists. Perhaps we were hoping to feel a pulse.

Erathiel blinked, as if when he reopened his eyes, the damage would be erased. Still, fate had claimed its victim, the wounds were all the same, it was undeniable; tragic, yet undeniable.

He blinked the tears from his eyes. *We were so, so close to peace. This could have been over.* He held my shoulders and looked to the side. He was unable to look at her corpse.

"She is gone," he managed to mutter.

Aestalios turned to Erathiel, appearing genuinely confused as his figure deflated. "She is not dead," he said indignantly.

I swallowed. "Aestalios, she–"

"No. What do you mean? She is not dead." Aestalios let out a cold laugh, then his voice rose to a shout. "She is not dead!" Fuming, he rammed his fist into the wall. *"She is not dead!"*

Erathiel, Stilis, and I slowly backed out of the room as Aestalios re-entered Godly Wrath. Once outside the castle, we ran as fast as we could.

A sick feeling rose in our stomachs as we mourned Haneræs, mourned peace itself, feeble as it may have been. It was as if the sun had vanished from the sky, and we were left tumbling through the dark, grasping around for something to hang onto.

I had seen a God die before me.

Why was even the immortal so fleeting?

A FEW WEEKS HAD PASSED, AND THE PAIN OF Haneræs's loss was no longer a deafening roar, more like a numbing dullness. Most of the time, the feeling was quiet, a sense of lypophrenia, if anything. Sometimes, the grief even allowed me to laugh again. Occasionally, though, the grief caught me off guard, and I would spend hours crying, reminiscing over our four years of friendship. It was hard to cope with, and I got the sense that it always would be. Things were getting better, though.

I got the sense that it would continue to.

The only thing holding me back, to my great surprise, was Erathiel. The loss had put a sort of strain on our relationship. It was unspoken, something outsiders were incapable of perceiving, but it existed, and my Gods, it stung.

Erathiel and I walked along a stony cliffside overlooking a bay in the Immortal Realm. I could tell that Erathiel, to some degree, longed for the Mortal Realm, but we both knew it was unsafe. Both the sprite and human armies were unrelenting, and the death tolls were ever-rising.

"Can I admit something?" Erathiel asked as he kicked a stone.

"Of course."

"When we were at the Village of the Blinded, I met a girl named Priya." He sighed. "She kissed me."

There was a dull pang in my chest, but somehow, the words did not faze me. "Was there a connection between you two?"

"No. If anything, the kiss only affirmed that my attraction lies solely with men."

"Good."

A bout of silence.

Erathiel let out a dry laugh. "Would it be horrible to say that I wished I felt something?"

Here, I froze. My head turned towards him slowly. "What do you mean?"

"Do not confuse my words; I did not desire Priya herself. She was a perfectly fine girl, but I only really bonded with her on an intellectual level. I almost—I..." He huffed. "I wanted to show myself that I am capable of loving a girl, that I hold some level of normalcy." He shrugged. "It amounted to nothing, I suppose. It is simply just another moment we must learn to move past."

I stared at him, feeling horrible. I shook my head in dismay. "After all this time, after all we have been through...you still view us as broken?"

"Not broken, not by any means, but–"

"Stop. You are wasting your breath." I advanced towards him as he backed away. "What could you possibly say to justify yourself?"

"It meant *nothing*, there was no emotion there–"

"You force me to constantly prove my love for you, then you say *this*, and I am supposed to see it as alright?"

"Is it such a crime that a fraction, a tiny fraction, of me wishes that I were capable of a typical relationship?"

"Perhaps it is!" I exclaimed. "I believed we had something! There, I said it. But, no, shame on me, I suppose, for believing in love!"

"Auroleus, you are being ridiculous. Of course I love you, with all my soul, I–"

"Alright, then. You love me? Stop acting as if it is some burden to bear, something shameful to carry!"

"I–"

I advanced towards him. "Do you understand how hard it is to be *so* in love, so publicly, so unashamedly in love, and have your partner, even if he loves you back, to view the relationship as 'incomplete,' or whatever you will!"

"Please, just understand that I–"

I let out a callous laugh. "Oh, please tell me, what can *I* do, Erathiel, what can *I* do to help you, what can *I* do to save this relationship, because clearly, I am the only one trying–"

"I don't know who I am!" Erathiel shouted. He took a step too far back, and the rock broke underneath him. There was a terror on his face as he fell from the cliff.

Immediately, I bolted over towards him and sent a gust of wind upwards. The wind pushed Erathiel up, but barely. When the wind faltered and he started to fall again, I shouted, "No!" and caught Erathiel by one of his flailing arms.

Erathiel and I stared at each other for a moment. There was wonder in his eyes, as if he was seeing me for the first time again.

I pulled up towards the surface, and we both retreated from the cliff. Once we were a safe distance, he remarked, "You saved me."

"Of course I did." Then, "You seem surprised."

He blinked. "I am."

Erathiel and I walked back towards the main street, and as we walked, I could not help but wonder:

If I am, as I say, the only one putting care into this relationship, then why is he surprised that I saved him?

Perhaps I need to show my love, rather than simply proclaiming it.

ERATHIEL AND STILIS WALKED ACROSS A stony bridge. They stopped at its keystone and stared out at the scenery: an azure river dotted with water lilies, a violet forest, and a small cabin in the distance (the home of Fluja, the Goddess of Rivers) with plumes of purple smoke releasing from the chimney.

Stilis let out a forlorn sigh. "We have stalled long enough," se admitted. Se outstretched ser hand, and Erathiel took it. Stilis created a rift, then the pair gave each other a forlorn nod as se led him in.

They reached the Lunar Library, which was brought to ruins.

Esolir and Lunix, hand-in-hand, walked through the ruins, searching for scraps that remained intact. They did not speak; rather, they were in quiet reminiscence of the palace of learning that used to be.

Auri was on the ground where the observatory used to be, crying and blubbering while holding scraps of the centre table. "It is my fault," she wailed. "I let them in, I had no idea they would destroy this much, they claimed to be loyalists–"

"They lied to you, sweetheart," Vesa said firmly, placing a hand on her wife's shoulder. "This is not your fault, it is theirs. They were the ones who managed to keep the rift open, after all. They were the ones who fired off the cannons."

"If I may," Stilis asked tentatively as se approached the pair. "Where are those humans now?"

"Dead," Vesa replied harshly. "At my hand, of course."

Erathiel nodded. "Ah."

Esolir and Lunix approached. "Erathiel...I believe this was yours." Esolir held out Erathiel's jade longsword.

A smile spread across Erathiel's face. "I am shocked that it was not stolen," he mused as he took the blade.

Auri's face lit up when she saw that Esolir and Lunix each carried a crate full of possessions, but then her expression fell again. "Is that all that was salvageable?"

Lunix nodded, and Auri crumpled.

"Do you intend to rebuild the Library?" Stilis asked.

Lunix dabbed her eyes with an embroidered handkerchief, then shook her head. "No, no, it would not be right. The Library's purpose has been served."

"Will you two simply retire, then?" Vesa asked, shocked.

Esolir shook his head. "No." He glanced at his wife, offered her a soft smile and kissed her lightly, then said, "We will simply find our next dream."

The six of them turned back to look at the Library, picturing its former glory. "This was a wonderful place," Erathiel murmured.

"It was a wonderful dream," Esolir added.

Lunix glanced at Esolir. "Can I create more dreams with you?"

Esolir took Lunix's hand. "For eternity, my love, for eternity."

Auri wrapped her arms around Vesa, and Erathiel wrapped his around Stilis. Eventually, the four joined together, and Esolir and Lunix entered the embrace. Entangled in each other's arms, they wept for the Library, for the icon of unity between the humans and Gods being levelled, for their losses and failures, but most of all, for a simpler, more peaceful time, when they were allowed to simply be young.

It was strange; Erathiel was pulled back onto the cliffside, but it still felt as if he was falling.

Chapter Seventeen

"WELCOME, COME ON IN!" AURI EXCLAIMED, ushering Erathiel into her cottage. It was a relatively small house by design, decorated with crystal wind chimes, homemade pottery, and shelves full of gemstones, all offerings from mortals. It was unusual that they kept all of the offerings, but he supposed that Auri and Vesa were sentimental.

Vesa and Stilis were sitting on an oversized green sofa, complete with a carefully woven throw blanket, and I sat on a yellow armchair. My eyes widened as I saw Erathiel walk into the room; we had not spoken since the day on the cliffside.

"Erathiel, I am deeply sorry, I–"

He met my gaze and offered me a smile. "As am I." I made room for him on the armchair, and he sat next to me, wrapping his arms around my shoulders.

Auri smiled as she sat between Vesa and Stilis. "Always the affectionate ones, you two."

"Have you two ever considered your own wedding?" Vesa asked. Erathiel and I looked shocked, then Vesa shrugged. "You two have been together for four years and have known each other for nearly twelve."

"Perhaps once this war settles down, we could consider it more closely," Erathiel replied, "but it may be on the horizon, yes."

"Can I plan your outfits?" Stilis asked excitedly. "Seeing as I clearly have the superior sense of fashion in this room."

"Stilis, did you *see* what Auri wore on her wedding day?" I retorted. "In this hypothetical, we would entrust her with this."

Stilis stared at me for a long moment. "Who do you think coordinated Auri and Vesa's ensembles?"

My eyes grew wide. "Really?" Se nodded. "Fair enough. Consider yourself hired."

"Oh, what could I do?" Auri asked excitedly. "I would like to help as well."

"Perhaps you could organise a few sprites to cook for us; you seem to be on good terms with them," Erathiel suggested.

"I thought we were going to let your brother cater," I joked. This earned me a jab in the arm from Erathiel. "Hey!"

"I would not want to intrude on your brother's cooking, of course," Auri immediately said, not grasping the joke.

"Can you cook?" Erathiel asked.

Auri blinked. "I suppose, yes."

"Is the food edible?"

She cocked her head. "Obviously?"

Erathiel grunted. "Hired."

"May I decorate the venue?" Vesa asked.

Erathiel and I exchanged a look. "To be honest, I did not expect you to be one for decorating," I admitted.

"I furnished this house perfectly fine; I can handle a wedding hall," Vesa snapped.

I was surprised; Vesa did not seem like the sentimental type. I expected Auri to have decorated their home. "Perfectly fair. You are hired."

"What shall we make Aestalios do?" Auri asked.

"Easy," Vesa responded. "Move all the heavy objects that I do not feel like lifting."

We all burst out laughing. After regaining ser composure, Stilis asked, "Where is Aestalios anyway?"

Auri clicked her tongue. "I haven't a clue. None of us have seen him since..." She trailed off, her eyes fixed on the floor.

"I worry for him," Stilis cerebrated.

"As do I," Erathiel said, biting his lip.

A knock came from the door, and Auri opened it, hoping it was Aestalios, but she only saw—

"Laphara?" Erathiel asked, confused. The Goddess of Stone rarely left her house, and even when she did, she was never seen without Ignos, her husband.

Vesa stood up, as if she expected this. "Ah, Laphara. Come." She and Auri led Laphara deeper into the house and closed the door behind them.

Erathiel, Stilis, and I were left alone. We made light chatter about our worries for Aestalios, but mostly, we sat in silent contemplation. Auri and Vesa stayed with Laphara. At one point, I could have sworn I heard Laphara sobbing, which was strange because she was always so apathetic and seemingly emotionless. I did not realise that it, in reality, was quite the contrary: Laphara had grown rather used to sobbing, but no one had ever heard her.

This was, of course, something I was unaware of at the time.

Finally, after an hour or so, Auri and Vesa emerged with Laphara. Erathiel noticed that Laphara's sleeves were rolled up and that her arms were covered in burn marks. Auri strode over to the front door and opened it to see Aestalios standing there, expression devoid of emotion. Laphara slipped out of the house, and Aestalios leaned against the doorway.

"I will not stay long," Aestalios said, his tone eerily dull. "I have been contemplating Haneræs's passing."

"We are very sorry, all of us are grieving, I am sure—"

"No," he said, cutting off Auri. "I decided that I will not accept an end."

206

Stilis cocked ser head. "Aestalios...I have already guided her soul to the Realm of the Dead, I–"

"I will attempt to revive Haneræs."

We were all dumbfounded. "Aestalios," Vesa said carefully. "It has never been done before, it is impossible."

"I do not care."

"Necromancy is a dangerous art," Erathiel remarked. "I cannot stress how dangerous this is."

"Please, Aestalios, sweetheart, sit down, we can talk about this–"

"No." His voice had a certain chill to it, something none of us ever heard from him. "I have work to do. If you'll excuse me."

He turned and left.

ERATHIEL AND AURI CARRIED CRATES FULL OF food through a village in Lenethaus. They stopped at every house, all of which were run-down looking, and delivered a parcel of food. Auri made sure to stop near the homeless families as well and personally deliver them the parcel. She wanted these people, the ones who were unwillingly most affected by the war, to see that the Gods were capable of doing good.

Erathiel looked out at the village. Families littered the streets. A cloaked peasant with blackened fingertips and buboes coughed while leaning against a building. A woman with a misshapen nose and bloodstained lips rocked back and forth while clutching a handful of dull green leaves.

Auri saw a woman shouting after a man in leather armour as he left their home. She approached the woman and handed her a parcel of food.

The woman eyed the food skeptically. "Why are you doing this?"

"I care." Auri looked after the man. "What seems to be the matter with him?"

"And why should I tell you?" she sniffed.

"I am not forcing you to," Auri said earnestly.

"He promised me he would not return to war, but..." She sighed.

"It sounds like you need a better man," Auri stated frankly.

The woman tightened at this. "Who are you to judge? I know what you are."

Auri's fingers clenched. "Yes, I have a wife, whom I care for dearly. What is it to you?"

The woman shook her head, lip pulled into a snarl. "Vile." She grabbed the parcel of food, stormed inside, and slammed the door behind her.

"Ungrateful, that one," Erathiel remarked as Auri made her way back down the front steps.

Auri shrugged. "No, we are giving her the very thing we took. After all, if I am being truly honest, the war is partially my fault." She stared at the woman's house. "Perhaps her demeanour was unwarranted, but I suppose you cannot please them all."

They continued handing out food. To Erathiel's great surprise, they only encountered a few hostile civilians, but one glance at the pair's blades seemed to shut them up. Many gave their thanks, and some simply stared, lost in some other dimension. The more food Erathiel handed out, the more of the village he saw, the greater the urge he had to help. Towards the end of the third street, he had the desire to personally deliver food to every village in Lenethaus. After all, you can only see so many children with their ribcages showing before feeling the urge to change something about the world that starved them. Either that, or you lack a soul.

Erathiel had seen plenty of the latter, especially within his own family.

One family in particular stuck out to him: a woman with three children. The children accepted the food gratefully, but the woman gave Auri a long stare. "We do not want this war," the woman said hoarsely. She did not seem angry, simply defeated.

Auri hugged the woman, who began to cry into Auri's shoulder. "Neither do we," Auri whispered. She sat there with the woman for about ten minutes, and she was prepared to stay forever, if that was what the woman needed.

Eventually, they ran into Esolir and Lunix, who were handing out books to young adults. "I had a feeling we would run into you two!" Esolir exclaimed.

Auri stared at him, dumbfounded. "You organised this event, you *watched* me sign up."

Esolir clicked his tongue. "Have a little enjoyment, will you? Believe in destiny!"

"Or believe in sign-up sheets and schedules, really your call," Lunix added.

Esolir and Lunix joined Erathiel and Auri. Eventually, Erathiel worked up the nerve to give out what he personally brought: small mechanical animals, which he gave to every child he saw.

After a while, Erathiel had an interaction that he would never forget.

A young, freckled boy, no older than fourteen, approached him nervously. "Are you Erathiel Karalor?" he asked tentatively. Erathiel nodded. "Can I ask you something in private?"

Erathiel glanced at the boy to ensure he was not armed, then said, "Of course."

The boy led Erathiel behind one of the homes, closed his eyes, and took a shaky breath, then asked, "Are you courting another man? Auroleus, if I am correct?"

Erathiel hesitated, then nodded. "Is that an issue?"

The boy immediately shook his head. "No, no, not in the slightest. Quite the contrary, I...I believe I desire a relationship like yours."

Erathiel nodded. "Alright."

"It feels refreshing to admit it aloud; I have never told a soul about this, and you mustn't either, alright?"

"I am glad you can confide in me, and believe me, this will stay between us. Out of curiosity, do you have a partner?"

"I do, but I wish I could have a relationship as openly as yours," he mused. "We only meet in private, if at all, and we usually communicate in letters that I burn, of course, just after reading them."

Erathiel stared at the boy for a long moment, seeing a bit of himself in him. "Why not be open about your relationship?"

"My father would beat me," the boy said simply.

"Well, then, allow me to take note of your father's address, so I can stab him in return." The boy giggled, and Erathiel placed a hand on his shoulder. "In all seriousness, though, do not give a care to what these people think of you. I can name at least twenty people on the other side of that veil," here he gestured to the sky, "that would fight for you, no questions asked."

The boy's eyes widened, and he nodded. "That means everything, you have no idea."

A smile tugged at the corner of Erathiel's lips. "I think I might be able to understand it." He glanced at Auri, who was staring after him. "I think I should return to my friends, but take this." Erathiel gave the boy a mechanical bird, identical to the one he and I had built years ago. "It should be strong enough to carry a letter. Use it to communicate with your partner."

The boy nodded, tears brimming in his eyes. Finally, he burst, and he hugged Erathiel tightly. Erathiel held the younger boy, picturing that he was embracing his younger self. "It is okay," he murmured, half to himself. "Things get better...someday, you will not only come to terms with who you are, but you will embrace it, and my Gods, the world will see the beauty of your love."

The boy nodded and took the bird. "I think I am going to go find someone."

"I think you should find him."

Erathiel turned and left the alley, feeling a new sense of belonging within himself.

He heard the sound of hooves on the ground. He turned his head to see who it was, and he felt a pit in his stomach when he comprehended that the man riding the horse was none other than his father, Chathan.

ERATHIEL'S EYES WIDENED IN TERROR AS Chathan approached. Lunix eyed the two, not quite comprehending the situation, then saw Erathiel's fearful expression and gently pushed him behind her.

Auri, however, recognised Chathan as Erathiel's father, and carefully drew out her spear. Erathiel mirrored her motion. Chathan stopped a few paces in front of Erathiel.

Esolir looked between the two. "What is this?" he snarled, noting Chathan's hostile stance.

"This boy has killed my nephew!" Chathan spat.

"He attacked me; I killed him in defence!" Erathiel shouted in response. "If he were not the brute of a man he was, he would have been spared!"

"You dared to leave your home and live among the Gods after you withheld information from your species!"

"So help me—you were the one who ordered me to leave."

"If I had no other option, I would kill you, boy," Chathan sneered. Auri crouched, entering an offensive position. "But we need you."

Erathiel sniffed. "How so?"

"You are a proficient swordsman. The human army could use you."

Erathiel paused for a moment, looked down, and let out a dry laugh. "Are you seriously implying," he muttered, "that even though you threatened my life, evicted me at seventeen, and neglected me as a child, you want me to help your cause?" Erathiel met Chathan's gaze, visibly amused. "Where do you get off? How deluded, how *impotent* could you possibly believe to think for a moment that I would join your cause?"

"So you stand with the Gods, then?"

"I refuse to choose sides in this frivolous war. I choose the people, regardless of species."

Chathan sniffed, drawing his blade from his sheath. "I may have a way of convincing you to obey."

"My Gods, how dense are you?" Auri asked. "You do realise you are single-handedly attempting to threaten a master swordsman and three Gods? Give it up, will you?" Chathan briskly shook his head, and the muscles in his neck tensed.

"You are a hopeless, pathetic man," Lunix sneered.

"He is *my* son, what he will or will not do is *my* authority, thank you!" Chathan exclaimed.

"Esolir is more a father to me than you ever were!" Erathiel bellowed. Everyone went quiet. Esolir looked perplexed for a moment, then placed a hand on Erathiel's shoulder and nodded firmly.

"Preposterous, I–"

"Are we finished here?" Auri asked, hoisting her spear towards Chathan's neck. Chathan's eyes widened, and he nodded. Auri nodded, satisfied. "I thought as much. Go."

As Erathiel watched Chathan ride off into the distance, becoming no more than a speck on the horizon line, Erathiel could not help but smile. He had the feeling that Chathan was out of his life for good.

ANIMA HAD REACHED HER BREAKING POINT.

At this point in history, it had been fifteen years since Pluvia's disappearance, and she had never seen Aques so apathetic.

He was cutting everyone from his life, even his Creations and wife. He absorbed himself in his work and often did not return for days. He spent an exorbitant amount of time with Luxheia and Tenedius. He was no longer able to banter with her, to scream at her, even to avoid her. He was simply going through the motions of life, hanging onto survival at its barest definition, on the precipice of complete emptiness.

It was like being wed to a void.

Anima could recognise that she was slipping away from the Goddess she used to be, but she could also understand that she had dealt with enough.

Perhaps it was time to take matters into her own hands.

So, one night, when Aques was out late, Anima gathered her things, glanced one final time at a painting of Aques, Pluvia, and herself, and ran away from the home she and Aques so lovingly built and had promised never to abandon.

She would never see the cottage again, not intact, anyway.

Where exactly she was going, she hadn't any clue.

Perhaps she was searching for home, wherever that was, because 'home' was certainly no longer there.

Chapter Eighteen

AURI RUSHED INTO THE QUIET BAKERY, HER demeanour frantic and eyes wild. Erathiel, Stilis, and I sat at a table, eating quietly. Vesa came in after Erathiel, a dazed expression on her face. Arberra dropped a tray of pastries in shock.

"What is going on?" Stilis asked, helping the poor Arberra clean up the fallen pastries.

"Ignos nearly died," Auri managed to pant.

Everyone in the bakery turned their heads in shock. There were shouts of confusion. Ignos, the God of Fire, brutal and undefeatable, upper hand in every battle, had a brush with death? The notion seemed impossible.

"How?" I asked.

"Laphara beat him to the point of near-death."

This, perhaps, elicited more shock. Laphara was apathetic, unresponsive to anything. While she may not have been inherently good, we were stunned that she was capable of such violence.

"Ignos was *lucky* Anima was nearby," Vesa added. "The healing water worked wonders on him, but since the water cannot replenish ichor, and he lost a substantial amount, he is still in critical condition. His vitals are out of control. Anima is watching over him as we speak."

A serious hush fell over the room. Finally, Erathiel was the one to ask, "Why?"

"Yes, why did she do it?" Auarae, the Goddess of the Breeze, asked.

"Do you all happen to remember that she would always cover herself fully in public?" Auri asked. Everyone nodded. "Underneath her extra layers were burn marks. Ignos had been abusing her."

"Oh," someone said quietly. The mood in the room, although still ridden with gloom, had shifted.

"She believed that it—whatever it was, she failed to provide too many details—was her fault. In her eyes, Ignos could do no wrong, so she blamed herself."

"It reached a breaking point," Vesa said, averting the gaze of everyone in the room, "and at last, she felt the need to confide in someone. She informed Auri and I about the situation, and we finally managed to convince her that she was not at fault."

"How did she defeat Ignos?" I asked. I felt heads in the room turn to stare at me, and I sighed and remarked, "Ignos could best the vast majority of Gods in a duel; if he nearly won against *Aques*, he would not lose to Laphara."

"No one was there," Vesa conceded, "but I would presume she entered Godly Wrath."

I nodded; it was a logical conclusion.

Vesa stared at the Gods, who were still transfixed on her and Auri as if expecting more. "Well?" she snapped. "That is all. Go about your day now."

Auri and Vesa pulled up chairs to the table, making chatter about how they were glad Laphara finally gained the capacity to stand up to Ignos, that they wished Aestalios was able to join them, had he not been desperately working on reviving Haneræs, and how "these fritters must be enchanted, I swear on Luxheia's name, this is the best thing I have ever eaten."

Elsewhere in the universe, a man lay in a hospital bed. His caretaker had stepped out of the room to allow a visitor.

A woman walked through the door. She stared at the man for a moment, expression unreadable. The man

216

outstretched his trembling hand, then murmured something to the woman. The woman's expression shifted, becoming very definitive, and she took the man's hand.

The next day, Auri and Vesa walked down the street. Imagine their surprise when, despite everything they had helped her through, they saw Laphara holding Ignos's hand, together once again as if nothing had ever happened.

Their one consolation in all of this was that Laphara was not nearly as heavily covered as before. Some of her scars had dulled or faded, and there were no signs of new markings.

Auri shook her head, and Vesa muttered, "Despicable." They walked away, and they silently gave up hope of helping Laphara; she was too far gone.

They had no idea why she had gone back to him.

Perhaps it was because she truly loved him.

But it cannot be that simple.

Nothing is ever that simple.

Perhaps it was out of routine. Ignos and Laphara, after all, had been married for centuries, and perhaps she felt the need to return to him, since it was all she had ever known.

Perhaps it was out of fear.

If he went into Godly Wrath, Ignos was undoubtedly capable of slaughtering Laphara.

Perhaps it was a mixture of the three.

Regardless, one thing was clear as day: Laphara was blinded, by love or fear or whatever else, she was blinded, and we in the Immortal Realm collectively predicted that Ignos and Laphara would not separate any time soon.

ERATHIEL AND I ARRIVED OUTSIDE A STONE house. It was a large structure, with mauve curtains shielding its inhabitants from its onlookers. The tides roared in the distance, an indigo sea stretching endlessly beyond our field of vision.

Erathiel approached the door, which was twice his height, and tapped the golden knocker against the smooth wooden surface.

The door opened on its own, and Erathiel and I entered.

We walked through a long hall. Our footsteps echoed off the walls, which were lined with frames, the paintings inside torn.

One singular oil lamp was illuminated in a small room. Erathiel and I tentatively entered. The room was full of crumpled papers and shattered vials. Aestalios crouched over a desk on the far wall, which sat near a panoramic window overlooking the sea. Books, portraits of Haneræs, and sheets full of jumbled handwriting cluttered the workspace.

Aestalios looked horrible. His hair was matted and dishevelled, his clothes were tainted, and he smelled atrocious. He had bloodshot eyes, dark circles, and trembling fingers as he turned the page of a book. His face was simultaneously manic and completely empty.

I had no idea what to say, but Erathiel seemed to find the words. In a stern, nearly father-like tone, he sighed and asked, "How long has it been since you slept?"

"Four days," he croaked.

"And how long has it been since you left the house?"

"I have no idea," he said, audibly defeated.

"You need to take care of yourself. Alleviate yourself of this, if only for a moment."

"I cannot," he sighed.

"Why?" I asked. "You will never accomplish anything in this state of exhaustion."

His voice was riddled with anguish. "I refuse to rest until Haneræs is revived. I will not accept an end."

"The dark arts are fickle, Aestalios," I said, raising my voice. "The chances you manage to bring her back are infinitesimal."

"It is a chance I must take," he said, tone dripping with anger. "Did you even know her?"

"Yes, and I know something about her that I doubt she ever told you." I took a deep breath. "She lived a difficult life, Aestalios, more difficult than you know. Let her have her rest."

"You are acting as if you are happy she is dead."

This broke me, and I began to shout. "Of course I am not *happy* about this. This grief is tearing me apart inside! I am only worried for you, can you not see? Necromancy will take a toll on you, you will *lose* your sense of self–"

Aestalios stood up, swept the items off his desk in a fit of rage, and shouted, "I will fight to the ends of the universe..." He clutched a portrait of Haneræs, and his voice grew weak. "...if only to see you once more."

Aestalios was brought to his knees as he trembled, clutching Haneræs's portrait. I made towards him, but Erathiel pulled on my sleeve. I let Erathiel lead me out of the house as I stared after Aestalios, who had collapsed and fallen asleep.

"I CAN SENSE IT," SE RUMINATED, EYES AGLOW. Stilis's expression was one of pain and deep contemplation. "Many souls are dying somewhere."

"Is there an ongoing battle somewhere?" Erathiel asked.

"I have no clue, I–" Se tried to conjure an orb, then the light and Symbol of Anima faded as se clutched ser temporal lobe. "It is getting worse. A God is in danger."

"Where–"

Stilis stood up abruptly. "I have to go." Se dissipated into light and vanished.

Erathiel and I jumped out of our seats, much to Arberra's discontent. "Always in *my* bakery..." she muttered.

"We must find Stilis," I said. Erathiel frantically nodded and took my hand. Our physical form collapsed until it was no more than a pale blue light, and we drifted downwards.

We sailed through the cosmos, swirling patterns of stardust forming and fracturing around us. I focused all my psyche on Stilis, pinpointed where in the universe se was located, and sent us to appear before sem.

Erathiel and I collapsed on the ground, gasping for air. After a moment, Erathiel regained his footing, and he pulled me up. We looked out at the scene before us.

A massive castle-like temple, the Temple of Seasons, was under attack. In the windows, we could see that Fisyn, Aedis, Auxra, and Hithar stood in the centre of the structure while shards of stained glass rained around them. Humans charged the doors and defaced statues, smeared the walls, and made a mockery out of the Gods.

Stilis ran inside the front doors of the temple, and Erathiel and I followed closely behind. A mass crowd gathered in the entrance hall, fighting off corrupted fire sprites that spawned from torches mounted on every wall. I pulled Erathiel away from a stray fireball. I used a dagger to fend off a human, and Erathiel managed to dissolve a fire sprite by attacking its solid parts.

I saw Stilis's coattail disappearing towards the right corridor. "There!" I shouted. We ran after sem, entering an overgrown hall full of flowers and ivy. Corrupted earth sprites grew from the ground, and Erathiel managed to kill a few before seeing Stilis run up the staircase at the far end of the hall.

Erathiel and I followed sem, and we emerged in an empty hallway. Stilis ran left, and we followed him, then climbed a spiral staircase until we emerged in the central chamber.

The central chamber was a large room completely enclosed in windows—while they were intact, they once depicted murals of Fisyn, Aedis, Auxra, and Hithar—and lined with trees and grass. The temperature in the room rose and dropped as the leaves grew red, disappeared, and regrew within a matter of seconds. The Gods in the centre of the room were all in a sort of trance, using their abilities as best they could to manipulate their surroundings; after all, their abilities did not exactly equip them for combat, so they opted to disorient their attackers.

Erathiel and I watched in terror as Fisyn's ichor was shed. Her wounds grew larger as more blades penetrated her skin, and the Goddess of Spring crumpled to the ground. The trance on the other three Gods was broken, in a sense, and they used their bodies to shield Fisyn from her attackers.

Stilis charged towards her, and for a moment, I was terrified that Fisyn had been killed, but se simply lifted ser hands and the Symbol of Anima appeared between them. "Anima, help!" se cried.

Within moments, Anima appeared. A swarm of corrupted air sprites appeared and cleared the area, save Erathiel and the Gods, since Anima was able to control the sprites. Anima withdrew a vial of healing water from her bag and poured it into Fisyn's mouth, which was slightly open. In an instant, Fisyn's wounds completely disappeared, and she was conscious again.

Aedis, Auxra, and Hithar immediately closed in around Fisyn, smothering her in kisses and affection.

"Not so fast," Anima chirped, slightly amused. "She needs to rest so she can replenish her ichor."

"That reminds me," Aedis said. "Is Ignos alive?"

221

"Yes, he is recovering rather well, unlike Ocari," Anima remarked. "Perhaps the healing water helps the process. If I may..." She took Fisyn in her arms and distilled into light. Fisyn's partners did the same, leaving Erathiel, Stilis, and I alone.

Stilis let out a shaky sigh, then slumped against Erathiel's shoulder. "Thank you," se managed to utter.

"We did nothing," Erathiel remarked, confused."

"You were here," se whispered, "and that means everything." Stilis sighed. "You cannot understand how difficult Reaping can be at times."

Erathiel and I exchanged a look, neither of us exactly knowing how to respond. Erathiel patted the back of Stilis's head and synced his breathing along with sers. "It will be okay," he muttered. "This war will be over soon enough."

His doubt was poorly masked.

I WALKED TOWARDS AURI AND VESA'S QUAINT cottage, tense after a meeting held by Aques. Every God of age was in attendance. We were discussing strategies as to how we would gain peace, and we all decided that we would abstain from using Temprysus's abilities. If a God attempted to convince Temprysus to manipulate time, the God in question would be renounced. A harsh punishment, I am aware, but the human army was growing more proficient, and we needed any chance at peace we could get.

I entered the cottage, and I was greeted by Auri, Vesa, and Stilis making light conversation. I had opted to walk to the house from Aques's manor; I needed fresh air, after all.

"Is Erathiel here yet?" I asked in a hushed whisper.

"No," Auri said, "but he should−"

There was a knock on the door. I let Erathiel in, and he smiled at me. Auri and I exchanged a panicked look, but quickly concealed it.

"No Aestalios?" Erathiel asked. Everyone shook their heads. "Shame."

"The man has been cooped up in his home for the last...I have no idea how long, months, at least," Vesa remarked.

"Let us speak of lighter matters," Auri suggested. She gave me a look, and we nodded. "Including..."

Stilis emerged from the kitchen, carrying two platters full of desserts. The platters were full of cakes, fritters, and jam tarts, which made me water at the mouth.

"What is the occasion?" Erathiel asked as Stilis set down the platters on the centre table.

Auri stared at him incredulously. "Your birthday, half-wit!"

"Right!" Erathiel exclaimed. "To be quite frank, I forgot. My family never celebrated those."

"Well, you are among the Gods now, darling," I remarked, sliding my hand around Erathiel's waist. "Although this may not be as grand as a coming-of-age ceremony, we always love an excuse to celebrate." I took a bite out of a tart. "Or an excuse to eat pastries, of course."

"Were these made by Arberra?" Erathiel asked.

"Yes, I had to convince her out of giving you twenty trays, seeing as it is your twentieth," Vesa replied. "She does not quite understand that humans eat substantially less than Gods."

Our conversation quickly fell apart as our hunger got the best of us, and we all dug into the pastries. Stilis ate slowly and carefully, taking utmost care to ensure that not a single crumb would fall on ser outfit. Auri accidentally spilt a bit of jam on Vesa's arm, causing Vesa to retaliate. By the end of the squabble, they were both covered in jam and somehow on top of each other, although I doubt that last part was a mistake.

"How did you manage to get powdered sugar in your hair?" I asked Erathiel incredulously.

He rubbed his hair. "Did I get it?"

"No, not at all, let me just–" I tried to rub the sugar off his wavy fringe, but it only spread.

"You are making it worse!" he exclaimed as he looked in a mirror.

"Okay, okay!" I pulled back.

Erathiel glanced in the mirror and groaned. "With this white hair, I look as if I am *sixty*, not twenty!"

The day continued with playful banter and unfortunate pastry mishaps (we managed to spill an entire platter on the floor, and by the Gods, we were not going to let that stop our craving for sweetness). Erathiel was lighthearted and jovial, but as he walked back to his temporary residence, my room in Ocari's manor, he could not help but feel a pang of emotions—not quite sadness, something else.

He felt out of place in the grand scheme of time.

He felt so much older than he truly was. Erathiel's eyes had seen more than most, and he had always been told he was wise beyond his years. Briefly, he imagined himself as a man whose hair had just begun to grow grey, laughing with his husband as he watched their child scamper around.

Simultaneously, he felt as if no time had passed at all since he was a child. In a sense, after all, the man that laid awake at night was the same person as the boy who wove grass anklets. Perhaps the man who laid awake wished he were the boy who wove grass anklets, even if only for a moment more.

Chapter Nineteen

STILIS AND ERATHIEL TORE OPEN THE DOOR to Aestalios's home. It had been a month since he left the house, and even then, he only left to purchase more materials.

Aestalios was passed out at his desk, his hand occasionally twitching. Stilis strode over to him, took a canteen of water off the desk, and poured it on his head.

"Gah!" Aestalios shouted as he woke with a jolt. He rubbed his eyes and comprehended Erathiel and Stilis's presence. "What are you doing here?"

"We are worried," Erathiel said softly. "We have not properly seen you in months."

"How many times have I told you?" Aestalios asked, voice devoid of emotion. "I will not accept an end."

"To what extent?" Stilis pleaded. "You have lost Haneræs, and you have lost yourself in the process of trying to save her!"

"I will do everything I can to revive her."

"Aestalios, you are only making this loss more painful for all of us," Erathiel remarked, taking a step towards Aestalios.

"Do you honestly believe that if I simply give up on this, I will *get better*? Are you out of your mind?"

"You seem to be."

Stilis paused, staring between Erathiel and Aestalios. Se knew Aestalios was right; if he gave up, he would simply be empty.

"We could help you clean up, at least," Stilis said softly. Se met Aestalios's stare. "It could help you think more clearly."

Aestalios nodded. "I would like that."

Erathiel and Stilis got to work. Erathiel cleaned up the piles of crumpled paper and broken vials, and Stilis organised the books alphabetically.

Stilis sensed Aestalios beginning to disassociate, so se began to talk. "Have I ever told you about my previous coterie?" Erathiel and Aestalios shook their heads. "Monsais," *the God of Mountains,* "Floratris," *the Goddess of Flowers,* "Palus," *the God of Swamps,* "and Glacies." Erathiel was surprised when se mentioned the God of Ice; aside from Aestalios, he was the Fourth-Generation God who garnered the most respect from mortals. "We were intellectuals. We hung around the Lunar Library, and we always got along rather well."

"I have never seen you there. What happened to your group?" Erathiel asked.

"Glacies and I started courting," Stilis mused, "and that was the beginning of the end, I suppose. We were together for a good while, then it ended about five years ago." Se shrugged. "Quite honestly, I forget how it ended."

"I would assume your group took his side?" Erathiel asked.

"They did." Stilis shrugged. "In all honesty, it was exhausting to socialise with them. You had to be at your best for every conversation, no matter what. I never felt at peace around them, if that makes sense?" Se smiled. "That is exactly why I appreciate the Starlight coterie; you all make me feel at home."

Aestalios faintly smiled, then his gaze dropped. "It is not the same without Haneræs."

"My Gods, how dense are you?" Stilis asked, storming over to Aestalios. Se shook their shoulders and half-shouted, "Do you realise: we are not the same without you either!"

To Erathiel's great shock, Stilis stared at Aestalios for a moment, then pulled him into a kiss.

Aestalios returned the embrace.

After a fleeting moment, Aestalios pulled away. "I must continue my work," he whispered, an inflexion of pain in his voice.

Stilis nodded, stepped back, and silently left the room, Erathiel following closely behind him.

Erathiel glanced at Stilis, desperately wanting answers, but Stilis seemed as if se was holding back tears, so Erathiel remained quiet.

Stilis and Erathiel approached the indigo sea, sitting down on the rocky coastline. Stilis clutched ser head and began to quietly weep. Erathiel said nothing. After a while, Stilis uttered, "I am terrified."

Erathiel leaned his head against Stilis's shoulder. "As am I."

AFTER A PARTICULARLY GRUELING DAY OF work, Aques returned home. He opened his door, awaiting his wife, but she was missing. He looked through every room, expecting to find Anima, or at least a note explaining her absence, but there was nothing. He began to hover with his Symbol between his hands, trying to communicate with Anima. However, there was only a low, nearly melodic, hum.

Aques began to hyperventilate, worried something horrible had happened to her, but then he found a loose sheet of parchment with a short message scribbled upon it:

I cannot go on like this. Do not attempt to find me. Goodbye, Aques.

Aques stared at the note in a trance of disbelief. His chest started to heave as breathing grew more difficult.

Eventually, his trembling hands were unable to hold the parchment, and it drifted to the ground.

Light surged up Aques's arms as his Symbol shone brightly upon his wrist. He grew in size, power surging through his veins. He was slowly, yet surely, entering Godly Wrath.

He rampaged everything.

Paintings were torn from their frames and ripped to shreds. Their bed was splintered, then broken into unrecognisable pieces. Books and scrolls were ravaged until they were no more than a pile of shreds and tattered bindings. Candles were thrown to the ground, incinerating several rooms. Aques had the innate urge to destroy everything in his wake. What he could not break by water damage, he shattered with his fists.

Within mere minutes, the cottage he had worked so hard to build had fallen before him, until nothing but the clutter from the destruction and the foundation of the house itself remained.

Aques crouched on the steps where the front porch would have been, deflating in size. He clutched his head and began to sob. The years flashed in his memory.

Once, when they were children, Aques and Anima were playing near an ocean. Aques found a unique stone, patterned with markings of blue and violet. He was excited to give it to Anima, but he dropped the stone, and it washed away into the sea. Seeing his disappointment, Anima swam after it, and she did not rest until she, eventually, found it.

Years later, Aques and Anima stood outside the Academy of the Gods. Aques took thirty minutes to deliver a five-minute speech to Anima; he stuttered and skipped over lines. He left off with a confession and a question. Anima smiled, simply said, "I know," and pulled Aques into a kiss. He supposed the question was answered.

During their wedding, Anima noticed that a bird had fallen from the sky. She halted the ceremony to find it, and refused to continue until she managed to heal the bird and got it walking again. She returned to the podium, expecting Aques to be angry with her, but he was only reminded of how much he loved her.

When they built their home together, Anima completely took over decoration, seeing as Aques was clueless when it came to colour theory. He complained that she cared too much about decorations, but secretly, he enjoyed the way she made their home feel.

As a young child, Pluvia was taunted by Itaria, the Goddess of Lava, who was around her age. Anima dismissed it as simple teasing, but this struck up an argument between Aques and Ignos, who was one of Itaria's Creators. Aques threatened to kill Ignos if the teasing continued. It was safe to say that Itaria never bothered Pluvia again.

When they raised Pluvia, Anima was confident that wherever Pluvia went in life, she was bound to be happy. Perhaps Anima was oblivious at times, but this was more than made up for by Aques's incessant fretting over their Creation. He always seemed to worry that he was doing something wrong when it came to raising Pluvia. She seemed happy with both of her Creators, despite their fears or lack thereof.

And for a few years, it was truly close to perfection, was it not? There were arguments here and there, a few too many nights spent counting sheep, but the genuine care and hope shared between Aques, Anima, and Pluvia was so strong that it nearly nullified all pain.

Their love was so powerful that, perhaps, they could almost be considered...

...a family.

Then, one fateful day, Aques saw black eyes when he stared at his reflection.

Everything fell apart.

The distance between Aques and Anima grew so vast that Pluvia disappeared in it, but no one could anticipate that Anima would turn her back on Aques entirely.

Even she herself was shocked at the notion.

And yet, after she weighed the cons and pros, after every alternative had played itself out in her mind, after all was said and done, leaving was just about the only action she could take.

Aques understood, in a sense.

As he knelt where his front porch once was, he was truly conscious of the fact that, perhaps, he broke everything the moment he expected them to be human.

After all, his greatest wish was to grow old with Anima, but he failed to realise that they did, in fact, have eternity; thus, it could never be.

He trembled, nearly convulsed, against the stone foundation. The family, the world he had built for himself, was gone. He felt so small, so insignificant, an isolated speck in the universe.

If he were human, he would have grown old with her. If he were human, they would not have left him: Anima, and Pluvia, and everyone else, in a sense. If he were human, he would be long gone, but if he were human, death was more than worth it. If he were human, he would have returned home, cooked dinner for his wife and his Creation—no, his *daughter*—and then danced in the rain with his family.

If only he were human.

Instead, there were clouds instead of rain, ichor instead of blood, a foundation instead of a home, existence instead of life.

So, he did all he could think to do, the only thing that could possibly prove his humanity.

He drew a dagger from out of his belt, brought it to the wrist upon which his Symbol was displayed, and watched as his ichor spilt out and tainted the grass around him.

He drew the blade deeper into his flesh, a stream of gold pouring from his arm. He felt dizzy, then faint, then nothing at all, simply a final echo in his mind:

Humans bleed.

Humans die.

Perhaps some part of me is human after all.

FLORIAN OPENED THE DOOR TO THE MANOR, letting Erathiel in. "Thank you," Erathiel said earnestly. He glanced around. "No one else is here, correct?"

"No, no, they are all off in battle. A group of corrupted stone sprites was spotted near the cliffside."

"Ah." There was silence for a moment.

"How are the Gods?"

"Ridden with drama," Erathiel groaned. Florian chuckled. "Everything is so romanticised…you grow tired of it fast."

"Understandable," Florian chortled. "How is that boy of   yours?"

"He is well," Erathiel said after a moment. "As well as we can be after the loss of a close friend, mind you, but even still."

"I recall you telling me," Florian said with a sympathetic expression. "The Goddess of Sand, was it? I am ever-so-sorry. Humans can be cruel."

"Indeed." Erathiel shrugged. "So can the Gods, of course."

"Staying neutral is easier, is it not?"

"Without a doubt," Erathiel agreed enthusiastically.

"You know, I always wished I were a God."

"Really?" Erathiel pictured the pressure every God was under to maintain perfection, and could hardly imagine desiring that for himself.

Florian shrugged. "Yes. I have always envied them."

"Alright, I will play along. What, if you were born a God, would you control?"

A thought came to Florian's mind, but he dismissed it. "I am not sure," he said. "I would want to be someone like Taarin, or perhaps Stilis. They both seem so free."

"Free?"

"Yes," he said, somewhat impatiently. "The Gods in general are so untethered to concepts mortals are forced into. Unfair, really."

"I suppose." Erathiel shrugged. "How has Ilyara been?"

"Quite well!" Florian exclaimed. "I am ever-so-glad I fell in love with her; perhaps Father has decent intuition after all. Oh, that reminds me, she has a request for you."

"And what might that be?"

"When you and Auroleus *finally* marry–" Erathiel rolled his eyes— "do not scoff, it has been years. When you and Auroleus finally marry, give us front-row seats to your wedding?"

Erathiel beamed. "But of course! So long as you come properly dressed, of course."

Florian sighed. "I may have to borrow a set of Ilyara's dress robes, then; heaven only knows I lack any formal attire."

"Preposterous, you have the best wardrobe out of any Karalor, and yes, that includes the late King." Erathiel considered it for a moment. "Has Crown Prince Orick been sworn in yet?"

"Yes," Florian sighed, "and somehow, he is less endorsing of peace."

Erathiel sighed. "When will this war end?"

"When indeed," Florian mused. His expression was

solemn for a moment, then he lit up. "Oh! I have prepared a meal."

Erathiel stifled a grimace. "Wonderful," he replied, masking a resentful tone.

Florian led Erathiel into the dining room, and a plate of meat and potatoes was laid out. It looked rather bland, but not outwardly revolting; improvement, he supposed. It did not provide Erathiel relief; it was suspicious, if anything.

"Eat up!" Florian smiled.

Erathiel carefully took a bite of the meal. The meat was most certainly overcooked and underseasoned, the potatoes had gone a bit cold, but other than that, there was nothing really to complain about. The meal was lacklustre, not necessarily inedible. Erathiel was proud of his brother.

"This is a nice meal, Florian. Do you still intend to open that tavern?" Erathiel asked, taking another bite.

"Of course!" Florian said. "I have been ecstatic, you have no idea. I even have a floor plan, here, let me describe it to you..."

As Florian and Erathiel ate, they discussed Florian's tavern. It was ambitious, certainly, but Florian's cooking skills were improving.

Suddenly, there was a voice that came from the sky. "Erathiel?"

Erathiel stood up. "Auroleus?"

"What is it?" Florian asked.

"Can you not hear—"

Erathiel was cut across. "Come outside." My voice sounded frantic.

Erathiel stood up. "I need to go."

"Wait, I—"

He left Florian and raced outside. I was waiting for him outside his manor. "Aques is sending an onslaught of sprites. People cannot keep up, they are dropping like flies."

"Has no God come to help them?"

"That, darling, is where we come in." I outstretched my hand, and he took it.

"Take us there."

We fractured into light.

WE ARRIVED AT THE BATTLE SITE, A SANDY coastline. Waves of corrupted water sprites, murky and shifting in appearance, attacked shambles of a human army. Neither side relented.

There were screams of terror from the human side as the water sprites filled their lungs with water. With a sputtering cough and a choke, lives were extinguished in minutes.

I sent out a wave of wind, tearing the corrupted sprites from the shore. Erathiel stood near me, ensuring that no sprites, nor confused humans, would shed my ichor.

"Is that a God?" a human shouted, pointing towards me, as Erathiel impaled a sprite with his blade.

"We are helping you, do you not realise?" I shouted as I sent ten sprites far out into the ocean.

The human nodded, and a smile spread across their face. The army raised their swords in vindication, a new sense of determination filling them.

The battle raged on, the humans managing to kill a few sprites here and there. I was their major weapon, of course, catapulting sprites into the water. For a moment, I thought we would win. We were truly going to win.

Then, out of nowhere, hundreds of sprites emerged from the water, each of them holding a sapphire-encrusted spear.

"Retreat!" I shouted towards the humans. They ran far away from the water, and about half the sprites tore after them. I could only hope they would be safe.

I turned my gaze towards the water, and around a hundred pairs of glowing blue eyes stared back.

They charged towards us.

I took Erathiel's hand, trying to dissipate, but I could not concentrate, and we were not fast enough, for the sprites had reached us.

I felt blades penetrating my skin, sinking deeper and deeper. I stared at my ichor-tainted hands in horror, feeling my power and life source slipping away. It was impossibly difficult to summon any wind. My energy was simply focused on my vitals, on keeping the steady, soft drumming noise inside my chest going.

With the last of my power, I cast a circle of wind around me, a forcefield around Erathiel and I sustained for a moment.

I fell to the ground, and he was already there beside me. I managed to turn my head to face him. He was bleeding out as well. His hand found mine, blood and ichor mingled together on our fingertips. Our gazes locked, and the world's greatest poets and wordsmiths could not replicate the raw emotion in our stare. I took a shaky breath and recounted our days of yore.

This was not some folktale love, and it did not have to be that way. Our love was true, painfully so; it stood through space and time and war and turmoil and anything the universe could think to throw at us, we would survive, we would resist, we would prevail. Our love was defiance, a whisper to mend a soul, a shout to shatter the sound barrier, a parallel voice in an echo chamber, a sound that could never be ignored. I do not mean love as in a gentle touch, not love as in a model or a perfectionist ideal, I mean love as in holding hands in a warzone, finding warmth in rigor mortis, a willingness—no, eagerness—to sacrifice yourself for the other. I mean love as in a shot or a swordfight, love as in second chances, love as in the first brick thrown to break a wall, love as in the beauty of ichor. I mean a love that transcends barriers, tears down borders, shatters expectations, exists 'in spite of', a love that fractures reality and moulds its own.

Erathiel and I stared out at the battlefield, and an overwhelming sense of rejuvenation flourished inside me. As the onlooking sprites watched, I pulled Erathiel into a kiss, and whether the mortals and Gods chose to see us as the paragon of beauty or the embodiment of abomination, we could not have given a care. After all, despite everything we had endured, we were alive, we were alive, we were *ALIVE, WE WERE ALIVE, WE WERE ALIVE*, and we were in love, my Gods, were we in love, and, damn time, damn fate, no person could dare strip that of us.

The forcefield around us dissipated, and I stared my demise in its many glowing eyes.

"So, universe, do with us what you will."

Before the sprites could strike us, rain fell from the sky, and we all stopped for a moment. As if on command, because of the rain and petrichor, the corrupted sprites retreated into the water.

I still could not manage to distil, but I sent a signal out to Anima for help. She quickly appeared, saw our lacerated state, and gave us each a dose of healing water.

Erathiel was fully healed quickly, whereas I was still lacking ichor. For several days, Anima and Erathiel doted on me, caring for my every need with no complaints. Internally, I felt horrible for wasting their time, but I could recognise that I was incapable of doing much in my bedridden state.

It was exhausting and rather painful to speak for too long. Erathiel often sat beside me for hours, and since I struggled to speak to him, I grasped his hand as tightly as I could. It turns out the words were not needed, because after all, by this time, our love went unspoken.

Although our dynamic had shifted and adapted overtime, I can say for certain that I had never loved Erathiel Karalor as much as I did after that battle. He had always been there for my highs, yes, but even at my weakest point, he managed to love me all the same. He stayed around, he protected me, he *cared*. I may have been incapacitated then, yes, but I was more than prepared to do the same for him. There was a sort of unspoken codependence between us. We needed each other, beyond anything, material or otherwise.

A smile spread across my lips.

We were alive.

We had gotten lucky; it was purely good fortune, but we were alive.

Chapter Twenty

TWENTY-ONE WAS A BITTER AGE.

I felt as if I should have grown up. I felt far too young for my body. Everyone else had aged, matured, and I was helpless in a sense. I was drowning in the belief that I was, mentally, so much younger than anyone else around me, and that I was incapable of anything worthwhile until I changed.

Simultaneously, I had grown too much. The things I had seen, the horrors I survived, they took their toll. I lacked smile lines and gained darker circles every day. Time was slowly breaking me down.

The war was ever-raging, and it could not have helped my state. My ichor may have replenished itself, yet I still felt an overwhelming state of weakness.

I was too young to be respected, yet too old to be carefree. Too young to be taken seriously, too old to be free of judgment, it was an exhausting emplacement. I needed a definitive place and purpose in the universe, not a void or null space. It was as if I were on a suspension bridge shrouded in fog.

I was drifting between here and there, trapped between two timelines, stuck in neutrality in an ever-raging war, and, damn the Gods, I was growing weary of it.

"COME," AQUES SAID, OFFERING ME HIS HAND. "I have something to show you."

I looked up from an orb, feeling it dissolve in my hands. "What?"

"Something I should have shown you after you came of age, but..." He sheepishly shrugged. "The war. You understand."

"Of course, it has only been...what, three years?" I responded dryly. I was in a particularly sour mood. "It happens to the best of us." I gestured to Erathiel, who was nearly frozen in place next to me.

Aques appeared conflicted. "This is a sacred Godly tradition—"

"That is all well and good, but I want him there."

I stared at Aques, defiance clear in my eyes. Aques paused anxiously. "Fine," he managed to let out. He extended another hand to Erathiel, who was visibly flustered.

The three of them distilled into a blue light.

We appeared on a stone path in the centre of a golden field. There was a mystic nature to the air, particle wisps dancing between the scattered trees.

Aques silently led us down the path. I picked a sky blue flower that was growing between a few stones and placed it behind Erathiel's ear. We chuckled lightly as my hand lingered near the side of his face, then we heard Aques clearing his throat. He appeared aggravated and beckoned for us to follow more closely.

"I must ask you, Aques," Erathiel queried, "how have the Gods managed to survive so long, yet you are so weakened if your ichor sheds? How can a human be capable of killing a God?"

"We have reached such a powered state that we can fend off disease, old age, most damage, but at our core, we are still human, and thus, we cannot fend off violence. Nothing can," Aques answered. "We separate ourselves, we create a veil, but we are destructible." Out of instinct, he ran his fingers along the cuff around his wrist. "Impossibly so."

Erathiel fell silent. Within a minute or so of walking, we saw the end of the path: a circular bit in the path with three stone pillars bordering it.

"Auroleus," Aques asked, "how long does it take until a God begins Ascension?"

"A hundred years," I answered.

"Until they become a Titan?"

"Ten thousand. Is this a test?"

"Not quite. Is time the only factor?"

I paused, genuinely unsure. "Yes?" I replied unconfidently.

He stared at me for a moment, then led us to the pillars. Aques gestured to the first pillar, which read: "First Cycle - Mastery." Several names were listed at the base of the pillar, including every Second-Generation God, as well as more recently Created Gods, such as Gala, Esolir, Ocari, and Lunix.

"This is the First Cycle of a God's life. If a God desires to Ascend, they must have full knowledge over their element." Aques tapped the pillar. "We call this Mastery. Mastery takes around a hundred years to achieve, sometimes more, sometimes less."

Aques strode over to the next pillar. It read: "Second Cycle - Wisdom," and only had two names inscribed: Luxheia and Tenedius. "This is the Second Cycle. If a God is to become a Titan, then they must gain Wisdom; this entails knowledge about the highs and lows of existence, and knowing how to use their power for the greater good."

Aques walked over to the third pillar. It only read: "Third Cycle," and the rest of it lacked any inscription.

"There are no other engravings," Erathiel remarked.

Aques nodded. "No God has ever reached this point."

Erathiel's eyes widened. "Even Luxheia and Tenedius? They are practically as old as time itself."

240

"Not quite," Aques corrected. "Luxheia simply harnessed life; she did not create it. The Ancients existed before the Gods did."

I stared at the pillars for a moment. "What was the purpose of this?"

"From this point on, you must work towards Mastery and train your abilities to reach their highest potential." Aques let out a trembling sigh. "If that is the path you choose, of course...no, I mean—" He fiddled with the cuffs around his wrists, and his many eyes blinked in shame. "I think I will depart now. Goodbye."

Erathiel and I watched in confusion as he distilled into light.

"What was this all for?" Erathiel asked.

I stared after Aques, recalling his past. "Perhaps...it is hard to explain, I suppose."

Erathiel spent the rest of the day weaving flower crowns for me, until there were too many to fit around my ears, so we decided to frolic in the golden fields instead, wasting the lucid day away.

"ARE YOU SURE THIS IS SAFE?" ERATHIEL asked, gripping the hilt of his sword. They were standing outside a set of glistening stairs that were similar in appearance to ichor. Clouds shrouded the stairs beyond a few steps, and neither Erathiel nor Aestalios could see what was beyond.

"No," Aestalios admitted. The stairs before them led to Luxheia's residence. No one had ever entered, and no one had ever seen her leave. It was impossible to distil into the area.

In Aestalios's months of research, he came to the realisation that the essence of Luxheia and an electric shock

241

would revive a soul. He planned to acquire a bit of the essence that surrounded Luxheia. It was dangerous, considering she was one of the most powerful Gods, but Aestalios refused to accept an end.

"Be safe, please," Erathiel pleaded. "Do not allow this to be your demise."

Aestalios gave Erathiel a simple nod, then turned to leave. In that moment, he felt inexplicably exposed. He was standing on the stairway to Life herself, completely armourless; the armour would not do much against Luxheia, it would only slow him down. He took a deep breath and walked up the stairs.

A strange sense of familiarity filled his mind as he walked through the cloud of fog. He nearly lost his way, but with a few more steps, he emerged and found himself in an entirely white void.

Although the void was completely empty, he had the sense of the area being overcrowded. A sense of alexithymia ran through Aestalios as his emotions were heightened. He felt everything and nothing all at once, and it was nearly sickening.

There were only two discernible figures in the void: himself and Luxheia.

Her form, or lack thereof, nearly filled the void, although the void itself seemed to span infinitely. She was too complex to fully comprehend, but she can best be described as the embodiment of existence. Resting above the vortex of swirling particles, there was one singular gigantic eye, which had two silky golden cloths bandaging it. She did not seem to notice him, but, oh, how she towered over him! If she wished, she could destroy his very being in a heartbeat.

If he could manage to feel something discernible, Aestalios would have been terrified.

With a quivering hand, Aestalios drew a vial out of his pocket. He took the cork off its lid, then trapped a few particles floating around her. He sealed the golden dust, then her blindfolded eye turned towards him slowly.

He ran for his life as she fired bullet after bullet of light towards him. He managed to dodge the light rays as he charged through tendrils of glowing fragments.

His life was on the line. Sprinting through the endless field of everything while light threatened to consume him, he could not help but wonder:

Is this worth it?

With a fierce nod, he continued to dart through the void.

At last, he found the fog from which he came. He ran towards it, determined he was going to make it, then he turned around to see Luxheia's eye right in front of him.

ERATHIEL STORMED INTO VESA'S COTTAGE, fuming. He had waited hours for Aestalios, and yet Aestalios did not return, so Erathiel assumed the worst. He was furious, and he needed a scapegoat other than fate.

"Vesa!" he bellowed. She was sitting on the sofa, sipping a glass of wine.

She set the glass down, looking concerned. "Is everything okay, Erathiel?" she asked.

"Aestalios is missing, Haneræs is dead, everyone is falling out of love, and all of this is your fault!" he shouted.

Vesa's expression grew hostile. "How am I at fault in any of this?"

"You Created the God of Time," Erathiel said beseechingly. "If it were not for Temprysus, this war would have never started, and everyone would have been spared."

"That is a terrible accusation," Vesa said, her tone dripping with iciness. "It is almost as if, and hear me out on this, I was not the only God to Create Temprysus."

"Auri has helped the humans. She has delivered food alongside me, she has spared countless human lives, whereas you...you are apathetic!"

"I—"

"No, let me speak. How could you not feel horrible, absolutely wretched, for all the damage *your* Creation's existence has caused? The war, the bloodshed, even your own ichor was spilt! How dare you—"

"Do you think I could have predicted this?"

"Yes!" he exclaimed. "Harnessing time itself? The humans were sure to riot, I—"

"I apologise, I have to clarify..." Vesa remarked, taking a sip of wine before letting out a light laugh. She stared at Erathiel, a mixture of apathy, amusement, and confusion in her expression. "...you really think we regret any of this?"

Erathiel was dumbfounded. He managed to find his way to the door handle, opened it, and started to hyperventilate after he left the house.

After everything we have lost, he thought, *how could she lack the capacity to care?*

Chapter Twenty-One

ERATHIEL AND I WOKE UP TO SEE A FIGURE standing over us. "What—" I sat up in bed, shaking awake Erathiel.

Aestalios was staring at us. "Hello."

Erathiel woke with a jolt. "Aestalios...you are alive!" he exclaimed. "What happened to you?"

"Never mind that. I discovered how to revive Haneræs."

My mouth dropped open. "Truly?"

"Yes. I would like you to be there for it."

Erathiel and I exchanged a glance. We could both tell: he did not seem excited or relieved, simply anxious. Still, we were thrilled to see Haneræs again—if the revival worked, that is.

We took Aestalios's hands, dissolved, and appeared in the hallway of his home. "Where are Auri, Vesa, and Stilis?" I asked. "Shall we wait for them?"

"No," Aestalios said suddenly. "I do not want to overcrowd her, and since you helped stand guard when I went to Luxheia–" he gestured to Erathiel– "I figured you should be the one of the first to see her."

"So why am I here, then?" I asked.

Aestalios shrugged. "You would not have let Erathiel go without you."

I nodded. "Fair, I suppose."

Aestalios silently led us down the hall, at the end of which was a grated metal door. Fulir stood at its frame, the light in his hair pulsating faster than normal. He and I exchanged a nervous look, then Aestalios opened the door.

Inside the room was a large coffin made of black stone. The coffin itself was standing upright, pushed against the back wall. The rest of the room was completely barren.

Aestalios opened the coffin, and I hardly recognised the corpse inside as Haneræs. She was hardly more than a skeleton, her skin sagged against her bones.

Erathiel's eyes widened in horror. Aestalios seemed unfazed by Haneræs's appearance as he gently opened her mouth. Her jaw clicked open, revealing a skeletal mouth devoid of a tongue.

"Ready your charge," he commanded Fulir. Fulir crouched, lightning surging between his hands.

Aestalios drew out a vial with a strand of golden particles—the essence of Luxheia— inside. "Aim towards her chest." Fulir took a deep breath.

Aestalios lifted the vial over where her lips would have been. "Fire."

He poured the essence into Haneræs's mouth just as Fulir struck her bosom with a bolt of lightning.

For a moment, there was silence. Aestalios's expression began to fall. He could not help but wonder: had all his work been for nothing?

Then, spirals of golden light emerged from the place where Haneræs was struck. Her skin slowly started to restore itself as her body began to convulse. Her figure was mended as the light surrounding her swelled, and a faint scream came from her heart. The light and shouting faded, and Haneræs was standing before us, breathing.

Her eyes darted around. "Where am–" She seemed to comprehend the situation, and she let out an exclamation of glee. "Aestalios, am I alive?"

Aestalios stared at her, not happy, really; he was more curious than anything. He stepped towards her, pulling her into a hug. She sobbed tears of joy and embraced him tightly, elated, relieved to be alive. He, however, only held her lightly. I looked into his eyes, and he appeared emotionally null.

It was as if he worked himself to death, but only his soul left him.

He pulled away from the embrace and stared at Haneræs dejectedly. He found himself weary of what he saw. He expected to feel something, anything, but there was only a void inside his chest. "I don't know what went wrong," he said just before storming out of the room.

Haneræs stared after him, confused. She reached for Aestalios lightly, then her hand dropped.

"We are glad to have you back, Haneræs," Erathiel said as I pulled her into a light side-embrace. "Infinitely so."

"He does not want me," Haneræs managed to utter.

Erathiel and I exchanged a look. "He will come around, I promise," I assured her.

"I saw the look in his eyes." She let out a forlorn sigh. "There is nothing left, is there?"

We were rendered silent. Haneræs lifted her hands and created a rift.

"Are you going to the Library?" I asked.

"Yes. If I am to live again, I would like to be reminded of happier times."

"I am sorry to be the one to tell you this...it was destroyed years ago," Erathiel said hopelessly.

Haneræs clenched her jaw. "Then I will wander among its ruins."

"Are you leaving us *permanently*?"

"Perhaps. I do not know."

"Aestalios will be distraught."

"I could not give less of a care to what Aestalios thinks of this," she spat.

"Haneræs, he will be *destroyed* if you leave, he worked to revive you for so long–"

247

"He brought me back," Haneræs said, "tore me from my eternal slumber, only to leave me loveless. He deserves this."

She made to step through the void, then turned to glance at Erathiel and I. He asked, "Can we go with you?"

"I need time, I think. You may visit me someday, I promise, just...do not tell Aestalios where I have gone, alright?"

Erathiel and I exchanged a glance, then nodded.

As Haneræs stepped through the rift, stifling tears, she shook her head and whispered to herself, "What went wrong?"

Time passed.

Haneræs always seemed to linger around the ruins of the Lunar Library. She said it evoked nostalgia, memories of simpler days. I think she needed that.

As for Aestalios? I hadn't personally seen him since. He arrived to see Haneræs gone, then was filled with the notion that he was not 'enough' for the Immortal Realm, and wanted to prove that he had a purpose.

So, he commanded a subsect of the human army trained to fight Second- Generation Gods. He channelled his ability and emptiness into the war, even though he was fighting for the very army that led to his and Haneræs's demise.

A tragedy.

AURI, VESA, AND I MADE HASTE THROUGH THE streets of an aristocratic village. The area appeared familiar—perhaps it was near Thyrin Cove—although it was fully shrouded in fog.

Our job? To start a fire in the forest near town. Ignos was still in a weakened state, so he had trouble creating fire.

He could manipulate it, and he could spawn corrupted spirits from it, but he needed someone else to create the fire itself.

Technically, it was only Auri who was given the assignment, but Vesa and I decided to join her as a sort of defence against any humans who noticed us.

We were lucky with the fog. Because of our cloaks and the mist dulling the streets, we were able to walk unseen. There were not too many passers-by, and they hardly spared us a glance.

We soon reached the woods, ready to start the fire. Seeing as she was a descendant of Ignos, Auri seemed to know what she was doing, so Vesa and I opted to stand guard.

Vesa nudged me and pointed towards an approaching shadow. The figure was lanky, too small to be a God. "Are they coming towards us?"

I examined the shadow for a moment, then took Auri's spear off the ground and threw it towards the figure. Shockingly, the silhouette collapsed, motionless once it hit the forest floor. I was shocked that I managed to hit them.

"Not anymore," I responded. Vesa chuckled.

The rest of the morning was calm, devoid of unwanted surprises. Auri managed to start the fire fairly quickly, and she spent the rest of the morning adding sticks and twigs to allow the flame to grow.

Soon enough, several trees were ablaze, and Auri, Vesa, and I stood far away from the forest, seeing as we were uninterested in catching fire. Corrupted fire sprites started to spawn from the flame, and we nodded, satisfied. There was a pang in my chest—I always hated getting involved in the war—but I was glad I decided to assist in defending Auri.

"I am going to examine that person you hit," Vesa told me as she stood up. She laughed. "Perhaps it was someone I held a grudge against."

Auri chuckled. "May I join you?"

Vesa intertwined her arm with Auri's. "Of course."

Auri and Vesa strolled over to the corpse. I lingered behind, not interested in seeing the death I caused, then froze when Vesa exclaimed, "Is this Erathiel?"

I ran over, heart racing, then calmed slightly when Auri replied, "No, this man has spectacles."

I sighed in relief, approaching Auri and Vesa. "You cannot frighten me so!" I exclaimed, leaning against Vesa's shoulder. "Not all humans look the same, you know."

"Have you spared him a glance?" Vesa gestured to the corpse. "You have to admit, they do look quite similar."

I examined the body, and my face went pale. The man's face was eerily similar to Erathiel's, as if they were—

"Erathiel had a brother, did he not?" Auri asked.

My limbs went limp. "He did," I uttered.

"Yes, yes, Florian, I believe," Vesa added. "You think it is him?"

"Certainly; I have seen Florian before, this is absolutely him," Auri replied.

They chattered away, lamenting on how the loss was 'a shame,' 'Erathiel will be distraught,' but they failed to realise the gravity of the situation. I knelt next to the corpse, clutching Florian by the collar as I began to sob. My heart was beating at an alarming rate. I struggled to breathe. My mind was racing.

I killed Erathiel's brother.

How could I have killed Erathiel's brother?

He will leave me for certain.

WHEN ALL SEEMED LOST, SHE WAS AT HIS side once more.

Anima heard the sounds of sobbing, and she found Aques outside their old home, covered in ichor. He was screaming, crying in pain, but he stabbed himself over and over until his arm went limp entirely.

In a heartbeat, she was kneeling beside him, tearing a dagger from his hand. "Stay alive!" she cried. "You cannot leave me now, Aques, not after everything we have gone through!"

She bandaged the wounds as rapidly as she could, trying to save as much ichor as possible. Once the wounds were fully bandaged, Anima pulled a pulpy green substance out of a pouch in her bag and shoved it in Aques's mouth.

After administering the substance, Anima rested her head against Aques's chest to hear his breathing. He was unconscious, and his face had gone pale. Still, his heart was beating and his lungs were moving, and in that moment, it meant everything.

A few minutes had passed, and Aques slowly blinked open his eyes. "What..." He looked up. "Anima?"

"You know my name," she breathed. "Thank the stars."

"What—"

"No. Stay still. How do you feel?"

"Lightheaded," he responded.

"As expected. Here." She pulled his legs onto her lap. "Keeping them elevated helps with the ichor loss," she explained.

"Ah." He nodded. There was a moment of silence. "Did I lose consciousness?" Anima nodded. Aques bit his lip. "Are you going to ask what happened?"

"I think I know," Anima replied grimly. She offered him a consoling look. "We can talk more about this someday. Now is not the right time, I think."

Aques was in disbelief. "You want to see me, after..." He gestured to the house, then back at Anima.

She smiled sadly. "It will take time for things to return to normal." He nodded. "But I can never seem to leave you, can I?" She gently took his hand. "Is there anything I can do?"

"Can you simply talk to me?" he asked softly. "It does not matter what you say, I—"

"I understand." She traced his fingers with hers. "I think I would like to become a healer someday, make it my mission to mend the Gods of their ailments."

"You would be wonderful."

"I think I would."

Anima raved about her plans for the future, and Aques listened, unable to speak much himself but taking in every word. Despite the circumstances, it was almost as if nothing had ever changed between them.

Perhaps there was hope after all.

The clouds above them broke, a gentle rain falling from the sky, washing away the ichor that tainted the grass. Aques and Anima locked gazes, and they began to sob. They sobbed for Pluvia, they sobbed for their home, they sobbed for empty hearts, for black eyes, broken promises, lost time, but above all, they sobbed for each other.

Everything had changed, but then again, had it?

After all, they were there, outside the house they built together with the intent of creating a family, standing in the face of everything that was wrong with the world, watching the rainfall, taking in the petrichor, and realising that, perhaps, there was something to fill the void.

STILIS AND I APPROACHED THE CLUELESS Erathiel tentatively. Erathiel was sitting on our bed, fiddling with a mechanical rabbit. "Erathiel..." Stilis began, hovering by the doorframe. "We have something to tell you."

Erathiel cocked his head. "Is everything alright?"

"I guided a soul to the Realm of the Dead today," se said, refusing to enter the room any further. "Impaled by a spear. A shame."

"Truly," Erathiel said, evidently confused.

"He was a dreamer, that one. He was genuine, more understanding than most. He said he wanted to start a tavern, if time allowed him to, that is."

Erathiel's expression dropped. "Stilis, who was it?" Stilis bit ser lip. Erathiel's voice rose. "Who was it?" Nothing. He started to shout, tears forming in his eyes. "Who was it?"

"It was your brother, Erathiel," I said, beginning to cry as well. "I am so sorry."

"No!" Erathiel wailed. He burst into sobs. "Who did this?"

"Neither of us were there," Stilis admitted. I nodded to confirm; Stilis had no idea of my involvement. "All I know is that Auri's spear was found in Florian's chest."

Erathiel's face flushed red with rage. "I vow never to speak to Auri nor Vesa again," he said through gritted teeth, seething with fury. "They are as good as dead to me." In his mind, they had caused this. If Temprysus had not been Created, if the war had not been started, then Florian would have been spared, as well as Aestalios, Haneræs, the *countless* human lives and drops of ichor.

Erathiel began to tremble. "My brother is dead!" he howled. He clutched his temples and sobbed. I rushed to his side, embracing him tightly, whispering words of comfort in his ear while stroking his hair.

Stilis mouthed, "I think I will leave now; I am not sure if I should be here." I nodded, then se stepped outside the room.

For hours, Erathiel sobbed, occasionally muttering something incoherent (something about demons, or at times, about a tavern). I simply whispered, "I know, I know," and continued to hold him.

Erathiel stopped sobbing—either that or he ran out of tears—then managed to lean into me and say, "I will be a mess of mourning for a while, I think."

I nodded. "Perhaps. This is by no means something you must 'get over,' let the grief run its course for as long as it needs."

"You are an amazing partner," he whispered. "Thank you for standing by me. I love you, even if I forget to say it at times."

"I love you too."

I felt sick to my stomach.

I was wretched.

Chapter Twenty-Two

ERATHIEL AND I LOOKED AROUND FLORIAN'S room, packing up boxes. Variton, Erathiel's uncle, had far more pity than Chathan, who refused to even acknowledge Erathiel when he arrived at the manor. Variton allowed Erathiel to gather Florian's belongings from his old room.

There was a large portrait of Florian on the wall. The canvas looked as if it had been ripped and mended. His bed, with champagne-toned pillows and mahogany red sheets, was perfectly made. Every item of clothing in his wardrobe was neatly folded, and based on the styling, Erathiel suspected that around half of it belonged to Ilyara.

The room was nicely lit, lamps on each nightstand of the large four-poster bed, and two larger, more ornate lamps near his desk. A few mechanical moths hung from the ceiling, courtesy of Erathiel. Recipes and drawings were tacked up on the walls. Even though I never met him, I got the sense that Florian felt at home in this room.

"He was always obsessed with organisation," Erathiel recalled. "A neat freak, that one. He would go berserk if there were crumbs on the table." He chortled. "Living with Tallis was difficult for him, I presume. The man was a raging mess."

"Was Tallis the cousin you mentioned?"

Erathiel rolled his eyes. "Yes." He huffed. "Can you believe he was closer in line to the throne than Florian? A crime, if you ask me."

Erathiel approached Florian's desk. His breakfast, an undercooked egg and overcooked bacon, sat out uneaten.

"He had dreams of opening a tavern," Erathiel explained. "I never had the heart to tell him that he was horrible at cooking."

"Would the tavern garner *any* acclaim?"

"I would dine there every day if it meant making him happy."

"And what of the apothecary? He practically ran the place."

"He enjoyed working there," Erathiel explained, "but it was Chathan's passion, not his."

Erathiel removed the plate from the desk, revealing a plethora of papers underneath. They were all ink drawings, with intricate detailing and a messy signature in the bottom left corner of each artwork.

"He could have easily been an artist," I remarked, examining one of the drawings. It was a depiction of a many-eyed monster with strange tendrils for limbs. "These are rather... *experimental* figures, but it is skillfully drawn."

Upon closer examination, every drawing seemed to be some sort of cryptid. There was a woman with rows of fangs, a small wolf-like creature that had a childish fear in its eyes, and two avians who appeared to be in love.

"He had a fascination with the mysterious," Erathiel explained. "He was entranced by it."

I finally noticed the drawing on top of the pile: a sketch of a God. The God was androgynous and mystical in appearance, and its face was akin to Florian's. Around its left eye, there were markings resembling constellations.

The drawing was labelled: 'Florian: Goden of the Unknown.'

"Goden?" I asked. Erathiel walked over and peered at the drawing. "Did Florian wish to be Tryan?"

Erathiel considered it for a moment, then slowly said, "If Florian said that se was Tryan, then I will refer to sem as such."

I nodded and smiled in return. Erathiel packed up a few crates of Florian's belongings, mostly clothing, recipes, and drawings. He took the sketch labelled as 'Goden of the Unknown' and stored it in his pocket.

Once everything was packed, Erathiel and I sat at the edge of Florian's bed. Erathiel rested his head in my lap, and I ran my fingers through his hair. "How are you feeling?"

"Lost," he answered. "Se was like a parent to me, more than either Chathan or Myrinai were, for that matter. The grief is impossible to cope with."

"Not quite impossible. You are here, are you not? It is difficult—I may not understand, but I can sympathise. You are doing wonderfully, though."

"Thank you." Erathiel took a shaky breath. "Can I ask something?"

"Since when have you asked permission?" I asked teasingly. I nudged Erathiel, who did not look amused in the slightest. I cleared my throat. "Of course."

"Could we name our daughter after Florian?" he asked, voice numb.

I hesitated, then nodded. "That would be wonderful. We could call her Flori, perhaps."

"Flori, the Goddess of Petrichor," Erathiel murmured. His fingers intertwined with mine. "I quite like the sound of that."

The image of our daughter was clearer than ever in our minds.

"I HEARD THE NEWS ABOUT YOUR BROTHER, Erathiel," Priya said as she rushed into the apothecary. She had gotten word of Florian's death and wanted to console Erathiel, so we decided to meet up at the apothecary. I tensed when I saw her enter—I was worried she and Erathiel had rendezvoused—but I did not dare let the fear slip onto my expression. After all, I had

"Se is not a brother, but a sibling," Erathiel informed her, "nevertheless, I mourn sem all the same."

"Ah." Priya appeared confused, yet respectful all the same. "Would you like to talk about the loss?"

"I have enough support," he said, leaning against me, "but thank you. I would like to speak of happier things."

"Of course." She smiled, then turned to me. "Are you Erathiel's partner?"

"Yes," I immediately said, placing a hand on Erathiel's leg protectively.

She found her way into a chair. "You are Auroleus, correct?" I stiffly nodded. She stifled a laugh. "Auroleus, I cannot say for certain what this hostility–" she gestured towards me– "was caused by, but if it is because of my time with Erathiel, I can assure you that I have long since moved on. I found a partner."

"Oh?" Erathiel inquired. "How is he?"

"'She,' actually. And, I must admit, I haven't a clue. We split up about a year ago."

"I apologise. It must be difficult."

She shrugged. "It was for the best. I–"

Just then, Stilis entered the apothecary. "Thank the Gods, I finally found you, Erathiel," se said, stumbling over to us. "Do you know how long I have been searching for–" Se turned to look at Priya. "Who is this?"

Priya appeared confused; after all, she could not see Stilis. "Is there someone new here?" she asked.

"Yes," I replied. "Ser name is Stilis, the Goden of Stars."

"Interesting!" she exclaimed. "You have quite the entourage, Erathiel. I am Priya Faye, a healer in the Village of the Blinded."

"A healer?" Stilis asked, taking a seat near Priya. "Fascinating. What do you specialise in?"

"Mostly surgeries, but I do dabble in matters of the mind. I find it riveting, the prospect of healing those who are manic. And what of your career?"

"Well, I control and chart the stars, obviously."

"Obviously."

"I also guide souls to the Realm of the Dead. I have always found death cold, yet fascinating, in a sense."

"As have I," Priya said excitedly.

"Can you believe that Tenedius once sent the souls to the Realm of the Dead without a proper send-off? Callous, if you ask me."

"It is lunacy! The poor souls deserve to depart once they are ready."

Stilis stared at Priya for a long moment. "I admire your intellect, Priya Faye."

"And I admire yours."

"Perhaps we should visit a tavern sometime. I would love to have a longer conversation with you."

"You intrigue me, Stilis." Priya smiled. "I would enjoy that, yes."

Erathiel smirked, eyes flitting between the two. "Should we leave you two be?"

Stilis appeared flustered, and Priya laughed. "No, no, I must leave soon anyway," Stilis said. "I simply wanted to tell you, Erathiel, that if you desire someone to speak to about Florian, I am here. I am well-versed in the matters of death, and I have helped many grieving relatives before."

"Thank you," Erathiel said earnestly.

"Leaving so soon?" I asked Stilis.

Se sighed. "There is a matter to attend to with Tenedius."

"Oh?" I asked, sitting upright. "Enlighten us."

"I am getting the sense that, and this may be incorrect, that I will soon bring two Gods' souls to the Realm of the Dead."

Erathiel's eyes widened. "Do you have any sense as to who?"

Stilis shook ser head. "Unfortunately, my ability does not span that far. I must go speak to Tenedius, but I will see you all soon."

"Goodbye, Stilis," Priya called. "It was wonderful to meet you."

Se smiled at her. "It was my pleasure." Se dissipated into a violet light, and Priya turned to us.

"Stilis is single, correct?"

Erathiel nodded, then he and I exchanged a look. "I sense a budding romance," I whispered.

"It is too early to tell," Priya answered. I sighed. *She must have superior hearing.* "Perhaps there is something there, though."

Erathiel and I glanced at each other and smiled. "Perhaps," he said lightly.

For hours, we made light conversation, as well as tidied up around the shop. Erathiel laughed for the first time since Florian's death. I had grown to miss the sound.

Once Priya bade us farewell, we climbed the ladder outside the shop to the roof. It was lopsided, its shingles shades of red, green, blue, and purple, and it gave the apothecary a nearly enchanted atmosphere.

"Do you think Chathan will keep up with this place now that Florian is gone?" I asked, leaning against the chimney.

Erathiel joined me. "No," he admitted. "This place will certainly go abandoned."

"Perhaps," I mentioned, my hand slipping into his, "once the world is safer, we can turn this place into our home. It would be a good place to raise our daughter."

He smiled. "Absolutely."

I glanced at him. "Your eyes are beautiful in the starlight."

Erathiel blushed, and I curled up against him. We gazed into the night sky, where two neighbouring stars seemed to stare back at us.

He pointed towards the glowing flecks. "It is us," he muttered. "Auroleus and Erathiel. Do you remember?"

I smiled and kissed him lightly. "How could I forget?"

Chapter Twenty-Three

"I NEED YOUR HELP," STILIS SAID, BREATHLESS, as se stormed into Erathiel's room.

Erathiel sat up. "What is wrong?"

"Turri and Fulir are under attack. I need you to help with damage control."

Erathiel nodded. "Of course."

Stilis took Erathiel's hand, and they dissipated.

They appeared at the battlegrounds: a long field with blood-stained grass. Humans fought off waves of corrupted earth sprites. Aestalios and Turri were in the middle of the battle, clashing swords together in a mighty duel. Fulir laid on the ground, ichor spilling from his mouth and a blade impaled in his chest.

Stilis donned ser cloak and ran off to collect souls from corpses strewn upon the ground. Erathiel raced over to Fulir, unsheathed his jade longsword, and slashed several of Fulir's attackers. Fulir conjured a bolt of lightning and struck a wave of mortals who ran towards him. He gave Erathiel a grateful nod, then continued firing at his attackers.

A man snuck up on Fulir from behind, and Erathiel used the pommel of his blade to bash in the man's skull. He threw Fulir's attacker off him, then received a particularly nasty stab wound to the knee from a soldier who ran past him. Erathiel was overwhelmed for a moment, then Fulir recharged himself and sent out a mass shock wave.

In the few moments of peace, Erathiel watched Turri's fight with Aestalios. She ducked under his legs and made to strike the back of his head with her battle hammer, then her posture slipped, and she fell to the ground. Aestalios struck her with his mace. Ichor poured from the wound, then she quickly drank a vial of healing water and battered Aestalios in the jaw.

Aestalios stumbled back, not expecting the hit. He shouted expletives towards the sky, and she shot him a triumphant look. He threw himself towards her, slamming her towards the ground. He struck her with his mace, pummelling her until she managed to writhe away from the assault. She spat out a lump of ichor and her tooth, then struck Aestalios in the eye, causing it to swell and grow a shade of gold.

They circled round each other, as if they were wolves preparing to pounce. Turri bared her teeth and spat, "I hope you are happy, now that you have turned your back on the Gods."

"How could I have 'turned my back' if there was nothing there to leave behind?" Aestalios roared in response. "Nought was left for me in the Immortal Realm!"

"You were meant to be my husband, Aestalios. I have grown tired of waiting for you," Turri said after a moment.

Aestalios readied his stance. "Then let us finish this."

Turri and Aestalios charged towards each other, weapons clashing as they both entered Godly Wrath. It was the fight of their lifetimes, ichor pouring onto the ground, and yet, they remained determined and carried on all the same. The humans around them stopped to watch in shock, causing the earth sprites to slaughter them. Stilis flitted between the corpses, reaping souls (which Erathiel could not see, as he was not a Reaper himself), then paused and stared at Erathiel. "Behind you!"

Erathiel jumped away as five attackers approached. He dropped to the ground and rolled, sparing himself of any damage. When he regained his composure, he realised that the soldiers were tearing into Fulir's skin, ichor pouring from his veins.

Turri escaped Aestalios and rushed over, hitting all five attackers in one mighty blow. She tore Fulir away, holding him in her arms.

"You cannot die, not now..." She pulled her vial of healing water out of her belt pouch, but it was empty. There was a wild, crazed look in her eyes. "No," she said, barely more than a breath.

Fulir, who seemed to have accepted his fate, moved his face closer to hers. "Turri..." He leaned in for a kiss.

Turri backed away. "Fulir, I cannot, not here–"

Fulir laughed bitterly. "Of course. Well." He clicked his tongue. "Now you will not have to worry that I'm not silent enough for you." He convulsed for a moment, coughing up ichor, then went still.

Turri let out a wail of grief. She collapsed with Fulir in her arms, sobbing.

Aestalios stood over, his manner not necessarily provoking; it was more infuriated than anything. "What in Luxheia's name..." Aestalios trailed off, shaking his head. "How could you, Turri?"

She paid him no attention. "I—I never got the chance to say 'I love you...'" Turri blubbered.

Aestalios stared at her with a deadpan expression. "If you had the chance, would you have taken it?" No answer. Aestalios let out a scoff. "We both know the answer, don't we?" He looked out at the humans. "I command my soldiers to retreat!" he bellowed.

With this, Turri stood up, enraged. "No!" she screeched. "This is not over, I–"

Aestalios gave her a sympathetic look. "Go home, Turri."

"It was *you*!" she shrieked, pointing at Erathiel. "You were meant to defend him."

Erathiel was affronted. He took a step back. "I was not meant to do anything–"

"You let him die! I will kill you–"

She attempted to charge towards Erathiel, but Aestalios caught her by the wrists. "He is someone's lover too, how can you not realise?" Aestalios scolded.

Turri scoffed. "'Someone's lover...' this romance of yours is doomed to fail, you know that?"

"What do you mean?" Erathiel asked skeptically.

She tilted her head and gave him a manic smile. "He killed your brother, Erathiel. The pretty little wind boy *killed Florian.*"

Erathiel froze. *Auroleus could not have killed sem,* he thought. *It is impossible.*

"You are lying, Turri," Erathiel responded as Turri began to cackle. He looked at Aestalios. "Tell her she is deranged."

Aestalios bit his lip and sighed. "I am sorry, Erathiel–"

"No." Erathiel's voice rose. "No! Auri's spear was found in Florian's side, Stilis saw–"

"He used Auri's spear." Erathiel fell silent as Aestalios continued. "He was with Auri and Vesa, helping Ignos attack a village, and he threw the spear at Florian. I am so sorry." He shook his head.

Erathiel searched their expressions, hoping this was some cruel jape, and found that there was no semblance of a lie in their gazes. He looked towards the sky and let out a roar of anguish.

He stormed over to Stilis. "Return me to the Hall of Ocari. Auroleus should be there."

Stilis appeared terrified, but nodded. Se took Erathiel's hand in sers, and they dissolved.

AND LIFE GOES ON.

Aques maintained a position of power. He was revered by both the mortals and the Gods, and he had a distant, purely transactional relationship with both. He managed to stay level-headed and fair, and although it was a mental struggle to see Luxheia and Tenedius as often as he did, it was worth it. He provided a voice to the Gods and was well-respected. He had a tendency to overwork himself, and he struggled to maintain relationships with many, even his own Creations. Despite floundering when it came to being personable, Aques had a special care for every single God, and truly wanted nothing more than to see them happy. He always seemed to worry, did he not?

Anima became something of a mass healer. She healed Godly wounds with expertise, and even treated mortals when it was needed. She often spared humans from the wrath of, say, Ignos or Prucaris, and she gained the reputation of a great protector. Anima was known for her empathy and bedside manner, and the Gods would often come to her in the event of any strife, whether physical or mental. She often grew stressed with her work—anyone would, being surrounded by disease, injury, and death so much—so she travelled to nearly undiscovered places in the Immortal Realm, planes of bounty that were seldom trodden, and hardly ever charted. She would run, climb, swim, traverse the areas, usually without using her Godly abilities. The obstacles and challenges did not deter her; rather, they only fueled her sense of wanderlust. She felt rejuvenated every time, as if her soul was reborn with each expedition.

Aques and Anima remained together. They were close enough, often only confiding in each other, but there was something detached about their dynamic. They could no longer speak for hours like they once had, conversations were often stunted, and half the time, their interactions were strictly professional. Their love for each other had not died, but for the most part, their passion did.

They had grown out of their old home, so they built a new one. This time, they used sprites to complete the job, so the handiwork was much more professionally done. It was a large, almost intimidating marble and gold manor. It was often mistaken for a town hall, or perhaps an academy, and they could not help but understand the confusion. It did not quite give the feeling of home, but it was large enough to sustain them and their endeavours, so it was enough.

The 'old house' and Pluvia were both sensitive subjects and were never brought up amongst the Gods, especially in the company of Aques or Anima. They refused to speak of Pluvia's existence, or that there ever was an old house, or that Aques had slit his wrists. The only time that these sorrows were ever remotely acknowledged?

Whenever it rained, Aques and Anima would go out on the roof of their house, and they would watch. They would look up at the sky, or perhaps spare the occasional glance towards the ruins of their old home, or maybe their eyes scanned the streets, searching for someone, knowing that they would not find her but hoping, praying, they someday could. After all, she would not willingly come back, not when Aques and Anima were in such an impersonal state. They never did see her again. Regardless, they hoped all the same.

When the clouds slowly shifted, rain fell from the sky, and petrichor filled the earth enough to wash a soul away, Aques and Anima would sit with each other and watch. They never talked, but they would sit in quiet mourning of everything they had lost. It was the one thing that never changed.

Overall, Aques and Anima were content. They may have lacked a family and a home, but at the end of the day, they had what they needed, and it was good enough.

Nevertheless, Anima would get out of her bed some nights, leave her house, and sob on her front porch. When Aques felt her leave, he would silently weep to himself. On a surface level, everything was alright, but something was so, so terribly wrong, and they both knew there was nothing they could do to fix it, but it hurt them all the same.

The pain varied from a bittersweet hum to a penitent gut punch, but regardless, it was omnipresent, and it clouded every interaction.

Their love was not the same as it once was, and they both knew. Still, it hurt all the same, and they hoped for change. They were sure they would, someday, for how could fate pull them together, only to tear them apart?

ERATHIEL ARRIVED IN THE HALL OF OCARI, completely silent. He lingered, unmoving, by the entrance.

I was cleaning off a table, sweeping silvery dust onto the floor. The sky outside was shades of crimson and orange, and the setting sun cast a shadow onto Erathiel. "Come in, darling, it is getting late! I am glad to see you made it back alright." There was no response. I glanced up at him, then gasped and nodded in understanding. "Shaken up from Fulir's death, I presume? I would imagine so. The whole ordeal sounded brutal. Would you like to talk about it?" Silence. "Or perhaps you are merely tired. Understandable; it has been a long day. Get some good rest, alright? We can talk more in the morning. I love you." There was nothing but an ominous quietude. I cocked my head in concern. "Erathiel?"

"You killed Florian," he said, barely more than a whisper.

My heart stopped beating. The ichor drained from my face as my mouth dropped open. I was nearly speechless. "Erathiel, I–"

"No. What could you possibly say to justify yourself? You murdered my sibling!"

"I am so deeply sorry, Erathiel, I am guilt-ridden to my core, you have no idea!" I exclaimed, my expression contrite. "I could not see who I struck, I did not know it was sem, I promise–"

"Even if that was the case," he hissed, approaching me, "we agreed to stay neutral in this war. You promised me we would stay neutral! You killed a person who did not provoke you. How *dare* you attempt to justify yourself?"

"I know, I know!" I wailed. "But, Auri and Vesa, they did not try to stop me–"

"How could they have?" he shouted. "You let Auri take the blame, you *lied* to me, you said you were clueless as to what happened!" We were standing face-to-face. "You comforted me, you spoke so kindly, you embraced me when I sobbed, all while knowing you caused this?" He looked at me, revolted by the monster he saw. "I feel disgusting for ever having held you."

I gasped. "You do not mean that."

He bared his teeth and turned up his chin. "With every drop of blood in my veins." Erathiel stared at me for a moment, expression distant. "We never had eternity, did we?"

He whisked away towards our room. I followed after him, and he sped up his pace. He slammed the door closed and locked it behind him. I pounded against the door, screaming apologies and pleas, but he did not respond. I leaned against the door, sobbing profusely.

Erathiel soon emerged with a bag slung around his shoulder and his sword in his hand. I glanced in the room, and all of his possessions were gone. "Where are you going?" I croaked.

"Away." He walked towards the hall's exit, shaking his head. "Goodbye, Auroleus."

"No!" I cried. I fell to the ground, desperately holding onto his hand. "Do not leave me!"

"What is there to stay for?" he snapped, pulling his hand away. He huffed, turned, and made to leave the Hall of Ocari.

Before he could leave, turn his back on our years together, I called out something that made him stop in his tracks:

"For what it's worth...it's always been you."

He stopped for a split second, then left the hall. Erathiel Karalor, the love of my life, stood at the entrance and lifted his sword in the air. He seemed to split the crimson sky, then I blinked, and he was gone.

I crumpled and began to sob. It was as if the world had collapsed in on itself. I rocked back and forth, hardly able to breathe, and I hoped with all my heart that he would return. I stared at the entrance to the hall until my eyes grew bloodshot and I was unable to stay awake, waiting for him to return. *How can he not return?* I kept telling myself, *how can he not return, when we are written in the stars?*

I held onto hope that Erathiel would come home to me, that we could have a chance to talk about this, that I could hold him in my arms once more. After all, we were fated to be together, were we not?

FATE WAS NOT STRONG ENOUGH.

Chapter Twenty-Four

ERATHIEL WANDERED, NOT QUITE KNOWING where he was going. He knew he was going away, and that was what mattered. Vengeance burned in his heart. He was consumed with the desire—no, the *need*—to avenge Florian.

He walked aimlessly until he found Esolir, who was willing to take him back to the Mortal Realm. Erathiel asked to be returned to his old manor. Once Esolir dropped off Erathiel, Esolir gave him a long look, grasped his shoulder, then said, "Be careful, son." Erathiel nodded, and Esolir dissipated into a violet light.

Erathiel maundered away from his old home, past the apothecary, and towards the hills. After hours, he was lost and had no clue where he was going. His eyes were sore, and his limbs were weary. He was prepared to give up for the night, but then he came over the crest of a hill and saw an army camp in the distance.

He breathed and smiled, then began to approach the camp. He began to see the scene more clearly: soldiers practising their swordsmanship, people huddled for warmth, a boy no more than twelve working on sharpening blades, women sewing leather armour, armymen trudging groggily towards their tents, and a lanky, black-haired man sitting at a desk in front of the fence that surrounded the camp.

"I would like to join your militia," Erathiel said once he approached the man.

The man pushed his spectacles up his nose, eyed Erathiel up and down, and shrewdly asked, "Name?"

He hesitated. "Erathiel Karalor."

The man looked at Erathiel skeptically. "You are a well-known traitor to the humans."

"I remained neutral throughout the war, actually," Erathiel said indignantly, "and, regardless, I have moved past the Gods now. I am more than ready to fight for your cause."

"Do you know how many loyalists to the Gods have arrived at this camp," the man hissed, "and stolen our food supply? We simply cannot trust you, given the circumstances."

"What is your name?"

The man eyed him for a moment. "Avis Daxidor."

"Well, Mr. Daxidor, I can assure you that I am a capable swordsman who will be wholly loyal to this army."

"We cannot allow your entry."

"But—"

"No."

"Let him in, Daxidor," a familiar voice said. Aestalios emerged from the camp entrance and offered Erathiel a light smile. "We can trust him."

Daxidor eyed him skeptically, then shrugged. "If you insist, boss."

Aestalios nodded, wrapped his arm around Erathiel's shoulder, and led him inside the camp. "I am glad you have joined us, old friend," he said, his eyes clouded with a familiar void. "You look exhausted. Let us get you set up with a tent, alright?"

For the next few weeks, Erathiel was a valuable asset to the human army. He specialised in fighting off corrupted earth sprites, and more often than not, he was on the frontlines of battle. Although he was often asked, he refused to utilise his mechanical animals for warfare. He had no clue as to why, but the notion felt morally wrong.

Throughout his time at the camp, Erathiel was very methodical, but between skirmishes with corrupted sprites, patrolling when needed, and tedious tasks like sharpening blades, he hardly spared himself any time for leisure. Aestalios was growing nervous that Erathiel was losing his sense of self, but he refrained from voicing these concerns; after all, doing so would make him a hypocrite, seeing as he himself slipped away long ago.

After a few weeks, however, Erathiel was growing restless of the militia's indirect approach. They always concerned themselves with the sprites rather than the Gods, even though they proved themselves capable of shedding ichor.

Erathiel could not quench the overwhelming thirst for ichor while he was at the camp, nor fulfil the desire to avenge Florian. He weighed his options and decided that he would leave the militia behind and slaughter a God himself.

His first thought, however fleeting, was to kill me, but he quickly abandoned the notion. However much he loathed my very being, he could not muster the will to take my life. Instead, his thoughts drifted to Ignos. Ignos, who burnt down Thyrin Cove. Ignos, who was especially cruel to the humans during the war. Ignos, who had sent Auri, Vesa, and I on the mission to start the fire anyway. Without him, Florian would have been spared.

Perhaps it was a suicide mission, but in Erathiel's mind, it was worth it.

He approached Aestalios one day, and before he could even speak, Aestalios gave him a knowing look. "Leaving?" he asked.

"How could you tell?"

He shrugged. "I had the sense that you were fleeting the moment you stepped onto these grounds."

"Could you take me to the Immortal Realm?"

Aestalios stared at him for a long moment. "Why?" Erathiel was silent, opting to stare at his weathered shoes rather than answer the question. "Fine. You do not need to tell me, as long as you swear to keep yourself safe, alright?"

Erathiel nodded, and Aestalios clapped him on the shoulder. "Atta-boy. Let's go, now."

He outstretched his hand. Erathiel took it, and they dissolved into a pale blue light and floated above the camp, past the clouds, and through the veil to the Immortal Realm.

A sense of confidence flooded through Erathiel.

Ignos will be no more.

ERATHIEL WANDERED THROUGH THE MAIN street in the Immortal Realm. There were places and people he recognised— Arberra's bakery, Aques's manor, groups of sprites playing music— but nothing filled him with comfort like the Immortal Realm used to, except, perhaps, a nearby cornflower and wisteria field, which incited an unmistakable sense of nostalgia. Erathiel approached the field for a moment, feeling wisps resembling dandelion seeds brush against his hands. For a moment, he almost considered staying.

He saw a bright spark out of the corner of his eye. He turned, then noticed a fire sprite—non-corrupted, of course—skipping down the road.

Erathiel approached it. "Could you point me in the direction of Ignos's cave?" The sprite cocked its head, confused. *Sprites cannot speak my language,* Erathiel thought, frustrated. He tried to think of a way to communicate with the sprite. Erathiel gestured to himself, made a walking motion, and then pointed to the Symbol of Ignos, which was borne on the sprite's chest.

The sprite let out an exclamation, then took Erathiel by the hand and led him towards Ignos's cave.

They traversed fields of silver and forests of bronze, walked past mountains capped with ever-shifting snow, and crossed swamps lined with cerulean willows and dotted with orchid-pink fey creatures.

At last, after making their way past a rocky coastline, Erathiel and the fire sprite saw a towering volcano in the distance. As Erathiel came closer, he saw the opening of a massive cave embedded into the structure. When he and the sprite arrived at the entrance, he took a shaky breath and handed the sprite his bag. "Hold this for me, will you?" It did not seem to understand his speech, but it held his bag and positioned itself just outside the cave. It smiled at Erathiel and let out a chirrup, and Erathiel weakly smiled back.

A breath in.

A breath out.

He entered the cave.

Erathiel navigated his way through the caverns, weaving around stalagmites. Soot smeared itself onto his face and arms. He walked through the winding tunnels, nearly giving up on finding Ignos, when he heard a deep snoring coming from inside the cave.

Erathiel followed the snoring until he reached a massive chamber. The ceiling rose to over ten times his height, and charcoal-red stalactites hung above him. Torches lined the walls. Other than that, the chamber was empty.

Ignos laid on the floor in the centre of the gigantic chamber. He was sound asleep, his snores shaking his entire body. Erathiel crept over to Ignos, drew out his blade, and stabbed it into Ignos's chest as hard as he could.

As streams of golden ichor poured from Ignos's veins, Ignos woke up, throwing Erathiel off of him. He stumbled as he stood, threw Erathiel's blade to the ground, and let out a terrifying roar that made Erathiel grow pale.

"You are dead, boy!" Ignos shouted. It was only then that Erathiel realised that not only was Ignos capable of controlling fire, but he was also around four times Erathiel's height.

Ignos raised his hand, and bolts of fire shot from the torches lining the walls. Erathiel crouched to avoid them. He dove for his shortsword, and he barely caught it as Ignos kicked him against a wall.

Erathiel scrambled up, regaining his posture, then charged towards Ignos. He managed to strike the God of Fire on the foot. Ignos's skin, however, was thick as armour, so it did not tear.

Ignos shot a rope of fire at Erathiel, which caused his clothing to burst into flames. Erathiel yelped in terror and dropped to the ground, rolling to extinguish the flames. He managed to put out the fire, then he jumped and impaled Ignos's leg with his sword.

Ignos roared in pain, ichor pouring from the wound. The blade was stuck in Ignos's leg, and Erathiel dangled limply, barely managing to hang on to the sword's hilt. Ignos's hand swept towards him, and Erathiel let go at the last second. He fell to the ground. Weaponless and ridden with burns, Erathiel realised he could, in no universe, win the fight, and he charged towards the exit of the chamber.

Just as he was about to leave, he felt something wrap around his stomach and pull him back. Suddenly, he was face-to-face with Ignos, who jeered at him. "You think you are capable of besting a God?" Ignos asked, voice dripping with mockery.

Erathiel, realising he was being held in Ignos's hand, was rendered speechless in his terror. He met Ignos's gaze, and in a defeated voice, he said, "I would like to pretend I can."

Erathiel's body was suddenly filled with heat, as if his insides were on fire. Ignos laughed as Erathiel squirmed, trying to break free of Ignos's grasp. He gritted his teeth as he accelerated towards his breaking point.

Finally, Ignos decided that he was done toying with him, so he threw Erathiel to the ground. Erathiel slammed against the wall, slumped against a crevice in the cave. Ignos pounded Erathiel three times with his fists. Erathiel was unable to move as blood trickled down his chin and flowed like a river against his bruised and beaten body. He expected a final blow, some mortal action that would make his world go dark, then, to his great surprise, Ignos backed away.

Erathiel stared at him in wonder. He huffed, a light smile appearing on his lips. *Has Ignos spared me?* he wondered. *Is there mercy somewhere in his soul?*

A wave of victory and relief washed over Erathiel as Ignos left the chamber, relenting. Erathiel had, it seems, made it out alive.

A few moments had passed, and he made to leave the cave. He was shocked that he was able to stand, let alone walk. He was about to exit when he stopped abruptly, hearing someone appear behind him.

Erathiel turned around to see Stilis, wearing ser cloak and holding a large scythe. Erathiel's smile dropped, his expression full of confusion. A bitter smile creased Stilis's face as se nodded. "It is time."

IF YOU GO AROUND THE LEFT SIDE OF THE manor of Aques and you walk a few paces, you will find that it borders a beautiful meadow. The grass, hues of cornflower and wisteria, is illuminated in the lights of the sky and glows a shade of turquoise in the twilight. Wisps resembling dandelion seeds ride the gentle wind, and trees of muted pinks and reds fleck the open field.

In the field, you may see bits of stone foundation, weathered and worn.

They were once a home.

In the centre of the ruins, there was a headstone, which was newly placed over a grave I had dug myself. The headstone read:

ERATHIEL
ETERNALLY BELOVED

I crouched over the gravestone, sobbing and struggling to breathe. My eyes were bleary and bloodshot. When Stilis told me Erathiel had been killed, I did not rest until I found his body.

"I love you," I whispered over the gravestone. "I am so, so sorry, Erathiel, I–"

I choked, unable to speak. I leaned my head against the grave, imagining it was his shoulder. I pictured him comforting me. He would have held me close, whispered in my ear that it was okay, that he still loved me, but I was only lying to myself, was I not? He died in hatred of me.

Stilis told me that Erathiel peacefully left. He quickly passed through the gateway into the Realm of the Dead. "Before Erathiel left," Stilis had told me, "he said that he regretted losing you. He said he still loves you."

Stilis had lied to me, I knew it. Se was simply trying to console me. How could Erathiel have given me his love? I had slaughtered his sibling, the last person in his family who remained. I deserved Erathiel's hatred.

Still, I loved him with all my heart, and I grieved for him, oh, how I grieved! It was as if a part of me laid in the grave alongside Erathiel.

I should have expected this. It was in his nature to die, was it not? Our love was fleeting from the start. We never could have had eternity.

I drew an object from out of my pocket: a mechanical bird, the one he and I built together. Aques allowed me to take it down from the clock tower.

As I laid it next to his grave, I began to speak. "I am sorry that this is not the burial you wanted," I whispered. "Atop the hill behind your childhood manor. It is not safe for me there." I looked around. "This place is nice enough for you, I think. Here, there used to be the kind of home I always imagined us in." I laughed bittersweetly. "Flori would have loved it."

I pictured him in the Realm of the Dead. I liked to think he was at peace with himself, something he could not find in the waking world.

I began to weep again. "Wherever you are, my love," I murmured, "tell me you are at peace. Tell me that, somewhere in the universe, you are happy, and all of this will have been worth it."

Chapter Twenty-Five

I LEFT ERATHIEL'S GRAVE, MY MIND RUNNING wild. I was furious. Erathiel's life had been stripped from him. Other Gods and several sprites jumped out of my path as I unknowingly entered Godly Wrath.

A single thought stood clear in my head:

I am going to revive Erathiel Karalor.

I instantly thought of Aestalios and Haneræs. He managed to bring her back. He may have slipped away, sure, but he figured out the cure for death in the process, so I would not have to redo all the work he had done. All I needed was the essence of Luxheia (if he could acquire it, then so could I) and an electric shock...

...no. Fulir had died, so it would be nigh impossible to obtain one. Besides, I had already buried Erathiel, and I would need his corpse.

I stopped in my path as my shoulders slumped. I could not revive Erathiel.

I numbly watched the world pass by, apathetic and expressionless. Auri and Vesa walked past. Auri stopped when she noticed me, then Vesa muttered something in her ear, and they sped away.

Auri and Vesa...

Temprysus.

Realisation dawned upon me. The God of Time could not only reverse Erathiel's death, he could erase Florian's death from history entirely. I would only need to convince him that Erathiel was worthy of being revived, and he would be brought back to life.

If I did utilise Temprysus's abilities, however, and if the other Gods found out, then I would be ostracised from society. We had all agreed long ago to never use Temprysus's abilities, lest we be renounced.

The other Gods would only find out if I failed, and I would by no means have let that happen.

The one issue? I had no idea where Temprysus was being held. The last time I had seen him was on Peace Day, after which Luxheia and Tenedius took him back into strict custody. No one had any idea where he was, except, perhaps...

I approached Laphara, who walked past the bakery. "Where is Temprysus?" I shouted.

Laphara's eyes widened. She struggled to remain apathetic. "I haven't a clue."

"Lies," I hissed. "Where is he?" I was met with silence. I held her by the throat against a wall. *Where is he?*

Laphara threw me off of her, then stared at me for a long moment. With a trembling hand, she pointed towards a small shack in the distance.

I nodded briskly and walked towards the shack, my Godly Wrath slipping away. I had no idea how Luxheia and Tenedius had gotten inside the structure. The tiny building looked as if it could barely hold an Ascended God, let alone a Titan.

I opened the door.

The building's interior was non-existent. Instead, there was only a void that seemed to stretch on forever. There was a narrow grey suspension bridge suspended mid-air. It seemed to be made of smooth, dark stone. The bridge led to a floating circular platform made of the same substance. A figure stood on the platform, completely unmoving, its back turned to me.

I took a step onto the bridge, and the door slammed behind me. A celestial choir sounded throughout the void, a melodramatic, melancholy cry filling the air with a sense of foreboding. Heart beating rapidly, I made my way across the bridge.

After a few steps, I must have slammed my foot down too hard, for a piece of stone chipped off from the bridge. The stone fell into the infinite void, and a blue light melted away the stone.

I stared at where the stone had melted, eyes wide, and tentatively walked across the rest of the bridge.

I came face-to-face with the silhouette on the platform. The figure turned around, and I hardly recognised it as Temprysus.

He was an amalgamation. Only parts of him were youthful and reflective of his true age. His body was creased with wrinkles, giving him an ancient appearance. He had multiple black eyes, a sign of Ascension, but he still had the body of a boy. One of his arms and bits of his torso were entirely made of particles, as if he were part-Titanic. There were parts of him that were entirely made of golden light left over from his Creation.

"Auroleus. Why have you come here?" Temprysus asked. His voice resembled multiple people speaking over each other.

"Are you capable of reversing a mortal's death?"

Temprysus raised his eyebrow. "Capable? Of course. Why, do tell, would I go against a decree of the Gods?"

I smiled at Temprysus weakly. "For your Uncle Erathiel?"

Temprysus did not seem to find that funny; I do not blame him, given the circumstances. "He was an unremarkable man. You do realise that if I am to revive him, we will both be renounced by Godly society. Auroleus, it is simply not worth it."

My voice rose to a shout. "He is worth everything!" Temprysus narrowed his eyes. I continued to plead. "If you think otherwise, you know nothing about him. Please, simply give him a chance."

He considered it for a moment, then shrugged. "I suppose I have nothing else to do." It sickened me how casually he thought of this, but I could not complain. "Enlighten me about this...*Erathiel* of yours. Tell me his story. Spare no details, lest he be lost forever. If I find him worthy, I may bring him back."

I took a shaky breath. "Thank you."

Temprysus stared at me for a moment. "Well? We don't have eternity."

Tears brimmed in my eyes. I searched for where to start, then smiled and nodded. "Ever since Erathiel was young, he had always liked to play pretend." I let out a bittersweet chuckle. "This is evident, through the stories of his childhood he told me over an autumn night's bonfire or through my own experiences with him, however fleeting they were. He would wander off, preferably somewhere quiet and colourful, and dream up whatever he could find in the expanses of his headspace."

I continued from there, sparing no details, telling the story of Erathiel, the story of us: two lovers who, amidst the darkness and in spite of their finite nature, never failed to take a moment of clarity, to breathe in the scent of petrichor as we found light in each other's embrace. It is certainly no epic poem, no tale of heroes and conquest, and I would know; I have read plenty in my time. Alas, it is the story that takes up the most place in my heart, so it must be a story worth telling.

I FINISH TELLING THE STORY OF ERATHIEL, tears in my eyes. Temprysus stands before me, his expression unreadable.

Suddenly, he closes his eyes and begins to levitate, and I stagger away from him. He is making his decision, the choice that will seal Erathiel's fate.

Runes of golden light scatter across the void as Temprysus's arms begin to tremble. His head whips around the room, and the unseen choir's song intensifies. I hold my breath.

Temprysus's head points towards me, and his eyes open. They glow hues of blue and gold.

He shakes his head.

My heart stops beating.

I STAGGER ACROSS THE BRIDGE AND EXIT THE void. I feel as if Erathiel has died all over again.

I take a shaky breath, and the thoughts rush in.

The Gods will find out that I attempted to use Temprysus's abilities. I will be cast off from the Immortal Realm; it is certain.

The mortals despise my existence. They will hunt me down, kill me for sport as if I am an animal.

The pantheon will turn on me.

My Creators are sure to reject me.

Auri and Vesa have sided with the Gods.

Aestalios has joined the mortal army.

Stilis cannot risk standing beside me.

Haneræs is broken.

Erathiel is dead.

What will I have left?

My fate is clear in my mind.

I see a silhouette I recognise as Stilis, strolling on the main street. I approach him, and se smiles when se notices me.

"Auroleus, how wonderful it is to see you! I wanted to discuss–" Se notices the expression on my face. "Are you alright?"

"Take me to the gateway."

Stilis stares at me for a long moment, then shakes ser head rapidly. "No, I–"

I draw a dagger from out of my belt and hold it to ser throat. "Did I misspeak? Take me to the gateway."

Terrified, Stilis holds out ser hand. I take it, then we dissipate into a violet light.

We appear on a floating island, the top of which is laid with stone. The only distinguishable object on the platform is a massive stony arch. Detailed engravings are present on every stone, but the most prominent is the keystone, which bears an etching of a human Tenedius drawing an arrow towards a First-Cycle Luxheia, who holds her hand out. The interior of the arch was a rift-like vortex, except this one had a more turquoise appearance.

Surrounding the floating island were swirls of stardust and a pure, uninterrupted expanse of the cosmos.

I stare around for a moment, then my gaze snaps back to Stilis. I tighten the grip on my dagger, brandishing it towards sem. "Go," I commanded.

Stilis stares at me for a long moment, then sighs. "Please...keep yourself from harm." Se dissolves into a violet light and disappears.

I turn around, facing the gateway. On the other side of that gateway is the Realm of the Dead. I cannot help but let out a laugh.

I am so, so close to Erathiel. I can almost feel him already.

I charge towards the gateway, more than prepared to feel the sweet embrace of death, then something stops me. Some sort of invisible forcefield surrounds the gateway, blocking me from entering.

I attempt to charge through the barrier a few more times, my desperation increasing with each attempt. By the fifth try, I cannot bear to run the full distance, and I crumple to the ground, sobbing.

I stand up slowly, another thought coursing through my mind. I draw two daggers from my belt, holding one in each hand. I take a shaky breath. *I may see Erathiel yet.*

Suddenly, Tenedius, the God of Darkness and Death incarnate, appears before me.

He is a swirling mass of black particles, incompre— hensible shapes being pulled towards and repulsed from his core. A single eye floats above the mass, its sclera black and iris purple. Black tears shed in a constant flow from his eye; he is famous for his ceaseless sobs.

"You truly believe you can abandon your status as a God?" Tenedius roars, his voice deep and menacing. "This action will not win you Erathiel. You think, after everything you have done, you deserve him? Even a *mortal* does not want you. Your soul is tarnished. Do you honestly assume he is waiting for you?"

Perhaps those were the final words to seal my fate; they were the daggers to my wrists and heart, the ichor pouring from my ventricles and veins as I look up at Death himself and, despite everything, manage a smile.

"There is nothing for me here. He is waiting. And I will be happy to see him."

The fallen soul of a God, plummeting endlessly through the Realm of the Dead. The hand of a mortal, despite everything, reaches for him. When the souls recognise each other, an unknown yet familiar force consumes the void. Somewhere in the universe, two neighbouring stars shine brighter. The souls, two broken halves, are whole once more.

"Eternity is ours."

Acknowledgements

I have a lot of people to thank, so forgive me if I forget anyone. Thank you:

To one of my best friends (you know who you are), to whom I constantly ranted about this book. You were the first person to read *Petrichor*, and you let me talk your ear off about Auroleus and Erathiel. It was so, *so* difficult not to spoil the ending for you, but I hope it was worth it. Thanks for being a great person to talk to about my creative works, and I cannot wait to rant about my next project!

To my family (both given and chosen) and my friends, for supporting me, not only *Petrichor* or my creative endeavours in general, but also for embracing my queerness. As a queer trans man, it is difficult to find support in this day and age, and I must have gotten lucky, because you all have been amazingly open. Thank you for everything.

To every music artist I listened to in the process of making this book. I cannot possibly name all of you, as there are too many to count, but your artistry fueled the creative process of *Petrichor*. If you, my reader, would like to get a taste of the music that I enjoyed most while writing *Petrichor*, I have an official playlist called *Petrichor* on Spotify, where there is a song for every scene in the novel.

To every person who silently struggles because of factors outside their control, you are not alone.

Lastly (but certainly not least), to all the dreamers who came before me, and the dreamers who will follow. Your ideas lead and shape the world as we know it, and we would be nowhere without you. Your creations are Gods in their own right. Never stop making art.

-Ezri Grey

Author's Note

If you're still reading, I'm glad you stuck around. I know not many people read through the acknowledgements and author's note, so thank you. I promise, I have something in store after all of this that will make the extra few minutes of reading more than worth it.

I'll admit, this was a difficult novel to write. Growing so attached to the characters, then having fate turn on them, was a challenging process to get through, and I am not quite sure if I will write another tragedy in the future. However, the writing process of this novel was more than worth it, because I believe this is the best work I have produced so far.

I would like to touch on one thing: these characters, however different they were, all seemed to have one thing in common: they were searching for home.

And that in itself is life, is it not? We try, and sometimes we fail, but we try nevertheless to find that person, place, or anything else that feels like home. We grow to not only accept challenges, but to embrace them, and we learn from our yesterdays, fight through today, and strive for better tomorrows. There is no perfect way to be a lover, nor a friend, nor a child, parent—all of this is to say that there is no perfect way to be a human, but perhaps there doesn't have to be. After all, despite our differences—our race, gender, sex, orientation, identity, religion, nationality, background, everything—we are all filled with the desire to find home, and that has to mean something.

One day at a time, we will live, and we will prevail. Champion your fate. Go find home.
-Ezri Grey

After The War

PERHAPS THE WORLD WAS RULED BY impermanence.

Ten years into the war, Tenedius was growing weary of the mortals' lack of respect for the Gods, so in a grand show of power, he strung his old bow for the first time in aeons.

He drew the bow and aimed it at the Mortal Realm. The arrow flew through the veil. It struck the ground of Lenethaus and brought destruction and demise to all of its inhabitants.

Furious, Luxheia abandoned the Immortal Realm, imprisoning Tenedius inside. She re-conquered Lenethaus from Tenedius's wrath, taking remnants and scraps of life and nurturing back civilisation.

The Gods and mortals were permanently separated. Tensions spiralled in the Immortal Realm, leading to near-constant conflict. Alliances were formed and betrayed, Creations and Creators turned on each other, and in time, the Gods had all passed on to the Realm of the Dead.

Aques, who was the final God in the Immortal Realm to die, staggered towards the ruins of his old home. Clothes tainted with ichor, he laid down next to Anima's grave. There were a few other gravestones there, one that he recognised, Auroleus, and one that he did not, Erathiel. He managed a smile. He quite liked that name.

In his dying breath, Aques looked up at the sky. "Tenedius!" he bellowed. "Luxheia! I urge you to make peace, lest the universe itself falter!"

As darkness consumed Aques's vision, he had the sickening feeling that they would refuse to find peace, that the world would forever be in a state of imbalance.

After all, there is no mercy at the hands of a God.

TWO SWIRLING MASSES DRIFT THROUGH THE universe. They both seem in search of something, but neither of them knows exactly what.

One mass, entirely made of light, tears through the remnants of a broken veil. It finds another mass, this one made entirely of darkness.

The two forms amalgamate.

Two people stand facing each other, suspended in a swirling void of light and darkness.

Luxheia and Tenedius.

In the void, they are not their Titanic forms. They appear as they were before she harnessed light, before he drew his bow.

They are simply human.

After spending so long in the Mortal Realm, Luxheia's form had begun to wilt. She stands before Tenedius in a withered state. A limp smile pulls at the corner of her lips as she says, "I believed I would go eternity without seeing you, Tenedius."

"We both know that is impossible, Luxheia," Tenedius responds, voice clear and coherent through his sobs, which never seemed to cease.

They lock gazes and are silent for a long moment. Perhaps in another life, they could have been functional. Perhaps in another life, they could have been lovers. In this life, they are simply Titans, who at their root are only humans with power who lost sight of why they had become powerful in the first place. If they want to prevent their kingdom from falling into ruin once more, they would have to forget their privilege as Gods, and relearn what it means to be human.

Luxheia lets out a bitter laugh, which sounds like the croak of a dying bird. "We have grown so distant. What have we become?"

Tenedius steps closer to Luxheia; not by much, but enough. "I have been pondering those boys, Ocean Winds and his human. Perhaps...perhaps we could learn something from them."

A look of nostalgia spreads across Luxheia's face. She seems to be recalling a simpler time. She murmurs, "The rulers and Creators of everything."

The crying God takes the hand of the weathering Goddess, and they feel a rain falling from the sky. They bask in the droplets, taking in all they have created and destroyed. They decide they have done enough in the world, and realise they have completed the Third Cycle of their lives through a single action:

Resolution.

They distil into the essence of nature, and the universe is at peace with itself once more.

ONE GOD REMAINS.

After Auroleus and Erathiel found each other in the afterlife, after every other God had died, after the Titans themselves distilled into the universe, after all was said and done, after fate failed itself time and time again, Pluvia stands.

She emerges from a cave in the Mortal Realm, in which she resided for decades after her disappearance. Throughout her time there, she went unbothered, except for a few frogs who resided in the cave (who were never really a

292

bother to see), and the occasional sound of two boys laughing outside, although they had not come back for decades. She wondered where they were.

She looks around at the world, seeing the destruction wrought upon it.

She understands she cannot save it.

She understands, somehow, that she is the last one left.

She understands she must do something, and she does all she can think to do.

Pluvia lifts her hands to the sky and sends a cleansing rain upon the kingdom of Lenethaus. The gentle pour of droplets sweeps through the kingdom, washing the land of its ichor and bloodstains, gold and red splatters fading until the world looks almost normal again, whatever that may be.

She hums a familiar lullaby, then closes her eyes, waiting for the wistful scent of petrichor. At first, she does not notice it and opens her eyes, concerned. Next to her, a girl stands. She appears to be a spirit, with freckles, blue skin and hair, amber eyes, short ears, and a playful smile.

Pluvia can tell that this girl is a dreamer.

The girl holds out her hands, and petrichor fills the land. Pluvia smiles, taking in the scent.

She and the girl sit outside the cave and watch the rain, the world healing and breaking itself until nothing remains but the numbing scent of petrichor.

Guide to the Gods

AEDIS - God of Summer
Third Generation God
Ascended
Created by Aques and Ignos

AESTALIOS - God of the Tide
Fourth Generation God
Created by Ocari

ANIMA - Goddess of Air
Second Generation Goddess
Asccended
Created by Luxheia and Tenedius

AQUES - God of Water
Second Generation God
Ascended
Created by Luxheia and Tenedius

ARBERRA - Goddess of Trees
Third Generation Goddess
Created by Taarin

AUARAE - Goddess of the Breeze
Fourth Generation Goddess
Created by Gala

AURI - Goddess of Dawn
   Fourth Generation Goddess
   Created by Esolir

AUROLEUS - God of Ocean Winds
   Fourth Generation God
   Created by Ocari and Gala

AUXRA - Goddess of Autumn
   Third Generation Goddess
   Ascended
   Created by Ignos and Taarin

ESOLIR - God of the Sun
   Third Generation God
   Pre-Ascension
   Created by Anima and Ignos

FISYN - Goddess of Spring
   Third Generation Goddess
   Ascended
   Created by Aques and Taarin

FLORATRIS - Goddess of Flowers
   Third Generation Goddess
   Created by Taarin

FLUJA - Goddess of Rivers
   Third Generation Goddess
   Created by Aques and Taarin

FULIR - God of Lightning
   Fourth Generation God
   Created by Prucaris and Itaria

GALA - Goddess of Wind
    Third Generation Goddess
    Pre-Ascension
    Created by Anima

GLACIES - God of Ice
    Fourth Generation God
    Created by Hithar

HANERÆS - Goddess of Sand
    Fourth Generation Goddess
    Created by Lacaos

HITHAR - God of Winter
    Third Generation God
    Ascended
    Created by Aques and Anima

IGNOS - God of Fire
    Second Generation God
    Ascended
    Created by Luxheia and Tenedius

ITARIA - Goddess of Lava
    Third Generation Goddess
    Created by Ignos and Laphara

LACAOS - God of Lakes
    Third Generation God
    Created by Aques

LAPHARA - Goddess of Stone
    Second Generation Goddess
    Ascended
    Created by Luxheia and Tenedius

LUNIX - Goddess of the Moon
    Third Generation Goddess
    Pre-Ascension
    Created by Laphara

LUXHEIA - Goddess of Light, Life
    First Generation Goddess
    Titanic

MONSAIS - God of Mountains
    Third Generation God
    Created by Taarin and Laphara

OCARI - God of Oceans
    Third Generation God
    Created by Aques
PALUS - God of Swamps
    Third Generation God
    Created by Aques and Taarin

PLUVIA - Goddess of Rain
    Third Generation Goddess
    Created by Aques and Anima

PRUCARIS - God of Storms
    Third Generation God
    Ascended
    Created by Aques and Anima

SOTIS - God of Soil
    Third Generation God
    Ascended
    Created by Taarin

STILIS - Goden of Stars
  Fourth Generation God
  Created by Esolir and Lunix

TAARIN - Goden of Earth
  Second Generation God
  Ascended
  Created by Luxheia and Tenedius

TEMORIS - God of Earthquakes
  Third Generation God
  Created by Taarin and Laphara

TEMPRYSUS - God of Time
  Fifth Generation God
  Created by Auri and Vesa

TENEDIUS - God of Darkness, Death
  First Generation God
  Titanic

TURRI - Goddess of Cyclones
  Fourth Generation Goddess
  Created by Prucaris and Gala

VESA - Goddess of Dusk
  Fourth Generation Goddess
  Created by Lunix

Made in the USA
Monee, IL
24 June 2025